Something About the Stars

Book Six of the
Coming Back to Cornwall
series

Katharine E. Smith

HEDDON PUBLISHING

www.heddonpublishing.com
www.facebook.com/heddonpublishing
@PublishHeddon

Katharine E. Smith is a writer, editor and publisher.

An avid reader of contemporary writers such as Kate Atkinson, David Nicholls, Helen Dunmore and Anne Tyler, Katharine's aim is to write books she would enjoy reading – whether literary fiction or more light-hearted, contemporary fiction.

Something About the Stars is her ninth novel and a continuation of this popular Coming Back to Cornwall series, which was originally intended to be a trilogy.

Katharine runs Heddon Publishing from her home in Shropshire, which she shares with her husband and their two children.

For Rosemary Rogers

My wonderful mum

Something About the Stars

Opening the front door, I am met by a gust of wind which feels like it could bowl me over. I step back into the hallway.

"Having second thoughts?" laughs Sam from the lounge.

"No way!" I say. I pull my hood up, tightening it and pushing my fringe safely under its cover. "I'll be back in an hour."

"Take your time. We'll be fine, I promise."

I shut the door behind me, treading tentatively into the street, where the rain is forming streams on either side, catching the fat drops which plummet from the gutters and windowsills, bubbling and tinkling down the hill, to the town. To the sea.

My wellied feet feel progressively lighter as I increase my speed, splashing through the rainwater, kicking up spray from the little streetside channels. It is blessedly quiet in town, with all but the hardiest of holidaymakers staying put, staring hopefully out from windows, keeping fingers crossed that the weather will change, and change quickly, as is often the way by the sea.

As for me – I welcome the wind, and the rain, as I find a spring in my step and feel my shoulders, which I had not realised were tensed up, begin to relax. It's a strange feeling, no doubt about it. My first time out of the house without Ben.

When Sam had suggested it last night, I wasn't sure. Not that I don't think he can look after our son; he is more than capable. An old hand at parenthood, in fact, and far more experienced than me. But could I bear to be away from my boy? After carrying him for nine months, then two months of spending every waking – and sleeping – moment together, I felt like I might not work properly without the warm bundle of loveliness tucked into the sling on my chest, or lying close by, his beautiful little lips puckered as he sleeps and breathes softly in and out, in and out.

I've done it. I've become a mad mother. I worship my child. I can't imagine life without him. *Was* there life without him?

But now, despite the atrocious weather, as I round the corner onto the harbourside, and see just the tiniest chink in the clouds across the sea, with a shimmer of sunshine and a hopeful suggestion of blue sky, I realise I am still a person in my own right, and that an hour away from my son will be good for me. In fact, now I come to think of it, an hour doesn't seem long. I check my watch. I've already had fifteen minutes!

Take your time, Sam had said. Maybe I should. Maybe I will.

Despite that promising break in the forbidding clouds, the grim weather stays. After a long, hot and dry summer, it's a welcome change for me, but I do feel for the people who are only here for a week. Holed up in their holiday cottages, flats, bed & breakfasts... digging out yellow-paged books, or crumbly and dog-eared board games in a bid to pass the time... irritable tempers flaring over trivial misdemeanours. I can feel the frustration.

But as I head along the harbourside I really couldn't care less what the weather is like. Head down against the wind, I tread determined steps until I reach the Mainbrace pub, where I take a left turn up the small cobbled street, which is sheltered from the wind but also runs with rivulets of rainwater. A lone flowerpot swirls slowly around the top of a drain, and I spy a child's face pressed against a cottage window.

Up I go, feeling my body perspiring inside my

waterproof layers. It may be windy and rainy but it's not really all that cold. I trudge up through a myriad of streets, passing and greeting occasional dog walkers; we toss pleasantries to each other about the weather, in good old-fashioned Britishness. At the turn to the surf beach the wind gets me again and I laugh out loud. I feel alive.

I check my watch. Fifty minutes have passed. How can that be?

I phone Sam.

"I can't hear you!" he shouts, although I'm not having any trouble hearing him. "We're fine. Ben's asleep upstairs. Don't hurry back, unless you want to."

"Thank you!" I shout back to him.

I end the call then I text him:

I'm at the beach. I'm going to get a coffee but just call if you need me xxx

We'll be fine. He's sleeping now. If he wakes and he's hungry, I'll try the bottle. If he doesn't like it then he'll have to hang on for you. Have another hour, at least, unless you're cold and miserable xxx

I'm not. Thank you Sam. I love you xxx

I love you too. Now get back to the beach and the shit weather! Xxx

I do as I'm told, running down the slipway and onto the sand. It's not easy, running in wellies, or running on sand. Running in wellies on sand is near impossible. I decide to take them off, along with my socks. I sigh at the feel of the rough grains on bare skin. The beach is wet, and my feet will be coated in the stuff, but who cares? Not me!

Will the Beach Bar be open? I don't know, but I would love a coffee so I decide to take my chances. Tucking my socks into my wellies, I carry the boots one in each hand, swinging them as I go.

The sea is a swirling mass of dark grey-green right now and dotted with surfers, who may also be grateful for the day's wild weather. I can see that the lights are on in the Beach Bar, though the windows are shut. It's a never-ending job, cleaning those – even on the calmest of days, they end up sticky with salt spray and sand.

I leave my boots upside-down on the decking, push the door open and go in. It's not as quiet as I'd expected. There are a few sandy fair-weather surfers sitting around on the beanbags, and a family with three young children all looking at screens. The dad is reading a paper and the mum sipping a large coffee, just staring out of the window. It's quite a peaceful scene.

"Alice!" I hear Andrew's voice. "Where's Ben?"

"I escaped!" I laugh, pushing my hood back. "Just for a while. It's the first time I've been anywhere without him. It is kind of strange," I admit.

"Well, you'll be back with him soon enough, I'm sure. So make the most of this time, I say! What can I get you?"

"Please can I have a large decaf latte, and a glass of water?"

"Of course. Take a seat. I'll bring it over."

I move to one of the high seats at the end of the room, then change my mind and take a place on one of the comfy sofas, right by the window. The local paper is on the table in front of me, alongside a couple of magazines, but I place my phone down in clear view, just in case Sam needs me, then I ignore all sources of reading in favour of following that other mum's lead, just gazing out towards the sea. I quietly take long, deep breaths, sink back into the seat, and try to let the craziness of the last few weeks wash over me.

1

I couldn't take my eyes off Ben as he lay wrapped in his blanket, a soft yellow hat on his head, in the clear-sided hospital cot. At this point, he wasn't definitely Ben. Sam and I had compiled a shortlist, of boys' and girls' names, not knowing what to expect. We had both wanted a Cornish name, we knew that. And the moment I'd seen Ben, I'd known that was the name for him – but for a while I hadn't mentioned it, wanting to work out if Sam felt the same. We had both like Jago, too; but I had wondered if it sounded too posh – and it was also very close to Jacob, Kate and Isaac's little boy. It could be confusing for Sophie, who was already having to come to terms with having been an only child to now, in the space of one year, having two baby brothers.

Benesek, our boy's full name, seemed perfect. It could be shortened to a 'normal' name, but he could grow up knowing his Cornish heritage: Benesek is the Cornish form of Benedict, and means 'blessed'. What more could we ask for?

I was truly in a little bubble of happiness that day as it sunk in that I had really and truly become a mum. My parents came to see us, with hugs and soft exclamations, both with tears in their eyes, and a cuddly toy elephant under Dad's arm. He had nearly walked out with it.

"Phil!" Mum had exclaimed, gently extracting the elephant and placing it at the foot end of Ben's cot. She had taken my emotional dad's arm and led him away, turning to smile at me just before they were out of sight.

Ben's other grandmother, Sam's mum Karen, had also come, bringing a soft, floppy toy giraffe with her. She placed it next to the elephant. Sam drew the line there, keeping a strict limit on visitors.

"They'll see you both soon enough," he said. "You've got to rest now. And just get used to it all. So have I, come to that." He'd looked most put-out when one of the ward sisters had told him that he too would have to leave. I'd felt it, too. He'd been so fantastic throughout my labour, and I'd cried quiet tears when I'd seen him holding our son. It seemed cruel to make him leave, just when we should have all been together. But when the visitors were cast out, the maternity ward took on a different feeling. All women and babies; not a man in sight. Us new mums began to look up, towards each other, and ask tentative questions. Is it your first baby? Is it a boy or a girl? What's his/her name?

At lunchtime, we were encouraged to eat in the communal area, while the nurses kept an eye on the babies. That did feel strange, leaving my newborn son just when I'd finally got him in my sights. And I don't think I was the only one who rushed their way through lunch. Food didn't seem important. I just wanted to get back to my baby.

It was funny sitting with Becky – already knowing somebody who was there.

"Ben and Jasper!" she grinned. "My god, they already sound like a pair of trouble-makers! I'm going home after lunch, and I can't wait. Not that they haven't been great here but I just want to get back, be with Andy. Sleep in my own bed."

By the time afternoon visiting hours were upon us, I was desperate to be back home, too. It seemed as though Becky's words had triggered something in me and I didn't want to spend the night in hospital. Sam came with a bunch of flowers for me, and a handful of cards.

"Can you hang on to those, please? I want to come home," I said to him.

"Well, do then," he said. "If you're sure. Once you're out, you're out, you know."

"No, I definitely want to be home."

"OK. I'll go and get someone."

A midwife I hadn't met came to us shortly afterwards, and asked me lots of questions.

"Is he feeding ok?"

"Has he had a wet nappy?"

"Are you happy bathing him?"

"Did you have any stitches?"

She checked Ben over and seemed satisfied. "Do you have any questions for me?" she asked.

In my dazed state, I thought not. "I can always call the health visitor, can't I?" I asked, suddenly nervous, acutely aware that once we left the hospital the responsibility of this brand-new bundle of life was all mine – and of course Sam's.

"Yes, and you can call this ward if you need to. And the community midwife." She had smiled. "You're not on your own, Alice. But if you want to stay here tonight, you can."

"No, that's fine, thank you. As long as I know what to do if there's a problem, I'll be fine."

"OK, then – well hopefully Dad's brought the car seat with him?"

"I have," Sam smiled.

"Right, well get yourself packed up, and let us know when you're ready. Somebody will come to make sure the car seat's in OK and off you go!"

"Sophie's at home," Sam told me in quiet tones while I put my belongings in a bag. "She's going to be so chuffed you're coming back today! I told her you might not be able to."

"Your big sister," I said to Ben. "You're going to meet her. We're taking you home!"

I said my goodbyes to the other women in the bay, as Sam gently fastened Ben into the seat. A rush of doubts washed over me. What if I couldn't fasten him in properly? Or forgot to attach the seat correctly in the car? What if he forgot how to feed when we got home? Or he got ill and I didn't realise? After all, though he'd been in my belly for so many months, I had yet to know him as his own independent being. And I'd never looked after a baby before.

Sam had seemed to sense my anxiety. He'd straightened himself up, put his arms around me and pulled me into him. His familiar smell and warmth soothed me, and he kissed my forehead. "You are going to be great," he said. "*This* is going to be great."

Exhausted and elated, I'd smiled into his chest, knowing I wasn't alone.

***

My fears have so far proved unfounded; I quickly learned how to strap our little boy into his car seat, though we go out and about on foot more often; I've found that both he and I love using the sling, but that gently bumping him over the cobbled streets in his pram sends him to sleep. As for feeding; it's more a case of him not being able to stop. It's quite exhausting, particularly at night, and I've tried expressing my milk so that Sam can give him a bottle, but

Ben is having none of it.

I don't mind, mostly; it feels like a privilege to feed my baby this way, and I know it does not come easily, or at all, for everyone. But I do sometimes worry that he may never want to stop. And although we have everything covered at Amethi, with Mum and Jonathan doing an incredible job up there, as time moves on I find my mind is moving back there, just a little. I miss it. I miss the place, and my work, and I miss Julie more than ever. Sometimes I can't believe there are still another six months until she's back. If I think back to a year ago, we were battling that horrible situation with Tony, with his nasty campaign against us; or me, to be precise. Yet again, I think, my world has changed entirely in the space of twelve months.

Kate and Isaac have moved to Devon with Jacob; Sophie has moved in with me and Sam; Julie and Luke have gone to India... and that is not all. Bea has left Cornwall for a life in America with Bob, while Karen has returned here from Spain. Mum and Dad have taken over the Sail Loft; David and Martin have adopted Esme; Jonathan is covering for Julie at Amethi, and he's going out with Sam's sister, Janie. Sam, Sophie and I are living in Mum and Dad's house – which used to be David's – back in town, while Jonathan is in the little cottage at Amethi. Oh, and I've become a mum. In just one year. That is ridiculous.

I seem to remember hoping that after all the stuff with Tony things would settle down. I've learned my lesson there. Maybe we will have a quiet and settled time now, but I'm not taking anything for granted.

***

When I return from my wind-blown walk by the sea, that little glimpse of blue that I'd spotted has widened, and the rain has stopped. Though it is still blowy, the wind has died down, too. Nevertheless, my hair is sopping, and I'm glad to be inside, pulling off my boots and coat, and shaking myself like a dog.

Sam appears in the lounge doorway. "Shh!" he smiles. "He's still sleeping."

"Still?" I ask, suddenly scared. Ben does not sleep for this long. Before Sam has had a chance to answer, I am on the stairs.

"He's fine," I hear Sam say, "I've been to check on him, more than once."

Nevertheless, I have to see for myself. I swing round the landing, up to our son's room. I open the door slowly and gently, and flood with relief as I see his chest moving up and down rhythmically with his breath. I smile at the sight of his chubby, dimpled legs and arms. I feel Sam behind me, his hands on my waist.

"See?" he asks quietly and I can feel his smile; hear it in his voice.

"Yes, OK," I say, and turn to move out of Ben's room. Sam is still standing there. Very quietly, and gently, he kisses me. I feel invigorated from my walk; refreshed by some time to myself. The touch of Sam's hand and lips reawakens something in me, which I haven't felt for some time. I kiss him back, slowly and carefully, and I push my fingers under his t-shirt. He jumps, as goose pimples break out over his skin.

"Your hands are freezing!" he exclaims softly into my ear.

"I know," I laugh, kissing him again and gently pushing him away from the doorway towards our room.

He looks at me, as if to check my meaning. I smile. He opens the door.

The baby starts crying.

"Bloody hell," Sam says, kissing my neck and wrapping his arms around me. "If that's not just typical…"

But the sound of my son has prompted another reaction in me and with the briefest squeeze of Sam's hands I extricate myself from him and move into the soft sunlight of our baby's room, exclaiming softly to him. I pick Ben up, careful to keep those cold hands away from his skin, and press his warmth to me, kissing the soft top of his head and feeling the milk flow fill my breasts, ready to go again.

2

"How was your walk, Alice?" Mum asks, settling herself at the dinner table. Her slightly wistful looks around the house have not escaped my notice. With her and Dad living and working at the Sail Loft, plus her filling in for me at Amethi, I think she is in need of some space, and some time to herself, as much as I have been.

"Oh, it was lovely, so lovely. Even though it was raining, and windy, and grey."

"Tell me about it! We've got a hotel full of grumpy guests at the moment."

"At least it is full," Dad says.

I look at him. "Are you having problems?"

"No, no," he answers, a little too quickly for my liking. "I think we just have to build up our reputation. You know, Bea was there for so long, people were coming back to see her as much as the hotel, I think. It's definitely put a few people off."

"But you've still got Stef to keep things on track," I say.

"That's true. And he is brilliant." Mum says firmly, then changes the subject. "So how about that baby group you said you were going to try?"

I squirm slightly uncomfortably. "I haven't been yet."

"Alice…"

"I know I said I would. And I will. But I like being home with Ben. And we see Becky, and Jasper, don't we?" I look across at Ben, who is propped up contentedly in Dad's arms, like a buttery Buddha.

"But it will do you good to get out a bit, you know. And

Ben, too. Meet some more mums, and babies."

"And dads…" Dad suggests.

"Yes, and dads, Phil. Not that I remember you going to any baby groups when Alice was little."

"I was at work…"

"As was I! Anyway, let's not get into that. I just think it would do you good, love. Give that one at the church hall a go. It's only an hour or two. If it's awful, you can just leave and not go back again."

"Alright, alright."

"Excellent. Now, I was wondering if we could get Ben one of those bimbo seats. Have you seen them? Ben will be able to go in it when he's three months. Then he can sit in it on the table while you and Sam eat. And there are ones with little activity stations…"

"Sounds expensive, Sue," Dad says.

"Also, they're called Bumbos, Mum!"

"That's what I said!" she protests. "Anyway, the price isn't too bad, I've been researching them. And you can buy them second-hand, though I don't really think I'd want our little Ben in a second-hand one."

"It's fine," I say. "Sam and I are really happy to have second-hand stuff, but don't worry about buying one for us, Mum, I'm sure I can pick one up from eBay, or the local Facebook group or something. Tell you what, I'll ask at the baby group on Wednesday."

"You'll go?" Mum asks, a wide smile on her face.

"Yes, I'll go," I say grudgingly. "But that doesn't mean I'll like it."

"I think it's a good idea," Sam says later, after my parents have left. "You never know, you might meet some new friends."

"I don't want new friends," I say, feeling like I'm

Sophie's age. "I've got perfectly good ones already. Becky and David cover the friends-who-are-also-parents angle, and Julie will be back soon, too. I don't want to be friends with somebody else just because they happen to be a mum. Or a dad," I add.

"There won't be many men at those groups," Sam laughs. "Or at least there weren't when Soph was a baby. I took her to the Sure Start, a couple of times, and I was the only bloke there. None of the women wanted to talk to me."

"You see?" I exclaim triumphantly. "They're horrible things, those groups."

"It wasn't all bad. The people who worked there were excellent and gave me and Kate loads of support. Shame it's closed now."

"But the church one's going to be different, isn't it? What if we have to say prayers, and listen to Bible stories?"

"It won't be like that!"

"How do you know?"

"Just give it a go!" he says.

"Fine," I mock-huff. Ben gurgles. "Don't know what you're laughing at," I say. "You've got to come with me."

On Wednesday morning, Sam goes to work and I pack the changing bag with spare nappies, cotton wool, Sudocrem, a babygro and vest (I have learned my lesson from going out entirely unprepared, having had to put Ben back into a dirty bodysuit when his nappy had failed to contain its contents. I felt like a bad mum that day).

Summer has returned in full force, so I slip the sling on over my t-shirt – no need for a jacket – and away we go. I feel slightly nervous, which is silly, I know. I run an award-winning business, for goodness' sake, with new guests every single week, and I host courses. I have to be sociable. I have to be confident. Yet somehow I feel unprepared for Baby Group.

The minute I walk in, however, a kind-looking woman of about my age comes over. She looks familiar, as most people do in this town.

"Hi there," she smiles. "I don't think we've seen you here before. Although I think I know your face…"

"I was just thinking that about you," I smile. "I'm Alice, and this is Ben." I peel the sling back slightly so his face is visible. He is awake and looks at me, unimpressed.

"Hi, Ben. I'm Sarah, and those are my two over there." She gestures towards a pair of small identical boys, playing with a big red plastic car.

"Twins!" I exclaim.

"I know!" she laughs. "It took a bit of getting used to. But then I think becoming a mum does, anyway. Here. Would you like a cup of tea? If you'd like, I can hold Ben while you sit and relax a bit."

"Thank you," I say, and follow her to the kitchen area. I am suspicious that once she has Ben in her arms she will start to try and talk me into coming to church. But I would like a cup of tea, so I sit on one of the plastic chairs set against the wall and extricate Ben from his sling, turning him so he is resting his back against me, looking at all the goings on in the church hall. There are about twenty toddlers and crawling babies in all, and their parents (OK, mums, Sam was right about the lack of males) are sitting in groups, chatting or playing with the kids on the floor. The sunshine outside makes the windows glow and it feels nice in here. Sarah brings out a mug, exchanging it for my baby.

"Hello," she smiles widely at him, "aren't you beautiful?"

I'm not about to be won over that easily, with

compliments to my baby. Although, he is beautiful.

"And what do you do, Alice, when you're not being a mum?"

"I'm a small business owner," I say, quite proud that I am able to tell people that, whilst also scared of sounding a bit pompous.

"Oh yeah?"

"Yeah, me and my friend, Julie, run a place just up out of town. It's a sort of self-catering place. We do yoga retreats and…"

"You don't mean Amethi?"

"Yes! You've heard of it?"

"I know it well! Or in its previous guise. My friend grew up there, and I used to go for sleepovers! Then they had to sell, unfortunately, and I think it changed hands a couple of times before you and your friend bought it."

I still find it amazing how everybody seems to know everything around here. And yet I know so little.

"I can't believe that! You'll have to come and see it as it is now," I find myself suggesting before I've even thought about what I'm saying. I don't know a thing about Sarah yet. But she does seem nice.

"I would love that!"

"So what do you do, Sarah?"

"Oh, all sorts. I mean, not really, at the moment… I don't really have time for anything, with these two, and their dad's not on the scene anymore, so it's just me and them. But I try, when I can, to do a bit of writing, if Mum can have the boys, about interior design, which is something I should actually be *doing*. But it seems like nobody wants to employ a single mum of twin toddlers."

"That sounds about right," I sympathise. "Though the writing sounds interesting."

"Ha! Yes, it can be… depends what it's about. I shouldn't complain, though, it means I can be a mum during the day and still get to do some work and earn a bit of cash."

"And your time for yourself is…?" I think of Sam's insistence on me going for a walk at the weekend.

"Well," she leans towards me slightly, conspiratorially, "I shouldn't say this because it'll almost certainly jinx it, but I've somehow managed to get them into a routine of napping at the same time in the afternoon. I give them their lunch, then I give them a bottle each, and we watch a bit of *In the Night Garden*, and I pop them in their cots and off they go."

"What, they just go to sleep?"

"Yes!" she laughs. "I take it Ben's not quite as easy to get off?"

"You could say that."

"It'll happen. They were a nightmare – Rory in particular. But we've got there, over time. And once they're napping, I'm on that settee, got a movie lined up, might have a doze. Possibly a cup of tea. But that is it. My time."

"Sounds pretty great," I say.

"It is… till they wake up again!"

We both laugh. "So, do you… go to this church?"

"Me? No! I'm a non-believer. Did you think I was trying to entice you into becoming part of the congregation?"

"No," I say too quickly, and look at her laughing brown eyes. "Well, maybe," I admit. "I did have my doubts about coming here."

"I get that, but honestly, these groups are a life-saver. We're all in the same boat, you know. And yes, you get the yummy mummies, and the ones who've read every book going, but most of us are just making it up as we go along and it really helps – especially if your kid's not sleeping. Or he's poorly. Most of us will have been through something similar. And at the very least, you get to drink a cup of tea while somebody else holds your baby."

I look at my cup. It's empty. "That was good," I admit.

"There you go, then. Stick that on the counter, and I'll introduce you to some of the others."

I do as I'm told and I follow Sarah to a small group of mums and babies. Sarah makes such quick introductions I can't remember anyone's name but I kneel on the floor, Ben on my lap, and I see how interested in everything he is. And I realise how friendly these people are. And what a wide-ranging group of people. There is a teacher, a doctor, a stay-at-home mum, a supermarket shelf-stacker. We are all different people, yet we all share the same slightly shell-shocked reality that no longer are we just ourselves; now we are responsible for these little people in our arms, or playing around us. A little boy pushes a toy car into my leg.

"Sorry!" says his mum.

"No problem," I smile at her, and the boy, and I push the car fast so that he laughs.

I feel like I am quite quiet, as a newcomer, but the others are friendly and I'm surprised when I see that it's 11.30. Time to go home.

As we walk through the sunshine, I feel really pleased that I went. I liked Sarah, and the others, and even if we might not be best friends, I can see now how good that camaraderie is. On the way back, though, I can feel Ben becoming restless and when we get in I know he is desperate to be fed. I wriggle him out of the sling and take it off. It's a relief to both of us when he begins to feed. I watch as he sucks greedily, then more slowly, his eyes closing briefly then his mouth working again as he remembers what he's doing. But before long he is fully asleep and I gently detach him from me, carrying him up to his room and laying him gently in the cot.

Going back down the stairs, I think of Sarah's 'me time' and I put on the kettle, make a cup of tea and a sandwich, and go back into the lounge. I can't face daytime TV so I put on Netflix and choose something new. *The Good Place*. Once I've eaten my sandwich, and drunk my tea, I lie back on the settee and just relax into this very special, very much needed, time to myself.

3

In September, the town is still humming with tourists and I find myself out and about much more – with Ben, of course. We are now regulars at the church hall baby group, and have even been tagged on to a weekly get-together of mums who take it in turns to have the rest of the group round to their house. This largely consists of coffee, cake, nappy-changing, and swapping stories either for everyone else's amusement or as a shared experience which we might all learn from.

It's my turn to have everyone next week, and I am looking forward to it. Maybe even a bit excited.

"You see!" Mum had said, smiling. "I don't mean to say I told you so but…"

"Yeah, yeah!"

I can't help but think of Julie, though – how she would see these cosy mother-and-baby chats, and might feel left out to know I'm in a particular social group that she, at present, has no place in. But that's not to say she resents me being a mother, no matter how hard it might be for her. Whenever we speak on a video-call, I love showing Ben off to her, because I know she wants to see him.

She's already set me straight on this: "Alice, Ben is the most important thing in your life. You are one of the most important people in mine—"

"Only 'one of'?" I had tutted.

"Look, of course you are the most important person in my life, don't tell Luke," she'd grinned across thousands of miles at me. "But what I am *trying* to say is that I am one hundred per cent happy for you and I need to know Ben; I want to know Ben. I can't believe I can't meet him in person yet."

"Julie, are you tearing up?" I could see her looking a bit emotional.

"Maybe." She had sniffed and smiled. "It's just been so long since I've seen you. And you've gone through this huge thing – are still going through this huge thing, which I feel like I should be part of."

"Wherever you are, my friend, however long it's been since we've seen each other, you are always part of whatever I'm doing."

"You're tearing up, too!" she'd exclaimed gleefully.

"Oh god, I am, aren't I?" We had both laughed, and I'd been grateful to her that she didn't want me to hide Ben away or tread on eggshells around her. Not that I'd ever expect Julie to be like that but I feel so strongly for her, in wanting to have a baby and not yet having been able to. I can only begin to imagine what that must be like.

Still, despite what I know is her very genuine interest in, and care for, Ben, and me – and Ben and me as a pair – I can still imagine what she might think about these new social situations I've become involved in. I think I know, because I know how I felt before them. But that was before I became a mum.

I could never say that to Julie either, though; we used to laugh at that one: *You'll understand when you've got kids.*

People love coming out with stuff like that. It's so rude, and presumptuous. Like assuming a single person must be looking for a partner. It's the smug side of being a parent and I often check in with myself to make sure I'm not heading down that road.

But Julie is in India, and I am here. She is living a very

different life to mine right now and we both have to do what we have to do. She is due back in February and that can't come soon enough as far as I'm concerned, yet at the same time that means Ben will be eight months old, and I'll be heading back to work and these beautiful days at the very start of his life will already be over.

Oh no, I'm getting all misty-eyed again. That's another thing since becoming a mum. I've become so emotional. And when I hear horrible things on the news I apply them to Ben, and it strikes fear into my heart. Sam laughs at me when I turn the news off.

"It's all real, though, Alice. You can't pretend it's not happening."

"I know that. I just don't want to think about it right now. Not when he's so small, and new, and untainted by any of that."

Climate change, knife crime, terrorism, people-trafficking. The list goes on. How can those things and my tiny, perfect boy possibly exist in the same world? I want to hold him to me forever and never let any harm come to him. Ever.

*****

In late September comes the Autumn equinox and Lizzie is running a yoga residential to celebrate this. Since the winter solstice week, last December, we decided to run four yoga weeks a year, falling on the solstices and equinoxes. It may seem a bit pagan, but people from all walks of life seem to enjoy it. I love the focus Lizzie puts on nature, and giving people a chance to step outside their normal lives, into the stripped-back, real world.

I am starting to sound like Lizzie, I think, but that's not

necessarily a bad thing. I remember when Julie and I first met her; she became Kate's maternity leave replacement and I think it is fair to say we both had our doubts. In appearance, Lizzie is slightly wild; all frizzy hair and woolly ponchos – and she does have a tendency to cast wise-seeming sayings about, which can make it hard to keep a straight face – but she has taught me such a lot, in her outlook on life and the world in general. She is relaxed and open to all sorts of people yet does not mind that not everyone will be as open-minded towards, and accepting of, her.

"Why don't you join us for the week, Alice? You and Ben come up for the days."

"I couldn't do yoga with Ben about…"

"Why not? If he starts crying, you break off, pick him up. Or someone else will."

"My pelvic floor…"

"Exactly! Your pelvic floor! Let's get it back to how it was, shall we? And give yourself a break. It'll be just what you need, I promise."

And so here I am, up at Amethi. And I'm so glad to be here. I step out of the car. There is still the subtle salty tang of the sea on the air up here but there is also an earthiness which isn't present in town. As Ben is fast asleep in his car seat, I take a moment to walk to the fence and look across the wildflower meadows, which have taken on a deeper colour now than in the spring, but which are still teeming with insects, the sun catching their iridescent, translucent wings as they flit and crowd busily across the tops of golden grasses. The trees which mark the boundary of Amethi are a darker green now than their lush spring vibrancy and I can hear the jackdaws squawking in their branches. I lean against the rough wood of the fence and breathe deeply.

"Alice!" I hear Mum's voice before I see her. She is rounding the corner into the car park.

"Hi Mum," I go across to see her. "Are you OK?"

"Yes, I'm fine," I can see she is slightly flustered, "I've just been making sure everything's all set for the yogis."

I think sometimes that Mum has taken on too much, what with the Sail Loft and covering here. It seems ridiculous that she and Dad are employing Stef to manage their business, while Mum is effectively managing mine. And we can't afford to pay her what they are paying Stef, so they are losing money.

"You look tired," I say.

"Thanks!" she laughs.

"You know what I mean. Are you sure you're alright?" Mum had some heart problems a few years back and, while she assures me she is fully recovered, it's hard to forget this. I know Dad worries about her.

"I'm fine, I promise. Now where's that little boy?"

"He's sleeping," I find myself whispering for some reason.

We tiptoe together towards the car, as quietly as it's possible on the crunchy gravel. I don't know why we're bothering; though he might not be easy to get off to sleep, once he is there is very little that will wake Ben. I can't help smiling as we look together through the car window. I'm so proud of him and feel like I'm allowed to be fully so when I'm with Mum because I know she loves him almost as much as I do.

"Oh, look at him," she says.

"I know."

"I wish I could have a cuddle."

"Well I'm going to have to get him out so I can go and see Lizzie."

"You don't have to do that. Tell you what, why don't I sit in the car with him while you go and find her? If he wakes, I'll bring him to you. Seems a shame to disturb him."

"Weren't you about to go back home?"

"Oh yes, but that can wait."

"Are you sure?"

"Yes! Go on, Lizzie's looking forward to seeing you, and I know you'll want to cast your eye over everything."

I grin. She's right. Not that I don't trust her, but it feels important to me that this is still my place. That I take the responsibility for making sure our guests are happy.

I hug her. "Thanks, Mum."

I try to tread lightly as I walk away, while Mum very carefully opens the car door and climbs into the passenger seat. I pass the little two-bed house that came with the business, where I lived with Sam, and then Sam and Sophie, and where Jonathan now lives.

My aim is to get to the Mowhay. This is the new name for the communal area, inspired by Hilary, one of the writers from the last course we ran.

"Don't you think 'communal area' sounds a bit awkward and clunky? Why don't you call it something that fits with Amethi? Something Cornish?"

I spoke to Julie about it and we asked Sam and Luke for suggestions. In the end, it was Karen who came up with the winning word. "Mowhay. It means barn, I think."

"It sounds like a dance," said Julie when I put the name to her. "I like it."

"Me too." And so, the name has stuck.

Before I get there, though, I see that the door from the kitchen is wide open and I can hear the rhythmic sound of chopping.

"Hello there!" I poke my head inside.

"Alice!" Jonathan looks round and smiles. "How are you?"

"I'm very well, thank you."

"You look it." He looks me up and down, and I feel slightly shy. "You'd never know you'd just had a baby."

"What a line!"

"I know." He has the good grace to look sheepish. "But it's true. You look great."

"Why, thank you."

I notice he doesn't ask about Ben. I don't think he is at that point yet, where the natural thing would be to wonder where somebody's baby or kid is. Jon and Janie – Sam's sister – are still in the fledgling days of their relationship. It's lovely, actually. After Jon had his heart broken by Lydia, which I secretly think was payback for him messing around countless other women over the years (but don't tell him I said that), he became quite down. This time last year, he was harbouring thoughts of leaving Cornwall. But much has changed since then and I hope he's going to stay, although come the new year, Julie will be back and his work at Amethi will be over. What will Jon do then? And what will we do, with the cottage? Could he stay on there and work somewhere else? I don't know. I did think it worked, me being on site, and since Sam and I moved into town, it's been great to know that Jonathan is here. Julie and Luke have a beautiful big house in town so there is no way they're going to want to live here when they come back. But there is even less chance of my family of four fitting into the cottage.

Now we have Ben, I can't believe I ever thought that might have been a possibility. I mean, of course, people do live in much smaller places; we are ridiculously lucky to have the chance to live in Mum and Dad's huge house in town, I know that. Let's just say it wouldn't be ideal, for the four of us to try and squeeze into a two-bed house. Sophie is fourteen; she can't be expected to share a room with Ben, and nor should she. She is struggling enough with being apart from her mum. Co-habiting with a screaming baby might just finish her off.

I shake the thoughts from my head. This is not for now. Though it can't wait much longer.

"I'd better go and find Lizzie," I say to Jon.

"Of course. She's just setting up in the Mowhay."

"You going to do any of the yoga?" I ask, smiling.

"Nah, not really my thing."

"You might surprise yourself."

"Yeah, I might, but… nah."

"Suit yourself! I'll catch up with you in a bit."

I find Lizzie making the place look beautiful. A long string of fairy lights hangs above the bifold doors, and almost every surface bears a battery-powered candle or lantern. On the floor are fourteen yoga kits – a rolled up mat, a blanket, a block and a bolster. I watch from the doorway as she moves one of these ever so slightly, standing back and looking around then moving the one behind it so that they are in a near-perfect line with each other.

"You're not getting OCD, are you?"

"Alice!" Lizzie turns, smiles and comes to hug me. "Where's Ben?"

"In the car, with Mum."

"You've got a few minutes to yourself, then. That's nice. Isn't your mum fantastic?"

"I'm quite biased on that one but yes, she is."

"I've been trying to convince her to join us, too."

"Good luck with that! Though I think it would do her good."

"Yes, I've noticed she's got a lot of weight on her shoulders at the moment."

"I'm glad you didn't say my hips." Mum appears at the doorway, Ben in her arms. "Sorry, I wasn't earwigging… I just came to say this little one's woken up, and I think he wants his mummy."

Ben's face is red and angry but he's already spotted me and is kind of twisting towards me, urgently, as if he can will my mum to walk this way. As it turns out, he can.

"Alright, alright," she laughs, and brings him over.

I take him into my arms, feeling that familiar sensation of all being right with the world now I am holding my baby. I also feel the all-too-familiar sensation of my milk coming in, and I move to the seating at the edge of the room so I can sit in comfort and feed him.

Once he's latched on, I look at Mum, who has come to sit next to me. "*Are* you alright?"

Lizzie is back to busying herself with the already perfect layout of the room so I feel I can talk to Mum quietly.

"I'm fine, Alice," Mum pats my knee. "It was always going to be tough, starting a new business."

"The Sail Loft? Are you enjoying it, though?" I feel a strong tie with the place where I used to work but I know the difficulties involved in managing it – and from Amethi I know how hard it is, starting a new business.

"Yes, mostly!" she laughs unconvincingly.

"I think you're doing too much, Mum. You shouldn't be working here when you're trying to get your own business started."

"But it's not a start-up. Bea did that. It's an established business. And besides, I love it here."

"I'm glad you do," I smile, "but you're going to end up split in two if you carry on the way you are." I notice the dark circles under her eyes. "And you do look tired. Dad does, too – when I see him." It strikes me that it's been a while since I have seen Dad, and that when I do it's usually because I have gone to see him at the hotel. He's become the breakfast chef, which I think he loves, though Mum says she has to shoo him back into the kitchen because he enjoys talking to the guests.

"We are tired!" she laughs again. "But that's to be expected. I didn't go into this with my eyes closed – neither did Phil. This is a tough year, for sure, but that's OK."

"As long as you're not making yourself ill, though, Mum. And I've been thinking, I'm going to try and get up here a bit more now that this little one and I have settled."

"You're not coming back to work yet, though, Alice. This is your one chance to have these baby days with Ben – make the most of them."

"I will, and I do, I promise. But I need to be planning ahead, for next year, and for Julie coming back, and to be honest, I miss it. It always hits me, just how much I miss it, when I come up here."

"It is a special place," Mum says, looking around. Lizzie has stepped outside and we can see her on the gravelled area, now shifting the tables, chairs and benches about. "I should go and help her," Mum says.

"No. You just sit for a while. Lizzie's strong as an ox. She'll be fine."

"OK, I'll do as I'm told," Mum smiles and sinks back a little in her seat. "And maybe I will try and join in the yoga when I can. But won't you need somebody to take Ben if he's crying?"

"It's fine, Mum. If he's crying, I'll take care of it. He's

my responsibility, and I'll take him off to feed him, or go for a walk or something whenever he needs me. Whatever Lizzie says, I don't think our guests have paid to come on this course only to have it ruined by a screaming baby!"

"OK," Mum says again, and I feel pleased that she's listened to me. That for once it's me helping her.

I am really happy to be able to greet the guests when they arrive, and to send Mum back into town, to see Dad and hopefully put her feet up for a little while.

There are a couple of familiar faces amongst the course participants but most are newcomers. I'm able to give them the tour of Amethi and show them to their accommodation, all with Ben strapped to my front in his sling.

I love people's reactions to Amethi. Mum is right, it is a special place, and I feel like with every event like this it becomes a bit more special. Aside from the writing retreats, for the rest of the time the accommodation is just holiday rentals, with the bonus of a chef onsite (usually Julie, currently Jonathan) and somebody to help organise and plan days and evenings out. Sometimes Lizzie comes to do private yoga classes, too.

I have said it before, and I will no doubt say it again, but to run a business with the sole purpose of making people feel good is quite a privilege. But also a huge responsibility.

Luckily, Cindy, our housekeeper, is incredible, reliable and thorough. As I take Mandy and Ruby, a pair of friends who are here for the first time, up to their rooms, they are full of compliments and admiration.

"This is so nice," says Ruby.

"And not a spot of dust," Mandy runs her finger along the top of a picture frame. "You'd do well on *Four in a Bed.*"

"I couldn't think of anything worse!" I laugh.

"How do you do all this, with your little one?" she gestures towards Ben.

"I don't, not really. I've got a great support team, who are doing pretty much everything at the moment. But I like to be here, too, when I can. It doesn't feel like work, really."

"No, it's definitely different to sitting at a computer all day," Ruby wriggles her shoulders. "I cannot wait to get into the yoga, I feel like all my muscles need a holiday."

"Lizzie can work you pretty hard!" I warn. "But she's also excellent at the relaxation and meditation parts. You're going to love it. Now, I'll leave you to get settled in, and I'll see you over at the Mowhay whenever you're ready. There's an official welcome for you all from Lizzie at five, and you'll get to meet the others then, too."

"Thanks, Alice," Mandy calls from her room. I can hear the bed springs as she falls onto the mattress. "Oh my god, this is so comfy. I might not make it to any yoga. I might just stay here all week."

"That's completely fine, too," I laugh, "though I promise you won't want to miss out on Lizzie's classes. She is brilliant."

I blink as I exit the house into the daylight. Ben is curled into me and as I always do, I check he is breathing, that his little face isn't pressed too hard against me. Every day he is getting stronger, and while he still relies on me – or Sam – for his every need, it's good to see him growing, and strengthening; using his strengthening neck muscles to hold his head up. Reaching for things that he wants (though it can be painful when he's got a handful of my hair) and, best of all, smiling and laughing, and beginning to make sounds of his own volition. I cannot begin to explain how lucky I feel to have him and, even though having a child is one of the most natural things in the world, just how special this feels.

It makes me think about Julie even more, and hope that it's her turn soon.

I've spoken to Kate a lot since having Ben – or, more correctly, we have messaged each other frequently. Sophie's mum, she's already been there and bought the t-shirt when it comes to having a baby, but she has started again with Jacob and with her and Isaac starting their own business in Devon, we can trade advice and support. I can put her mind at ease about her daughter, too.

I have been really impressed with Sophie and how she's coped with her mum being a couple of hours away, and of course becoming a big sister. I know it is not easy, though, for her or for Kate.

Kate will ask me every day how Sophie is and I've learned to be honest. If Sophie is having a bad day, I'll tell her. Early on, I made the mistake of trying to cover it up but as it turned out, Sophie had been really horrible to Kate on the phone so while I was there trying to say Sophie was happy as could be, Kate was wondering why, in that case, her daughter was being as she was. When Sophie came to me in tears, saying she had been mean to her mum, we called Kate back, and straightened it out.

I'm sorry, Kate, I'd messaged her later. **I didn't want you worrying about Sophie but I could tell she'd had a bad day at school. I realise now that it would have been better if I'd told you that. She was obviously just taking it out on you.**

Ha, well that is something I definitely have experience of! I can't believe I've done this, sometimes. I mean, I love it here. And I love Isaac and Jacob, of course. But I miss home. And I miss Soph like you wouldn't believe.

I completely believe it. Don't worry. She'll be up to see you at the weekend. And she misses you, too. You know that. But I will make sure she is safe and well – and Sam does that, of course. Any problems, I promise I will let you know xx

Thank u Alice, I appreciate that. I feel like such a bad Mum xx

You are far from it, I promise xx

When Isaac had made the shock announcement that he and Kate had bought the business in Devon, there had been no time to process it properly, as it was at almost the exact moment that Kate's waters had broken. She and Isaac – and Lizzie! Isaac was three sheets to the wind – had been whisked off to hospital while Sophie had stormed off, Sam following her. It had later been put to Sophie that she could choose whether to go to Devon with her mum, or stay in Cornwall with Sam and me. She had chosen the latter – but I wouldn't say she chose us over Kate. I think wanting to be with her friends played as much of a part in her decision, including her new boyfriend, Josh.

When I was Sophie's age, if I'd had a boyfriend it would last about two weeks before fizzling out, and nothing would happen differently except that we were boyfriend and girlfriend in name. No dates. No hand-holding. No kissing. Which wasn't the same for all my peers, including Julie – already an experienced kisser by the age of thirteen – but I don't think I felt ready for anything else at the time. With Sophie, it is different. I have seen her holding hands with Josh but it's not so much about that as about their strong friendship. They spend every Wednesday evening together, with Josh coming to us or, more often, Sophie going to his place. And when we went to the tourism awards ceremony in Bristol, Josh and his mum Sharon came with us.

At weekends, they hang out in a large group of teenagers, in the park, on the beach, or at one of the cafes. It's hard for them, in a way – everywhere is so expensive, but the beach is free. It does get incredibly busy, though. Sam has cautioned me – and Sophie – about the very specific risks to teenagers growing up by the sea. The dangers of clifftop parties and crazy activities like 'tombstoning'. I remember very well how invincible you can feel as a teen, and how the world just begins to open up. There is more freedom, and so many hormones flowing that it's not always easy to make good decisions. But I am happy Sophie has Josh, and they seem to be pretty sensible, as do most of their friends. I just worry that their relationship can't go on forever; well, it could, but it seems the odds are against them. I know a few people who have been together since they were fifteen or sixteen, but thirteen… It seems unlikely, somehow. Although anything is possible, I suppose. What happens if they split up? We will just have to deal with that if and when it happens.

For now, if I see her and her mates out and about around town, I try to avoid them; give her some space. But if I am spotted, she will give me a friendly wave. I guess it's a bonus of being an almost-stepmother. I'm not embarrassing in the way I might be if I was her actual mum. Although there is nothing embarrassing about Kate, who is tall and slender and always so well turned-out.

When I met her and Sophie, she'd been very much concerned with her appearance but while her attitude has mellowed somewhat, there is still a bar below which she wouldn't dream of dropping. Sadly for me, I think at my highest standard I can probably barely reach that bar, even if I stand on my tiptoes.

Over the few years I've been back in Cornwall, my family has grown and I consider Kate, Isaac and Jacob family, as well as Sophie, of course. Sam and I have added our own little contribution in the shape of Ben. When Karen came back to Cornwall, I gained a mother-almost-in-law, and a sister in Janie. I feel very lucky to have all these people, not to mention my friends. Life is good right now and I don't want to take anything for granted.

4

"Josh has dumped me," Sophie sobs into my shoulder. I'd heard her familiar sounds on the doorstep – largely rummaging around in her oversized bag for her keys – just as I was bringing Ben downstairs from his nap, so I'd opened the front door for her and she'd practically fallen in, her face grief-stricken and streaked with tears.

"He's… what?" I shift Ben onto my left shoulder, so I can put my right arm around Sophie. "Oh no, Soph. I am so sorry."

She is crying like I've never known before; not even when Kate left for Devon.

"Come on," I say, shepherding her through to the lounge, aware that Ben is restlessly trying to manoeuvre his way down to the source of milk but also aware that right now I need to give Sophie my best attention. She doesn't need to feel as though she's not my priority.

In her heartbroken state, she is easily led and obedient. She comes with me and sits next to me, heavily.

"Soph," I say, "I am really sorry, let me just get Ben feeding then I can give you my full attention and we won't be bothered by him, OK?"

"OK."

She is so subdued, I'd rather she seemed annoyed with me. What can have happened to split them up? Have I somehow brought it about by casting doubts on the longevity of their relationship?

The familiar relief, as Ben starts to feed, greedily. I look to Sophie again.

"So, what happened?"

"He said… he said it wasn't me, it was him."

Ah, that old chestnut.

I wait, while she calms herself enough to talk some more. Her blue eyes, which are eerily like Sam's despite the fact he has no biological claim to this amazing girl, are spilling tears. I want to put both my arms around her, let her sob into my shoulder until she has no tears left to cry, but Ben has staked his claim on me. Instead, I hold her hand with my free one, gently stroking her soft skin with my thumb.

"I asked if there was somebody else and he said no but I've seen him, this summer, seen him with Annabel Fenwick. She's a Year 9," she says in disgust.

I am tempted to say that Sophie herself was a Year 9 until July, and has only been a Year 10 for about two weeks, but now doesn't seem the right time. And I feel like any righteous indignation she has will be good for her.

"But he didn't say he was with her?"

"No." She sobs again, clearly the words being spoken out loud, a suggestion of Josh being with somebody else, are too much to take.

"Then believe him," I urge, although I am not sure I do. "Soph, I'm so sorry. I remember just what this all feels like. It is awful. It feels like the worst thing in the world, and I know it won't just go away. I remember the first time my heart was broken – I was a little bit older than you, at fifteen – and it completely floored me. It knocked my confidence, I felt unwanted and horrible, and like nobody would want me again." Am I saying the right things, or just putting ideas in her head? Those blue eyes meet mine again. She is listening. "I know how annoying it is when adults say they've been through what you're going through. I'm not trying to say I know it all. I just know how you feel right now. And I can tell you that I did get through it; I did have other boyfriends – not too many of course," I add on behalf of Sam, "but I did. And then of course I met your dad, when I was eighteen."

"And you fell in love," she says and I think I see her eyes glimmer in hope.

"We did, but," I caution, "that wasn't altogether easy. Remember, we didn't see each other for ten years. And you know what happened a few years back, when your dad was away in Wales. We didn't think we'd make it through that." Do not allude to the role Sophie played in that, I think. Don't make her feel any worse than she already does. "But even after we'd first met… you know I used to live upcountry, quite near Birmingham?"

"Yes."

"Well, I met Sam one summer, down here, and then I had to go back home. And go to university. I mean, I didn't have to, I wanted to. But I also wanted to stay here with your dad."

There is a small smile on Sophie's face.

"That was the autumn when he had that accident, and ended up in hospital. And I didn't know what had happened. I didn't hear from him. We did have mobiles then, but not like the ones we have now. He had lost my number when his phone was damaged in the crash and I just thought he wasn't interested any more. I was completely heartbroken."

I feel Ben pulling away from my left breast; I need to swap him to the other side but I don't want to let go of Sophie.

However, the brilliant girl knows the drill. She's seen Kate do this with Jacob many times, too. "Does he need to swap?" she says, keeping her eyes strictly averted from

Ben. She's not so grown up that she wants to inadvertently see her stepmother's nipple.

"If you don't mind, sorry."

Sophie obligingly stands and comes round to the other side of me, sitting close and leaning her head on my shoulder. I manage to plant a kiss on the top of her head. Ben gets going again and we sit in peace for a while. I wonder what Josh is up to? I feel righteous anger at him for breaking Sophie's heart. But he is fourteen. He is entitled to end a relationship if he isn't happy in it anymore. He could have come up with some more original words but I guess it's his first time dumping somebody.

My heart goes out to Sophie, who seems smaller than usual, somehow. I can feel her body quiver every now and then, as she tries to suppress her sobs.

"I tell you what, Soph. I know this isn't going to change anything but once Ben's finished feeding how about me, you and him go out to the beach? Then stop and get pizza on the way home? We can watch a film tonight if you like; your choice."

Her head lifts from my shoulder. "I don't know…" she sniffs.

"I know," I interject. "You probably don't feel like going out anywhere. You might want to go up to your room and cry it all out. Which isn't necessarily a bad thing. But it is a beautiful afternoon out there and it's going to start getting colder soon. The clocks change in a few weeks. And do you know what? Getting some fresh air, and having a bit of a mooch on the beach might be just what you need."

I can see she's thinking about it. It doesn't normally take much to get her down to the beach. Like Sam, she is a keen naturalist. The first time I met her, she'd been rock-pooling and accidentally managed to splash half a bucket of water over me. It seems incredible to me, how much she has changed in those few years. From nine-year-old to fourteen-year-old. It's amazing how much children change and develop while adults stay more-or-less the same.

"OK," she says, doubtfully.

"That's great, Soph. You won't regret it."

***

The walk down to town is through streets still busy with tourists. Now we have a slightly different crowd to the main stretch of summer. Mostly older couples – no kids – or young ones, with babies and toddlers. The first lot walk slowly, leisurely, often hand-in-hand; popping into shops or a pub (for a swift one) just as they please. Gazing into estate agents' windows dreamily. The second lot, meanwhile, look done in. Happy, for the most part, but traversing the cobbled streets with a toddler in tow and a pushchair is no mean feat. They are hampered by members of the first group stopping to admire an old building, or point out something in a shop window. Also impeding their efforts to get places are the small, sticky-handed toddlers, who also want to look in the windows, but not at old buildings, and want fudge, or an ice cream, or don't know what they want but just know they want something. Causing them to break down as their tired little legs, not used to so much walking and so many hills, just want them to sit on one of the stone doorsteps and rest for a bit. Of course, to do so would mean being in the way of other people, and would also mean their parents having to stop in the busy street through which every now and then a vehicle tries to squeeze. Stopping to rest is not an option.

I am grateful for my sling, and for teenage Sophie, who

knows the streets at least as well as I do. Without saying much, we slink through the crowds at twice their pace and head determinedly for the beach. It's the surf beach; it always is. It's where we met and it is the wildest of all the town beaches, facing the Atlantic head-on, not tucked into the open mouth of the bay like the others.

Ben is awake, and now he is a bit bigger he can face front-on in the sling, getting to look at his surroundings, but as we are heading to the windiest beach in town I've tucked him in facing me instead, to keep him warm and shield his eyes from the wind and any sand that is blown about.

He doesn't seem to mind; he snuggles against me and I smile. I can't help but smile. My heart fills with love, as it so regularly does. But right now is about Sophie, not Ben. Her pace quickens once we are through the main thoroughfare, and I follow her past the tranquil terraces. We are in the heart of the town. The road is layered with a thin scattering of sand, blown in by the wind, piling up in little corners and crevices like miniature snowdrifts.

As we reach that corner where the street opens up and the beach reveals itself, Sophie gasps. I follow her gaze. I gasp, too, and I kick myself, for making her come out here. For there, right ahead of us, is Josh. Holding hands with a girl who I have never seen before but can only assume is Annabel Fenwick.

5

"The little…!" I exclaim in a half-whisper to Sam, when he's back from work, and Sophie is installed in the lounge with a box of tissues. When I heard Sam outside, I left Ben in his bouncy chair, eyeing his crying sister with interest. I opened the door to Sam's smiling face…

"Where have you been?" I hissed.

His face fell. "At work. Of course. Why…?"

"I've been trying to call you. It's Sophie, it's… she's fine, physically." As we were right next to the lounge, I beckoned him through to the dining room. Our resident seagull was on the back doorstep, looking through the patio window. He flapped a little and strutted off guiltily, knocking into one of the planters. "Josh has dumped her," I announced unceremoniously. Sophie had asked me to tell Sam but I hoped she couldn't hear us talking about it.

"Oh no," Sam looked sad, but not surprised. "I guess it was bound to come to an end someday…"

"Yes, but that's not all. He's going out with Annabel Fenwick."

"Who's Annabel Fenwick?"

"She's in *Year 9*," I said disgustedly.

"Alright, alright, start from the beginning."

So I did. "I just can't believe I made Sophie come out with me, only to see them together. He only finished with her today, for god's sake. The little…"

"Shall I go in and see her?" Sam asks now.

"I think so." I look at my watch. "It's Ben's bathtime anyway. I'll do it tonight, you go and have a chat with

Sophie. I had promised her pizza for tea but we came straight back here and now she says she's not hungry anyway."

"I'll see what I can do." I follow him into the Farrow & Ball hallway, where he knocks gently on the lounge door before going into the lounge.

"Daddy," I hear Sophie say, and he goes to her, putting his arms around her while she begins sobbing anew.

I tiptoe over to the bouncy chair, where Ben is looking like he's had enough anyway. He clearly has no sympathy for his big sister's evident heartbreak.

"Hello," I whisper to his beaming face. Oh, if only everybody looked as pleased to see me as Ben does. If every person began the morning with a huge smile. Why do we have to lose this when we get older? I'll tell you why, it's because of people like Annabel Fenwick.

I don't mean that, of course. It's Josh who has behaved badly here. Annabel, Year 9 or not, is no friend of Sophie's that I know of. She owes her nothing, and she is also very young. Josh, however, has been part of Sophie's life – all of our lives – for quite a while now. He knows that she has been getting used to life with her mum being two hours away, not to mention two new baby brothers to contend with. But, I accede, he is also very young. He doesn't get it yet. Still, *the little…*

I strip Ben to his nappy and lie him on the soft cream bathmat on the bathroom floor while I turn on the taps, put the plug in, and a small squeeze of Organic Baby Soft Baby Bubbles. We are still working our way through all the gift baskets we received when Ben was born. People were so kind and generous. I think it's because Ben is our first baby together. I have been warned by some of the mums at the church group not to expect the same if we have another. Another! Imagine. I am quite happy with just this one for the time being.

While the water is running, I intersperse raspberry-blowing on Ben's perfect, warm little tummy with checking the bath temperature with my elbow. I remember the first few baths I gave him; I had been so scared of making them too hot, or too cold; of dropping Ben or him slipping out of my hands somehow. I had an awful image of him sliding beneath the bubbles. I also imagined tripping on the stairs with him, or letting go of his pram on the steep street outside. Or if I hurt myself or became ill while he was napping and I couldn't get to him, and he was on his own, crying for hours. I was hit by all the awful possibilities there were now I had such an immense responsibility.

But we are three months in now and while my mind still taunts me sometimes, I have a tiny bit of experience behind me now to give me confidence. And as Ben's own strength grows, it helps a little, too. Although of course he is still dependent upon me and Sam for absolutely everything. It's exhausting to think about. But a few long, deep breaths help to pull everything back into perspective.

He giggles now as I kiss his feet. I can't get enough of his perfect little toes. I seriously am turning into one of those crazy obsessive mothers, but I think as long as I keep it to myself it will be ok.

I turn the taps off and I make sure I have everything laid out ready for after the bath… clean towel, clean nappy, vest, babygro. He has already outgrown those first impossibly small newborn clothes, and the next size up. While I am glad he is growing in strength and in size, I already miss his tiny days, too.

I slide off his soft bamboo nappy and put it in the

washbin. We are using reusable nappies during the day but treating ourselves to disposable nappies overnight. It's a source of guilt as I'd sworn I would use only the washable type but as Sarah has said, more than once, motherhood is fraught with guilt and as much of it comes from other people, we don't need to create more for ourselves.

Gently, I lift Ben into the water, supporting him with one hand while he coos at me and I use the other hand to softly swirl water around him, and over his skin. He hated baths at first, which didn't help my unease, but now he loves them. His little hands go into the water and he relaxes. I tumble a little water over his virtually non-existent hair, and I trace my fingers over his skin, singing softly to him about three little ducks who went swimming one day.

I try to make bathtime last a little longer, to give Sam and Sophie some time downstairs. When I lift Ben out of the water, I do Round and Round the Garden with him, then dry him off and put on his night-time nappy, then his vest, and his babygro. We go to Sam's and my bedroom for the night-time feed, and soon enough, Ben is fast asleep. I lift him gently and carry him into his room and over to his cot. His little baby sleeping bag is laid out there and I place him on it, zipping the side and clipping the shoulders over. His elephant and his giraffe look on from the other side of the bars, not allowed in for night-time cuddles until Ben is older.

Switching the monitor on, I creep out of the room and go downstairs.

All is quiet inside the lounge. I knock softly and push the door open. Sam smiles at me as I go in. Sophie is leaning against him and she doesn't look up.

"Hi, you two," I say. "How are you, Soph?"

She looks at me now and I can see how red-rimmed her eyes are. She doesn't need to say anything.

"Oh, Soph. I'm so sorry."

"S'OK."

"Do you feel hungry at all?" I already know the answer.

"No."

"I get it… I really do. But you do need to eat. I tell you what, I'll get those pizzas and maybe you'll feel like some in a little while. The usual?"

"OK," Sophie says in a small voice.

"Sam, I might just walk down and get them, it'll be quicker." I also fancy a little fresh air. It's a lovely evening out there, although pretty much dark by now. We are beginning the fast freefall through autumn into long, slow winter.

The air is still warm as I step into the street. And it still feels like a novelty, leaving the house without Ben, though I have done it a few times now since that rainy day in August. I decide to go to the pizza place by the harbour; partly because it's Sophie's favourite and partly because I fancy the walk. I go up the steep steps, place our order, then slip back out into the growing darkness, sitting on a bench at the harbourside, watching the small waves lapping lazily in the dark, the streetlights reflecting on them, creating shadows across the water. What lurks beneath, I wonder, when the tide is in? Nothing very sinister, I'm sure, but I'm always interested in what is below the surface. It's a different world down there.

The lights are on in the lifeboat station, the grand boat lit up proudly for all to see. Every now and then, Sam talks about volunteering for them, like his grandad – Karen's dad – once did. I'd be at once proud and terrified if he does. I always try to find a reason to put him off, while trying not to look like that's what I'm doing. Right now I have the perfect line: "Not while Ben's so little, please, Sam. We're exhausted as it is!"

"You're right, I know, but I do want to do it, Alice."

"Of course, and I wouldn't stop you. I think the RNLI are brilliant, you know that. But maybe just give it a year or so, just till we're getting a bit more sleep." *And till you change your mind,* the bad voice in my head whispered.

It is pure selfishness, hoping he will go off the idea. I don't want him putting himself at risk. But other people do, and they're dads and husbands, and daughters and sisters. There are no mothers on the lifeboat crew at the moment and as far as I know there never have been. It's interesting, I think, how men are applauded for their bravery – putting their lives at risk in any number of ways, be it volunteering for the lifeboat or extreme sports – while if a mother does the same, for an interest like mountaineering, for example – something she enjoys but which puts her safety at risk – it is frowned upon. Women like that are seen as selfish.

It's to do with our immediacy to our children, I think, but also centuries of ingrained sexism. We must put our interests after others'. We must halt our careers, take a step back, and a cut in pay, to keep our children safe and well. And I would never begrudge that. I would only ever want to keep Ben, and Sophie, safe and well. But they have two parents – well, Sophie has two parents and two step-parents – and I feel like men should be held equally responsible for their child's day-to-day needs. As well as anything else, they are missing out. Sure, looking after a baby does involve day-in, day-out nappy-changing, feeding, cleaning, bathing, etc. – and the prospect of baby groups is not an exciting one. Days can be long, and very much the same as the one that came before it. But to see it only from this point of view is missing all of the joy that comes with it. The smiles and the cuddles; watching your baby or child learn and develop; reading to them, showing them pictures; talking to them as you make lunch or carry them around the house; forming a bond so strong and a love so intense that it almost hurts.

Maybe I'm wrong. Perhaps women are genetically pre-disposed to these things. But I don't know. I am sure men are just as capable of all of this.

I am lucky with Sam, and I am fortunate to have my own business. Sam gets stuck in. I know he was the same with Sophie when she was a baby and he sees and meets most of her needs now she is a teenager, too. And while some of the mums I know have found their companies have 'coincidentally' had to lay them off when they were pregnant or on maternity leave, or found there was just no need for their specific job any longer, I have a job which I love, which I can't wait to get back to. If only it didn't mean the end of these baby days.

I check my watch. I'd better pick up the pizzas. It's been good to just sit for a while, let my mind drift, and breathe in the sea air. There is the slightest breeze, which chases a crisp packet along the pavement towards me. I stop the litter with my foot, picking the crumpled packet up and dropping it in the bin. Then I go back to the pizza place, collect our takeaway boxes (see, women can be hunter-gatherers, too) and I walk back home to my family.

6

The weekend is unexpectedly warm, like a return to summer. Holidaymakers out in shorts and t-shirts, on the beach, in the sea, walking the coastal path, spilling out of pubs and pub gardens, unable to believe their luck.

For Sam and me – and Ben – it is a chance for some family time. Poor sad Sophie has gone up to Kate's; it wasn't meant to be her weekend to do this but she felt that she needed her mum; and Kate felt she needed to see her daughter, having had her in tears on the phone, more than once, every day this week.

It's been a tough one for all of us but, of course, especially for Sophie. While she was sad and grateful for our sympathy on Monday, when what happened with Josh was still fresh, she has been in a foul mood since and taking out her pain and misery on me and Sam – especially Sam. I must admit, with no offence to Sophie, it's quite a relief to have a little break from each other. And it will do her good to see her mum. I feel guilty even saying that, though. It is part and parcel of having a teenager in the house and by and large Sophie is pretty easy, and a pleasure to live with. Just this week has been particularly difficult.

"I hate you!" she shouted at Sam; something I have never heard before and, judging by the slightly stunned look on his face, neither had he. It was in response to him not letting her stay up late to watch something on E4. She had stormed off, slamming her bedroom door. We held our breath – Sam perhaps out of shock, me out of hope that it wouldn't wake Ben. It didn't.

"Don't take that to heart," I'd said to Sam.

"I won't," he smiled slightly uncertainly.

"She's a teenager! And she's having a bad week. To be honest, I think we get off pretty lightly with Soph."

"I know, but…"

"It's a shitty thing to have shouted at you, I realise that. But you know she doesn't mean it. I know you know that. It's classic projection, isn't it? She hates what has happened this week. She hates Josh, or is at least very angry at him, but she can't tell him that, so you're getting the brunt of it."

"You know you missed your calling as an agony aunt."

"I haven't missed it. I'm waiting till I've got a few more grey hairs and a perm, then just try and stop me."

Sophie had calmed down pretty quickly, and come downstairs, apologising to us both. See… she did that all of her own accord, no prompting. She is a good girl.

I gave her a hug. "Thanks for coming back down. We know you're upset. And we hate seeing you so sad. But you are brilliant, and one day you'll feel better about this. For now, though, we just have to keep on going. But try not to take it out on your dad too much, eh?"

"Sorry, Dad." She'd put her arms around his waist and squeezed him.

"Ouch!" Sam had laughed. "Don't worry, Soph, these things happen."

"Would you… would you come and tuck me in?"

I had to bite my lip. How many years was it since Sam had tucked Sophie into bed?

"Of course, love, come on, let's go."

"Night, Alice."

"Night, Sophie." I stood and hugged her.

While Sam and Sophie went upstairs I put the kettle on and opened the door into the little garden. Barefoot, I stepped gingerly onto the gravel, which was still ever-so-slightly warm, and across to the bench. Sitting and pulling my knees up, I leaned back and looked up at the clear sky. There is a lot of light in the town so we don't get to see as many stars as at Amethi, but it was still a beautiful clear night. I breathed in deeply, exhaled slowly, one ear always listening for the baby monitor. Just in case.

In the summer, I would bring Ben out here when he woke for a night-time feed; it was so warm and stuffy inside, and I loved hearing the sounds of the town at night. Without the daytime traffic and the people traipsing up and down the steps behind the garden, it was incredibly peaceful, the air fragranced by flowers well-chosen by David and then Mum and Dad. Night after night, it was clear and still and I could turn my face up towards the stars, feeling Ben's small but definite weight in my arms, and if I was lucky the softest of breezes brushing my skin. One night in late summer, I counted eight shooting stars while I sat there. It was magical.

Now, Ben still wakes at night, but it isn't warm enough to take him outside and he's so much more alert now. I am sure it would just wake him up and he'd want to play. Instead, I sit on the seat next to the window in his room, and while he feeds I gently let the blackout blind up so that I can see across the town and, depending on how clear the night is, look up to the stars again.

This room is smaller than ours, but I envy its view. It used to be Julie's room and I like to think of her while I sit with Ben, hoping he will get his fill and go back to sleep quickly.

"Do you look at the stars and think of me?" she'd teased.

"No," I had said too quickly. I definitely do.

"You do!" she'd laughed. "You used to say that to me when we were kids, if we couldn't have a sleepover. If we looked up to the stars at the same time it would connect us."

"I never said that," I protested. I definitely did.

It's true; there is something about the stars which makes everything and everyone feel connected. Within the world and the wider universe. Maybe it's my sleep-deprived brain making me think like this. Or perhaps it's Lizzie's influence. But when you look up, and away from the world, you remember you're a very small part of something infinitely bigger.

All these thoughts streamed through my mind as I sat in the garden. I heard the kettle boil but I didn't want to leave my seat, not yet.

After a time, I heard Sam on the stairs. He came to the door.

"Hi," I smiled.

"Hi." Face dark against the light of the dining room. He sounded tired. "Want a cup of tea?"

"Just a herbal one, please. I did put the kettle on ages ago, sorry. I got distracted."

"Yes, you do look very busy."

"I didn't say busy, I said distracted."

He smiled. "I'll come and join you, if I may."

"Of course."

I heard the kettle go back on and the sound of Sam making the tea, then he was back, bearing not only two cups of tea but a packet of chocolate Hobnobs.

"Thank you, I would have got to it eventually."

"Course you would."

"How's Sophie?"

"Ah, she's OK. I do feel sorry for her. If I see Josh, I'll…"

"You'll do absolutely nothing as you're far too nice and he's just a fourteen-year-old boy?" I suggest.

"Yeah," he grins. "Something like that."

He sat next to me, pulled my legs over his, and we just sat, the silence broken only by intermittent munching of biscuits. I think back to a night that feels a lifetime ago; a similar time of year to now, when Sam was about to go off to university in Wales. We sat out here, our stomachs full of delicious food cooked by Julie, and we talked about the future. Having no idea that one day we'd be living in this house, together; a tight little family unit of four.

Unlike that night, when I seem to remember things becoming quite heated between us, tonight when we have finished our tea I kiss Sam's cheek. "Come on, let's go to bed. We need some sleep."

"I was hoping you'd say that."

How things have changed.

7

I am determined to make this weekend special for the two of us as a couple. With Sophie away, we will have our evenings, once Ben is in bed. I think of cooking something nice, and getting a good bottle of wine – when did I become so old? – but I have form when it comes to cooking nice meals. And I don't really want to spend the whole afternoon or evening in the kitchen so instead I place an order with the deli, for everything I need for a mezze board. "No meat, or fish, please, but anything else, just load it up. Thanks, Gordon."

We sometimes order from the deli for special events at Amethi so I know Gordon will have put together something lovely. I walk through the sunshine down into town to collect the order, stocking up on pitta breads, and tiny pastries from one of the bakeries in town. Yesterday I bought a bottle of pink gin, and a bottle of spiced rum – trying to rebel against my approaching-middle-aged liking for 'good wine' – and now I pick up tonic water and Coke Zero, along with a brown paper bag of juicy lemons and limes from the greengrocer.

This is all first thing on Saturday and when I get back Sam is lying on the lounge floor, next to Ben on his playmat. He is talking him through the various dangling toys. I smile and take my spoils through to the kitchen.

And now here I am, back in the sun-soaked town, Sam pushing Ben in his pram. It's still a novelty, walking out as a little family. People smile at us, and occasionally an old lady will peer in at Ben, proclaiming what a beautiful baby he is. I can't help but agree.

It feels like the height of summer as we walk, taking our time, doing the full tour of the town. The only problem is that we can't very easily go on the beach, with a pram to get stuck in the sand. But today is about long, lazy meandering. We stop at the café near the smallest beach, and our luck is in; a table by the window is free. I sit on the seat against the wall, from which I have a view of families, set up for the day, kids running in and out of the waves while parents play with the younger ones or lie back on colourful towels, making the most of this sun-kissed day, before autumn finally stops batting at us teasingly, like a cat with a mouse, and claims the land for real.

With the windows open, it's pleasantly cool in the café, and Ben mercifully sleeps on, his pram tucked next to the table. Sam and I order coffee, and toasties. He picks a paper from the rack on the wall and idly skims through it, remarking on anything interesting. I am happy to just watch the people on the beach, my eyes casting out to sea as well, in my never-ending watch for dolphins. Sometimes I am rewarded. Today is not one of those days, although I do see a dark, shiny face protruding from the water just a little way out. There is a seal who is a regular on this beach in quiet times but it has clearly seen how packed the place is and thought better of it today.

Other customers come and go but Sam and I sit for some time. I'm amazed Ben hasn't woken. Gratified, too. It does seem like sometimes we are thrown a little blessing like this – I like to think of it as a payoff for my broken nights' sleep, and the fact that my eyes constantly feel like they are coated with a thin layer of sand; my head packed with cotton wool.

Eventually, of course, Ben does wake, and I feed him, asking the waitress for a glass of water, which I guzzle down. Then we pay up and go, along the road past the surfer beach, which is also heaving with people, the sea invaded by what must be a hundred or more surfers, who stay further out from shore. Contrasting with the children and adults who paddle and swim in their everyday swimwear, braving the cold Atlantic water. A little wave of envy ripples across me, but I feel Sam's arm around me, and I look at Ben all happy and relaxed in his pram, his big blue eyes looking up at us, or the sky, and I know today is about us – not about me. The sea can wait.

Ben falls asleep again on the way home and when we get in we leave him in his pram in the hallway – he looks so content – and go into the lounge with the newspaper. It feels like an absolute treat to have this time to ourselves. I want a coffee but I don't want to risk waking Ben up. Without the radio or TV, the sound of Sophie giggling on the phone, or Ben gurgling (or crying), the house is so quiet. There is the occasional interruption from people walking down the street outside the window but for the most part the only thing I can hear is my stomach, which seems to be doing its best to fill the gap left in the absence of all the usual noises.

"Do you have to be so loud?" Sam doesn't look up from the paper and his face is very serious.

"Shut up!" I laugh and give him a little shove on his arm. "Actually, I think it's a cry for help."

"I thought you said you weren't cooking tonight."

"You'll be sorry for that."

"You are definitely cooking then?"

I say nothing but, ninja-like, I turn and I trap him, my

fingers dangerously close to his very ticklish ribs. "Shall I?"

"No, you'll wake Ben."

"I won't. I will be very quiet. If anyone wakes Ben it'll be you."

Sam takes hold of my fingers. "I'm sorry. You're the best cook ever. I only say otherwise to spare Julie's feelings."

"I knew it." I smile, aware suddenly of our physical proximity to each other. I kiss Sam on the cheek and he turns his head so our mouths find each other.

"Hello," he smiles, softly, and the smile touches my lips, making them curl upwards too.

His arms pull me to him, and his hands find their way under my top.

"I need to close the blinds," I say, and quickly I tiptoe to the window, pulling the cord so that the room becomes dim. I am desperate not to wake Ben, and to have just a little more time, just me and Sam.

Carefully, I creep back to him, and place one leg either side of his, moving so I am sitting on him and facing him. I kiss him deeply.

"I've missed this," he whispers.

"Me too." I haven't actually had time to miss it.

I pull my top off, and he takes his off too, revealing his warm, curly-haired chest. I smile.

Every sound we make seems magnified amid the quiet of the house. I think of Ben in the hallway. Push the thought from my mind, just for now. This is important, too.

Slowly, Sam moves me down onto the settee and kisses all the way up from my stretch-marked stomach to my neck. "You are beautiful."

I smile and reach for him, and he moves on top of me. I may not have had time to miss this, but right now it feels like I have.

As Sam and I lie in each other's arms, our heart rates and breathing beginning to slow, I hear Ben stir.

"Talk about timing," I smile, and suddenly I want nothing more than my little boy back in my arms. But I can't just up and leave Sam, not after that.

"Go on," Sam smiles. "I know you need to go and get him."

"Oh Sam, but that was amazing. That was so good."

"It was, wasn't it?" He kisses me and starts pulling his clothes back on. "Now come on, you don't want your son seeing you naked, do you?"

"I think he's a bit too young for mental scarring just yet." I too begin to dress. Ben is starting to murmur now. Once my clothes are back on, I creep to the door. Open it and peer around. I want to see what he does, in this time between waking and one of us coming to collect him. Those big eyes are casting about the hallway. Is he wondering why he's asleep in his pram, or is he far too young to think like that? Sam joins me, poking his head round above mine.

"I love him so much," Sam says.

It melts my heart and I turn to kiss him again, with feeling. "I love you so much."

We hold each other for a moment then I can bear it no longer and I am at the side of the pram, picking Ben up and bathing in the glow of his smile.

We spend the rest of the afternoon at home, in the garden for a while, with Ben on his playmat, the seagull watching distastefully from the wall.

I've heard tales of seagulls attacking babies (*Express* headline: 'A CAMPAIGNER has warned that seagulls could start killing BABIES if the Government fails to crack down on the boisterous birds') but I'm not convinced. I know it's not fashionable but I love gulls, and they have a bad press. They are definitely greedy and certainly not afraid to do what is necessary to look after themselves, at least insofar as getting some unfortunate holidaymaker's chips. They are also no stranger to eating other birds' eggs, and even baby birds (why do I leave fish out of this list? Poor old fish, as if they don't matter). The problem is, they have evolved along with humans, so that as we become greedier, so too do they. As we leave more litter and waste, they take advantage of it. They're endangered, too, many of them.

I'd be very sorry for anyone who actually is attacked by a gull, and I do really feel for the hapless kids I've seen having been taken by surprise by some sneaky gull swooping from behind and stealing their ice-cream. But gulls are big, beautiful birds, and for me the sound of them calling across the town is an integral part of this place. I love watching them glide above the rooftops and the cliffs, set against the blue sky.

With gulls, and other animals or birds that humans don't like, it often seems to be those which present that a threat to us – real or imagined – and they also share some of our characteristics. What is the greediest creature on earth? The most ruthless in fighting for its survival or to get what it wants?

I'd say humans, every time.

Still, I am not taking any chances, and I would never leave Ben unattended outside. The very thought of him, helpless and unable to move away, makes my stomach squeeze tightly in on itself. Today, Ben has both Sam and me to take care of him anyway, and it seems neither of us can leave him alone for too long.

Sam lifts him and holds him close, under the shade of our small stripy umbrella. I smile and take a photo of them, then another, then another.

"I hope Sophie's doing OK," I say.

"She's alright, been texting me. Kate's taking her out shopping today."

"Oh, she'll love that. They both will."

"Yeah, I reckon. I think they've got a new retreat beginning tomorrow so Soph's going to have to set off back in the morning."

"Poor girl. So rubbish having to go to school with Josh and *Annabel*."

I've started saying her name like this to make Sam laugh but I don't mean it really. I feel bad being horrible about a teenager.

"I told you Sharon called, didn't I?"

I had got to know Josh's mum fairly well over the time Josh and Sophie were going out, and she's always been so good to Sophie. She was mortified about what had happened. "I told Joshie he's behaved like an A1-idiot," she said, sounding more than a little embarrassed.

"Oh, no, don't…"

"Yes, Alice, he's been a total little shit to Sophie. I told him it's not on. I stopped short of telling him he's in danger of turning into his dad if that's how he treats women."

"Oh, Sharon, I'm sorry."

"Well, I was just so mad at him. I mean, I know they weren't going to be together forever, but that was no way to treat a lovely girl like Sophie. And you know what, I think I'm mad because I'm going to miss her, too. It's been nice having a girl around."

That made me smile. "Sharon, honestly, don't worry. Like you say, it couldn't last forever, really."

"Yeah, well, there's ways to do things and that ain't one of them."

"Look, it's happened now. Sophie will be OK. And I am sure Josh just hadn't thought it all through."

"He's certainly not having that Annabel round here like we did Sophie."

I suppressed a smile. "She's probably a really nice girl, too, you know. I agree, Josh could definitely have done things differently but he's a good lad really, isn't he? They're all just learning about this stuff."

"Well, I don't think I'd be as understanding as you, Alice, but thank you."

"No problem, Sharon – and keep in touch."

"I will. You take care now."

I lean on Sam. "Do you remember getting your heart broken at that age?"

"Nope."

"Were you the heartbreaker? Were you *Josh*?" I ask incredulously.

"Nope."

"Then…"

"Nobody would go out with me," he says and, looking at this beautiful man in front of me, I can't believe it. "I was skinny and lanky and had braces, and this crazy curly hair. I was not the bronzed hunk you see before you now."

"I can't believe I never knew that about you, Sam."

"What about you?"

"I wasn't a bronzed hunk, either."

"I mean, were you a heartbreaker, you idiot."

Ben laughs at this moment, and I pull a face at him. "No, that was always Julie. She was the heartbreaker. I was her wingman – if a teenage girl can be a wingman. Then I had my heart broken, when I was a bit older than Sophie. I told her about it the other night."

"You're good with her, Alice. She talks to you."

"She talks to you, too."

"But not in the same way. Which is fine. You're not her parent so she doesn't feel embarrassed talking to you. But she knows how much you care about her. She trusts you."

It gives me a bit of a glow, this conversation. I don't know what to say. "I love her, you know that."

"I do. And do you know she is still desperate for us to get married?"

"No, I did not know that!"

"Yep, she was on about it on the way to the train yesterday."

We've been engaged a while now, but the pregnancy kind of threw that to the back of my mind. I still can't imagine it, somehow. Not that I don't want to get married, but there is so much to do, and I am so desperate to get back to work, too. Once I do that, how much time will there be to plan a wedding? How much money? Still, I do want to marry Sam. I realise now I want it very much.

"It would be nice," I say.

"Nice?!" He nudges me, mock-outraged. "It would be amazing and you would without a doubt be the luckiest girl in the world."

"Exactly what I was about to say. What about you? Still want to get married?"

"Alice," Sam looks me in the eye, "I would marry you in an instant. I want to spend the rest of my life with you, and I would love to make it official, and most of all to celebrate it, but I know there's no hurry and I hope you know that, married or not, I am one hundred percent committed to you… and to our family."

I do know that. I lean forward and kiss him, feeling Ben's little hand in my hair as I do so. With the sun smiling down on us in our little white-walled garden, it feels like life couldn't get much better than this.

We eat in the dining room with Ben on the table in his Bumbo – yes, Mum did get him one – watching our every move. The food is delicious and I'm glad I decided not to cook. Although it would be easy to think that when you're at home with a baby there is loads of time – after all, you're not going out to work, and really, looking after somebody who just needs to feed and sleep can't be that time-consuming, can it? – somehow that time is sucked away. Each day can feel extremely long but at the same time I don't feel I have a spare moment.

My timetable is dictated by Ben. Feeding, changing nappies, playing with him, comforting him when he cries, washing his clothes (and ours), folding and putting clothes away. Getting him out for a walk each day, which is good for him and me. And still, put like that, it doesn't sound like a lot, but take it from me – days are filled without having to make the slightest effort to find something to do, and usually end with a list of things which remain undone. And it's not like Ben just lies there quietly while I get on with things. No, most things I do I usually have him strapped to my front, or I'm holding him, or trying to keep him entertained while he's on his playmat. I don't think people always get that about babies. They get bored. You can't just leave them to their own devices for hours on end. And all of this on night after night of broken sleep. I am so tired that I sometimes feel sick.

Mum was so right to encourage me to get out to the baby and toddler group. Like the list of daily chores, it is not exciting, but it's a much-needed break from the house, and a chance to chat with people who are in the same position as me. Who need a bit of social input in their day as much as I do. I need to get organised for them coming to me this week, but today is our day – Sam's, Ben's and mine – and that can wait.

Sam and I drink a glass of wine each while we eat; a dark, rich red. We've bypassed the gin and the rum. As I'm breast-feeding I shouldn't really drink much anyway, and we are both exhausted. Drinking doesn't hold much appeal. But this one glass of wine is delicious. I take a sip, in between mouthfuls of grilled artichoke, slick with garlic-and-chilli oil, sit back and sigh.

"Alright?" asks Sam.

"Yes. Very."

"Me too."

I can see he is stifling a yawn. "Tired?" I ask.

"Ha, yep, just a little."

"Me too."

"Why don't we go to bed when Ben does?"

"What, at seven?"

"Yeah… now I've said it, that sounds like the best idea ever. Can you imagine..?"

"That does sound pretty tempting. But what about watching a film?"

"We can if you want," I say.

"Only if you want."

"I think I'd just like to go to bed. Get some sleep. We could never go to bed early when Sophie's here."

"True."

"And we've had a lovely day."

"An amazing day," Sam smiles lazily at me.

"Shall we…?" It's like I'm suggesting something daring.

"Sounds bloody brilliant," Sam says.

And so we do. Sam baths Ben while I clear up downstairs. The red wine has gone to my head and I feel very sleepy, but content. I nibble on a chunk of dark chocolate while I put things away, enjoying its bitterness on my tongue.

Up the stairs I go and I can hear Sam singing to Ben in the bathroom. I go through to our room, change into my pyjamas, and climb into bed. I should have put fresh sheets on, I think – that would have made this even more perfect. As it is, it feels wonderful, sliding under the sheets before seven p.m. Even though I know Ben will wake at least twice during the night, it offers the possibility of hours of much-needed sleep.

Sam brings him through, hair soft and fluffy after his bath, already poppered into his sleeping bag.

While I feed Ben, Sam gets undressed and gets into bed, too. "I don't think I've even got the energy to take him to his cot," he says.

"I know exactly what you mean. Don't worry, I'll do it. He's going to feed for a while anyway."

Sam lies down, looking up at me from his pillow. "I love you, Alice. I love… this."

I know exactly what he means. "Me too."

"And I meant what I said; I do want to marry you."

"And I want to marry you, but as long as we both know that, it's fine. We will do it, but when it's the right time." I am speaking softly now, I can tell Ben is getting sleepy. "Anyway, what will it change, getting married? We're here, together, with Ben, and Sophie. We know we love each other. There's no hurry."

"But it's romantic, isn't it? It's something brilliant, what we've got it. I was thinking about it while Ben was in the bath. I want to celebrate it. I've never been so happy."

"Me neither."

"Then why don't we do it? Get married, I mean. It doesn't have to be huge. Just the people we love most. Let's do it, Alice. Let's get married."

These words make my heart sing. "Like… make a date?"

"Yeah! Why not?"

"Where would we do it?"

"I don't know. What about the chapel on the Island?"

"That would be perfect." It's my favourite place, and Sam knows it. It's also where Stefan and April had their ceremony. Not that it would bother me, getting married in the same place they did.

I picture the scene. It's already familiar to me as I've pictured it multiple times before, ever since I was eighteen. Does Sam know this?

"Alright," I say. "Let's find out about it. When it's available. How much it costs."

Ever-the-romantic, I know we have to be sensible with money. I am not taking a wage while Mum's covering for me at Amethi and statutory maternity pay is something I'm always grateful for, but it doesn't go a long way. Sam, meanwhile, loves his work but it's not going to make us millionaires.

Still, the thought is out there now. The words have been said and I want to do it. I want to get married. I smile. Look across to Sam for an answer but he is already asleep, a smile on his face.

Like father, like son; Ben is also zonked out. I climb carefully out of bed, with Ben in my arms, careful not to wake either of them. Pad across the floor and through to Ben's room. Officially, it's recommended that babies share their parents' room till they are at least six months old, but he is an incredibly noisy sleeper, this boy, as we soon discovered. We compromised by putting him in his own room next to ours but having our door and his wide open, and of course the baby monitor on at all times.

I place him gently in his cot and I smile at my son, my heart flooding with love for him, as it does multiple times a day.

Softly back to bed. I glance at my book on the bedside table. Should I…? It is very rare that I get any time to myself in the evenings. But no, I need sleep.

I switch off the light; it is barely dark outside yet, and I settle down under the soft duvet, moving next to Sam so that he stirs and puts his arm around me. In the next room, Ben gives a little snore and I smile to myself.

Then my mind turns to the conversation we've just had. Getting married. Could we do it? Of course we could. Should we do it? Financially, maybe not. But otherwise, yes! I can't think of anything better than proclaiming and celebrating our love, with our friends and family.

I picture myself being driven to the Island; Dad and Mum at my side, a gathering of friends and family peering down, watching for our arrival. Windswept and wild at the chapel, I would hang onto my veil. A veil? Really? That doesn't seem very practical. OK. Windswept and wild, I would hold my skirts to stop them blowing into the air and I'd make the walk up to meet smiling Sam. My one true love, waiting for me at the chapel. Hand-in-hand, we'd go into the little place of peace, thick stone walls shielding us from the weather. Say our vows, sign the book. Emerge into the sunlight and kiss on the steps, to applause and exclamations of joy. Sweet dreams.

8

On Tuesday, it is Mums Day. The old me still sits just below the surface, feeling slightly uncomfortable with the whole thing.

"It's such a cliché!" I say to Julie on a video call that morning. "All the little ladies getting together for coffee while hubbies are out at work."

"Or," my friend smiles at me, "it's a group of strong young women who are sticking together, sharing their knowledge, supporting each other, and helping their children learn to socialise."

She's good, this one.

"Alright," I smile, "I'll take that. But can you imagine it? I mean, they're lovely, all of them that are coming today, but I wouldn't say we have a lot in common."

"Except you're all relatively new mums. That is one huge thing which you do all have in common."

"OK!" I laugh. I want to ask her, could she imagine going to one of these things? Hosting a mothers-and-babies coffee morning doesn't sit right with Julie somehow, but knowing just how much she has wanted a baby, for quite some time now, I feel like it would sound frivolous and thoughtless.

"So how's Luke?"

"I'm fine thanks, Alice!" I hear his voice from somewhere in the background. Julie spins her phone round so I can see him lying in bed.

"What are you doing in bed? It's 10 o'clock in the morning!" I exclaim.

"Maybe where you are, my friend, but here it's half past two and the end of my little siesta."

"I didn't know they had siestas in India."

"They don't – but I do. Sometimes. When I can."

He looks thinner but happy and healthy. They both look happy. They always do. It's a relief after the anguish they've been through in their so-far unsuccessful quest to become parents.

"I can't believe you've only got a few months left now," I say to them both.

"I know, it's just amazing out here. And the kids are so great. So bloody great," Julie says with feeling. "But I am looking forward to seeing you, and meeting *your* kid!"

I swivel my phone now, so that Julie can see Ben, who is lying on the settee, idly sucking his fist, looking up at me.

"Oh my god, he's so gorgeous! And Alice, is that a homemade cake I caught a glimpse of then?"

"Could be."

I've made a chocolate cake, decorated with Smarties. It is in a plastic tub, on the table next to the settee. I hadn't planned on Julie seeing it, though.

"What have we said about you baking?"

"We said I should never do it again," I say, like a child being questioned by their teacher.

"Because…?"

"Because I always get stressed when it doesn't turn out the way I want it to and because I have more than once left something in the oven to burn."

"Well done. Having said that, I'm impressed – at least as far as appearances go."

"What can I say, Julie? I'm growing up."

"Well, don't grow up too fast before we get back, will you?"

"I'll try not to. I'd better go now. Love you, miss you."

"Miss you too, my friend. I wish I was coming round for a piece of that cake."

"I'm glad you're not. I mean, I wish you were coming round, but I wouldn't want you judging my cake."

"Rescued just in time!" laughs Julie. "Have fun at your coffee morning. Love you, miss you."

"Bye Alice!" Luke calls.

"Bye, Luke. Love you, miss you too."

"Whatever!" I just see his grinning face before we end the call.

It's such a great thing being able to speak to each other so easily but I often feel sad afterwards, and I miss Julie – and Luke – more than I do day-to-day. I suppose it brings it into sharp focus. But still, they look very happy. And it is only a few months till their return. That's not too long.

It is also, I realise, less than an hour till The Mums are due round here. We seem to have settled into a group of five: Sarah, with the twins – Rory and Ethan; Miriam, with Esther; Heather, with Markus; Lucy, with Matilda, and Suzie, with Delilah.

You quickly learn it's best not to judge other parents. Whether it's the baby's name; feeding (breast or bottle); if they are starting weaning younger than the recommended six months; using disposable nappies, and the easy-to-carry-but-bad-for-the-environment-not-to-mention-the-baby's-skin-according-to-the-health-visitor baby wipes, as opposed to sterilised water and cotton wool. These things are our choices, as parents, and it is not up to anybody else to tell us if we're doing it right. I bristle if I ever think somebody is judging me and believe me, as a first-time parent I am overly sensitive to anything which might seem like a criticism.

I pick Ben up and, swept up in a moment of unexpected joy, swing him gently round in front of my face. He giggles and puts his hands out towards my hair. He cannot get enough of pulling my hair. And he's surprisingly strong.

"Hey, you, stop picking on me." I carry him with me as I go into the kitchen to make sure that there are enough mugs out, coffee ready to make, tea bags immediately available and, for the twins, the oldest of the bunch, a couple of small sippy cups which I bought a couple of weeks back, even though Sarah said not to bother and she'd bring everything they need. There is also a box of gluten-free brownies, for Lucy – I would have tried to make a gluten-free cake but despite what I told Julie I am still aware of my limits when it comes to baking. Better not to risk everyone leaving with a bad taste in their mouths.

Soon enough, the doorbell goes. It's Sarah, with Miriam right behind her. Where on earth are the pushchairs going to go? I take Ben into the lounge and put him on his playmat then I take baby Esther, while Sarah frees the twins from their double buggy. Both mums fold up their pushchairs while the boys stand shyly by Sarah – I am well aware this shyness will not last long but it's cute while it does – and we lie the pushchairs against the stairs.

I see Lucy and Suzie coming down the street together, chatting merrily over the tops of their prams. I usher Miriam and Sarah inside. Sarah already knows the layout of the house, having been round a couple of times. "Ben's in the lounge, on the floor," I add, suddenly fearful of the little boys trampling all over him.

"We'll go through. I'll pick him up if that's OK?" She's seen the danger and already removed the risk.

"That would be brill!" I smile, waving to the others. They are followed closely by Heather, and with three pushchairs folded up and two prams wheeled through to the dining room, two adorable little boys becoming slightly less adorable as they refuse to stay in the lounge with us, not to mention one teething Markus, who won't stop crying, we are complete.

I had hoped to introduce Becky to this group but she has gone back to work already and although she has a couple of days off during the week, we (the baby group) tend to meet on Tuesdays, when she is at work. I quite like having Becky as a friend separate to this group anyway, and as she and Andrew were friends before the babies came along it's a different dynamic. Plus, Andrew and Sam like hanging out together so we can go for days out with them, as families. I often think they know the 'real' us – the ones from before Ben came along. Not the sanitised, baby-friendly version I feel I display at the baby and toddler group. I have found myself exclaiming in a child-friendly way: "Oh my goodness!" and, once, "Gosh!" Listening politely to discussions on sleep-training and how many words a child should be able to say by a certain age.

It would be unfair to say I am not interested in parenting conversations; often I will pick up something really useful, or just some reassurance that other babies do what Ben does (and other mothers do what I do) but I like to talk about other things, too. And maybe we're all the same, the mums at the groups. Perhaps it's just safe ground, the baby talk. It is, clearly, the one thing we do have in common. But it feels sometimes like it's what some people have been waiting for, preparing for motherhood for years. They've bought the books, they've watched the programmes. Is it wrong to say that there are some people who feel like they've achieved their ambition in life now they have their babies? I don't think it is, and again, no judgement. Being a mum – a parent – is by far the best thing I've ever done. But I wouldn't want to give up Amethi for it, or for it to become my sole topic of conversation.

Luckily, in The Mums I have found a group of lively, interesting people who do, of course, talk quite a lot about their kids and we do, naturally, discuss the ins and outs of parenting and any problems we're having, but we also talk about life in general and TV and books and films. People we know and places we've been, or want to go to. Life now that we are parents, and how it has changed. How it has changed our relationships.

Today, despite the rampaging twins (told you the shyness wouldn't last long) and the red-cheeked, unhappy Markus, we have a great time. Two hours pass in a flash. Suzie is a great story-teller and regales us with tales of growing up in a commune with her hippy parents. "I was brought up by all the adults; all the kids were. It was like they were all responsible for us, but we still had our own parents, if you know what I mean. We were meant to be like brothers and sisters, the kids, but when we were teenagers that changed. The adults would have been disgusted to know what went on between some of us! Or maybe they wouldn't, in fact I bet more than a few of them switched beds regularly. Mum says she can see why I've settled for a nice comfortable new-build and a normal husband, with a normal job. I think she's needling me, sometimes, but Alex is brilliant. He's just not a hippy. He likes his car, but he's no Jeremy Clarkson."

"I could never live on a commune," Sarah says. "I like my own space too much."

"That's a shame," laughs Heather, "I was going to suggest to Alice that we turn her place into one. What's it called, Alice?"

"Amethi."

"That's right – doesn't that mean farm? We could all live there, looking after each other's kids, working the land."

"Sounds like a total nightmare," says Lucy. "I mean, I love you guys and everything but I don't want to live with you."

I've been a bit shy till now, as it feels like there are more established friendships in this group. But I have an overwhelming urge to share with them, about the conversation Sam and I had the other night.

"I have to tell you," I say, "I don't know if you're aware Sam and I are engaged."

Sarah nods. She knows a lot about our history.

"I had clocked the ring," Suzie says.

"Yeah, well I'd kind of… not forgotten about it, as such, but, well Ben came along, and there was work, and Julie leaving…"

"Julie?"

"Yeah, she's my best mate. And business partner, up at the commune." I smile, thinking how funny it is that these people don't know Julie, who really is an integral part of my life. "Anyway, Sam and I were talking about it at the weekend."

"Oh yeah?" Sarah smiles.

"Yeah, and I think we might go for it."

"A wedding!" Miriam breathes. "I love a wedding."

"And a hen do!" laughs Lucy.

I hadn't thought of this. My new friends will want to be invited, too. In fact, will there be loads of people who expect an invite? And a hen do as well. When Julie married Luke, she just wanted a night away with me, which was lovely. I start to feel a little anxious. I hadn't thought this through. I imagine what a hen do might be like.

"Steady on!" Sarah laughs. I am grateful to her. "They might just want a small wedding. And they might not want to invite a bunch of people they've only known five minutes!"

"Of course," Miriam says. "I was only kidding, really."

"We should definitely have a hen do anyway, though," Lucy insists, "even if we don't come to the wedding."

"You just want a night out," says Heather.

"Yeah, course I do. Don't you?"

"I wouldn't say no."

And to my relief, the conversation turns quickly from my wedding to the (sort of) safer ground of a Mums Night Out.

The conversation changes again, to returning to work, and childcare, and I start to feel another little flutter of anxiety as I realise most of the others have already sussed it out. Heather's visited all the nurseries in town; Lucy has met a couple of childminders. Miriam's mother-in-law is going to look after Esther, and Sarah's mum minds the twins when she can.

"What about you, Alice?" Miriam looks at me. "And you, Suzie?"

Suzie and I look at each other. I'm glad I'm not the only one who hasn't quite got up this sorted.

"I don't know. I suppose I'd better get a move on," I say. "I'll be back at work in January. I used to think I could have the baby with me, and he'd sleep by my side while I worked." They all laugh. "Yep, I know… the things you don't know, eh? I suppose I'd better get organised. Maybe one of the nurseries. Which one did you like, Heather?"

"I've got Markus a place at Little Angels – but I start back next month, so I had to have something sorted."

"I might check it out then, it would be nice for Ben to

have a friend there."

"I might, too," says Suzie. "We could go together, Alice."

"Brill, let's sort that out."

I hadn't really thought how you need to plan ahead with these things. That nurseries and childminders have to plan ahead, too. It seems obvious now, but I'd kind of just thought I'd sort it out nearer the time.

Two hours is over in a flash, although when the house is empty and quiet once more, I realise it's completely drained me of my energy. Ben's been so interested in the other babies and children, it's kept his mind off being hungry. Now that they are gone, however, he apparently can't think of anything else. His fists are tightly balled as he begins to feed but they soon relax and so does he. He falls into a deep sleep and I carry him carefully upstairs, laying him down in his cot. I switch on the baby monitor, go back down to the lounge and lie half-reclined on the settee, my feet up on the footstool. Nurseries, I think. There is always something new to think about; never time to stop. And I want to think about the wedding instead. For it has now become 'the wedding'. From a nice idea to something which might actually happen.

I sit up and cut a huge slice of cake, half-disgusted with myself as I methodically munch my way through it, dropping crumbs on my top and resting my head on the cushions while I flick lazily through the TV channels. Escaping for a while into a world of antiques and people buying second homes, as if there wasn't enough of that round here.

9

"Are they getting on OK, your mum and dad?"

"With each other, or with the Sail Loft?'

"The Sail Loft, you imbecile," David cuffs my arm. Ben is lying prone in the crook of my other arm and somewhere in the kitchen I can hear the mischievous giggles of Tyler and Esme. I wonder what they're up to but it's David's kitchen, not mine, so I don't really mind. "I know they get on with each other. At least, I hope they do. They're my ideal of long-lasting happiness. They're not allowed to not get along or my dreams will be ruined."

"I know, and we're all living our lives with your happiness our central concern," I smile, then think about what he's asking me. I think they're OK but I do feel like they've been more tired, and less light-hearted, than normal. And we don't get to see them as much anyway; the most I see Mum is up at Amethi and Dad really only if we pop in to see him at the hotel. I feel uneasy and try to read David's expression as I ask, "Why? Do you know something?"

"No, I don't, and I would tell you if I did. But Bea said something that made me wonder."

"What did she say?"

"Well, something and nothing, really. I did wonder at the time though, when they said they were buying it, if your parents were doing the right thing."

"Why didn't you say something?"

"It's hardly my place, is it? Plus, there was something magical going on then, wasn't there? Everything falling into place just before Ben was born. And I know Bea wouldn't have let them buy the Sail Loft if she'd thought they couldn't cope. Your mum was looking for a new challenge too, wasn't she?"

"Yes, but she's also helping at Amethi. And when I say helping, she's doing an awful lot there, covering for me. I'm a bit worried she's bitten off more than she can chew."

"Well, at least you can relieve her of that soon. Have you decided what you're going to do with this little one yet?" He strokes Ben's cheek and Ben looks delighted.

"No, I'm going to make sure I look at a couple of nurseries soon."

"Better hurry up, girl. You know these things get booked up months in advance?"

"I didn't, till a couple of days ago," I say with chagrin. "Now I realise I'm about a year behind. I'm starting to worry about it. What if I have to leave Ben somewhere rubbish?"

"You've just got new-parent anxiety," David smiles. "In fact, it doesn't only affect new parents – it's part and parcel of being a parent forever, as far as I can make out. From nurseries to getting into the right school – not that there's much choice round here – to checking if your kid's developing at the same rate as everyone else's, secretly hoping they're developing just a little better. Are they speaking before the others? Feeding themselves? Walking? Running? Playing lacrosse?"

"It's true," I rub my eyes. They're particularly sore today and feel like they'd close of their own accord, shut me off to the world so I can sleep, if I'm not careful. "No matter how much you know that each baby, and child, develops at a different rate, and that you'll love yours no matter what, you want them to be doing well, and it's also true that there's a little part of you that wants them to be doing better than the others. Urgh, I can hardly bring myself to say it, how awful!"

"It's not awful. It's natural. And it's not like *you're* ever going to be one of those mums who wants their kid to be the best at everything. It's just fine to want them to do well, though, and knowing how they're doing in comparison with their peers is a good benchm…"

There is a crash from the kitchen. And a cry.

Tyler shouts, "Esme's crying."

David is already on his feet, and quick as a flash he is through the door. I follow, Ben still in the crook of my arm, Tyler passing us on his way out. In the kitchen is a very sorry scene, with a biscuit tin on the floor; lid off, cargo spilt and broken on the tiles. Esme sits next to it, her curly hair in her face and an ever-increasing wailing emanating from behind the curls. A chair is upended on the floor next to her. Tyler is nowhere to be seen. I can just hear some small footsteps speeding up the stairs.

"Are you OK, baby?" David picks Esme up and holds her. She presses her face into his shoulder and I think about how it took them a while to bond, these two, after Esme was adopted. You'd never know it now.

"Tyla… Ty…" she sobs, barely able to get any words out.

"I think I can see what happened," David says grimly, though he gives me a slight smile. "Tyler!" he shouts. There is no reply. "Alice, do you mind if Esme comes and sits on the settee with you and Ben? I need to go and have a word with her brother."

"Of course. Come on, Esme, come and sit with us. Let's look at a book, shall we?"

She wants more cuddles from her dad, it's obvious, but

David selects one of the least broken biscuits from the floor. A ginger nut. "Come on, darling, come and sit and eat this. Look, it's fine. I mopped the floor this morning." Another look at me, mouthing "I didn't."

I take Ben back to the lounge and sit facing the window, through which we can see glittering water; above it, fast-moving clouds scooting across the sky. Focusing my eyes, I can pick out a small group of black birds flying low over the water, towards the mouth of the estuary, with its shallow waters and expanses of sand at low tide. The year has long since turned and we are headed straight for winter. The days are shorter now and there are often skeins of geese moving noisily through the sky, returning to their winter homes. Down on the rocks and in the shallows there will be winter visitors like purple sandpipers; sweet little birds, similar to the turnstones we see around the harbour in town. I remember Sophie telling me earnestly all about the winter avian visitors, back when Sam had gone off to study in Wales. My heart contracts slightly at the thought of that sweet little girl and what she went through then; what she is going through now.

David places Esme next to me and I try to point out the birds to her; I can see a gannet diving out in the deeper water, too. But Esme isn't interested. Instead, she wants to look at Ben. She pushes herself up onto her small, chubby knees.

"Why doesn't he talk?" she asks, scattering biscuit crumbs over him.

"Babies can't talk. But he's trying, sometimes. They have to learn, by listening to us. Look, he's looking at you. Shall we read this book to him?" I pick up a slightly dog-eared book from the table next to the seat. *The Snail and the Whale*.

"Mine," Esme says, snatching it off me.

"I know it's yours!" I laugh. "I just wondered if you'd mind me reading it to you and Ben? We don't want to take it."

She's not sure. The book remains under her arm.

"Look, why don't you read it to me?" I suggest. "Show Ben the pictures. He can't read, of course, but I bet you know some of the words."

"I know them all."

"Well, brilliant. Let's see what happens, then."

As it turns out, she does know all the words. Is she reading, or has she just remembered them all? She's two, so surely too young to be able to read? I realise I need to get to grips with how these kids are meant to develop.

While Esme is showing the pictures to Ben, very endearingly, I am aware of some less happy sounds upstairs.

"No!" I hear Tyler shout, more than once, interspersed by the firm but indistinct voice of David. "It wasn't me!" I am not convinced that Tyler wasn't the mastermind behind the biscuit-stealing scheme.

In time, David and a sorry-looking Tyler come downstairs. David's mouth is set in a hard line, though this breaks at the sight of the three of us.

"What have you got to say to your sister?" he prompts Tyler.

"Snem."

"Pardon?"

"Sorry, Esme," Tyler's voice is so small it is hard to hear. But his sister hears him and, all thoughts the book forgotten, she jumps down off the settee and hugs her brother. He puts his arms round her. It is very sweet.

"But Esme," David crouches down, taking one of each child's hands so they turn to look at him, "you should not have been on that chair, and neither of you should be taking biscuits without asking. Do you understand?"

"Yes, Daddy," she puts her arms around his neck. "Sorry."

"That's OK. But now you both have to pick those biscuits up and do you know what? Now they're all broken, we're going to have to get rid of them. We'll give them to the birds, but we won't have any biscuits left for ourselves."

Both children immediately break down into hysterics and David casts a very small smile my way, over their heads. "You should have thought of this before you decided to take the biscuits without asking," he chides. "Now go on, I'll help you. We'll just have to wait a day or two before we can get any more." He winks at me.

I smile. He's very good. I have much to learn from this man. "We might leave you to it, David, if you don't mind. I think I might pop up to the Sail Loft and see Mum and Dad."

"Of course, no worries, Alice, we'll be round to see you later this week if that's OK. How about a little trip to the beach, kids, with Alice and Ben? And Sam and Sophie?"

Both children cheer up at this idea. It seems to me that each day with small children is full of ups and downs. Extremes.

"Bye, Tyler. Bye, Esme." They run up, each hugging one of my legs. I laugh. "Right, you're going to have to let go now. I'll see you soon, OK? Be good."

"I hope I didn't worry you about your folks," David says as I'm strapping Ben into his baby carrier.

"No, no, it's fine. I just realised I haven't seen them for a few days." I step outside, baby changing bag across my body and Ben's weight heavy in his car seat. The air is definitely colder than it has been.

I fix Ben's seat into the back, kiss him, then get into the driver's seat. It will be good to see Mum and Dad, make sure they're OK. Despite telling David I'm not worried, I can't seem to shake the feeling of unease that has settled over me.

10

On the way back, Ben starts crying. I try to sing to him, and talk to him softly, but nothing distracts him from his determined misery. It is hard to concentrate; all I want to do is brake sharply into the side of the road, whip him out of his seat and feed him. It's a physical reaction as much as emotional.

We arrive back in town, parking in the closest free space we can find, at the top of the hill, almost a halfway point between home and the Sail Loft. I decide to go straight to the hotel. When I lift Ben from the seat, he quietens a little at my touch and, I suspect, the prospect of being fed. When I go on to put him in his sling, he is outraged. The crying begins, tenfold, and I feel like everybody is looking at me as I make my way to the hotel. I can't bring myself to look at the view as I normally would; head down, I march on.

"Little Ben, whatever is the matter?" Mum smiles at her angry grandson as we come through the door. She is behind the reception desk, sifting through a sheaf of papers.

"Urgh," I slip him out of the sling, and hand him to her while I take it off. He is not best pleased to be handed to Grandma. "He's been doing this all the way back from David's."

"Oh Ben, where are your manners?" Mum asks, rocking him. His fists are tight little balls of frustration. "Poor little boy, you can't tell us what's wrong, can you?"

"I've got a pretty good idea," I say, grimly. "Do you

mind if we use the office so I can feed him without scaring any of your guests?"

"Of course. You go on through, and I'll get you a drink. Do you want a decaf tea?"

"Just a glass of water will be brill, thank you Mum." I retrieve my red-faced son from her, and he shifts to check who's got him now. He moves his head towards me. "Just a minute, young man."

Mum opens the office door for me and I slip gratefully into the peaceful room. Bea left her office furniture, having no need for it, and I sit in the big leather desk chair, where I used to sit when I managed this place. Ben is desperate and I sort myself out to he can begin to feed – which he does, immediately and intently, his little hand finding me as well. I could cry with our shared relief.

Instead, I look around the familiar room, silently greeting the ghosts who I half-believe live here. I used to imagine them, the spirits of past owners, no doubt wealthy and respected in society, now indignant and disgusted by the constant tide of guests – sometimes sunburnt, most in shorts and t-shirts (*What are those awful people wearing?* I imagine the spirits asking each other), sometimes rolling in merrily from a night on the town – who move in and out of the place, treading sand up the stairs and into the bathrooms.

All is quiet as I sit back in the chair, holding Ben to me. I close my eyes. Hear the tick of the clock and the soft sound of footsteps in one of the bedrooms above.

Where is Stef? I wonder idly. He would normally be here now. I ask Mum when she comes in, smiling, with a glass of water for me and a cup of tea for Dad. She looks uncomfortable.

"He's at a job interview."

"He's… what?" Stef joined the Sail Loft as night manager when I was working as the manager here. He's a good friend but I realise I haven't spoken to him in a long time. I hope he's OK.

"Yes, well I suppose there's not much point trying to hide it from you, Alice, but your dad and I are having a tough time of it. With the business, I mean."

So David was right. "Oh Mum, how bad is it?"

"It's OK, we're not on our knees… yet. But Stef can see we're not getting the bookings we were, or that Bea was, I should say. He has been perfectly honest and upfront with us. He says he doesn't want to leave but can see that we could do without the outlay of his wages. He's right, really. And to be honest, there is less for him to manage anyway."

I'm floored. The Sail Loft was never less than thriving when I used to work here. We often had to refer people to other places in town. I stroke Ben's hair with my free hand. He pulls his head away, looks up at me. Mum continues.

"We've spoken to Bea… a lot. She says it just takes time. That although we have an established business, it's up to Dad and me now to establish ourselves. She's right, I think she herself has been a draw to the place, for the people who have been coming here for years. They don't know us and I think people – some people, at least – come to rely on the familiar for their holidays. Of course, Jonathan isn't here anymore, either. So it does feel like everything has changed." Mum rubs her eyes. "I just feel so tired."

"Oh, Mum." It is very rare that Mum lets anything get her down but it looks like this is one of those times. "And you're spending your time up at Amethi."

"It doesn't matter," she says firmly. "I promised you I would do that. And I really enjoy it. Plus, it's more income."

Things really can't be great for her to be saying that. And she and I both know her wages at Amethi don't match Stef's at the hotel. "But you're never going to be able to build up your reputation here, Mum, if you're at Amethi all the time. I think… I think I should go back to work."

The words are out before I've really had time to consider them but I realise it's something I've been thinking about for a few weeks now. I miss it. I love being with Ben but I miss work. Does that make me a bad mum? I really, truly hope not. He's finished feeding now so I pull him up on my lap, lean him against me. Mum smiles.

"You can't do that, Alice, you've got Ben."

"I know, I have, but I've been thinking about nurseries and childminders a lot, and all the mums were talking about it the other day. It depends on what they're like, and how long their waiting lists are, but I'll sort something out. You need to focus on your own business now, Mum. Especially if Stef is going somewhere else."

I see a range of emotions cross Mum's face. Relief, and regret, amongst them. "Well, you talk to Sam about it. See what he thinks."

She hasn't tried to talk me down from it anymore. This in itself is telling. Now that I've made the suggestion, I can see it's the right thing. How did we ever think she and Dad could take on a new business and she could stand in for me running Amethi? Especially with Julie away. While Jon is covering Julie's work there, it's the catering side of things. He doesn't do the extra managerial work that Julie, as co-owner, does.

"I can't believe you haven't said anything before now," I say.

"Well, you've been busy," she gestures to Ben. "And a promise is a promise. I wouldn't let you down."

"No, I know that, Mum."

At this moment, Dad comes in. "Alice!" he says, delight written all over his face, more at the sight of his grandson than me, I suspect.

"Hi, Dad."

"Alice and I have just been having a chat," Mum says.

"Oh yeah?"

"Yes, I've told her… about Stef."

"Ah."

"And the situation here."

"OK."

"She wants to go back to work. At Amethi."

"But… Ben…"

"I know," I step in. "But it'll be OK. I don't think I will be able to do it immediately as I need to sort out childcare, but when I have that sorted I can do it. I promise, and I promise it'll be OK."

I hope it will. I don't really want to leave him just yet. But I have to sometime. And in all likelihood this will only be a few weeks earlier than planned. Besides, Becky works, and Jasper is fine. In fact, even though Becky doesn't like her job that much she says she does like having a bit of time to herself – even if she's working. "It's the lunchbreaks," she says. "I have a sandwich from home, and I treat myself to a coffee, find a quiet place to sit and have nearly an hour to myself, to read, or just look at my phone or whatever. No interruptions."

"You two need to focus on yourselves, and this place," I say firmly to my parents now. "I'm really sorry I hadn't realised what a tough time you've been having here."

"We're hoping it will pick up," Dad says. "Christmas is looking busy, and New Year, so that's good news."

"That is positive," I agree.

"It's just the four months either side of them that are proving difficult," he says ruefully. "Your mum and I won't be having a holiday in January, that's for sure."

That was one thing Bea always did. Although I imagine in her early days she wouldn't have had that luxury.

"You don't… you don't think you've made a mistake, doing this?" I ask.

"Sometimes, Alice. Sometimes I do."

"But that's natural, isn't it?" Mum steps in quickly. "I don't suppose many people can take on a new business, and so much responsibility, without some doubts."

"No, that's true." I stop and think for a while. Dad puts his hands out and I pass Ben to him. Dad's smile says it all.

"Maybe you need to make this place your own," I say, thoughts forming alongside my words. "I mean, the Sail Loft is Bea, isn't it? It's her place, which she built up from scratch. The decorating's to her taste. The breakfast menu… still hers. She did brilliantly well with it, and maybe there will be people who would have come from loyalty to her but it's yours now. You can find your own loyal guests." I am starting to warm to the idea. "Change the menu, even change the times breakfast is on, even if it's just by half an hour. Maybe redecorate, though I know that means additional costs."

"This has crossed my mind," Dad says. "We've taken on the business running pretty much as it was. The only real change is no evening meals and of course no Bea, or Jonathan."

"But you and Mum are lovely, and people will enjoy coming to stay here because of you. And you do a mean breakfast," I say. "I know you can't do evenings too but I don't think that's a huge problem for most people. There are plenty of places to eat out."

Mum looks a little brighter. "I always said you were a smart cookie," she smiles. "But really, you need to talk to Sam, before making any decisions about going back to work."

"Why? It doesn't make any difference to him; he's at work anyway."

"Just talk to him!" Mum smiles. "It's Ben's welfare, isn't it? Who looks after him when you're at work... and that you both agree on not just the childcare but whether he's ready for it."

"OK, you're right." I look at Ben, who Dad is jumping up and down, dangling him above his face. Ben is laughing his little head off.

I feel a wave of doubt wash run through me. Do I really want to leave this little boy? It will be the end of these unique weeks of just me and him. But needs must, and Mum and Dad need my help now. They've certainly helped me enough. Also, there is a little swell of excitement growing deep down in me, at the thought of getting back to work. I love it. Not as much as I love Ben, of course, but I do love it. And I think that's OK.

"Changing the subject," I say, when Ben is sleeping soundly, worn out by Grandad's over-excitement, "Sam and I have been talking about getting married."

"I thought you were already engaged?" Dad says.

"Engaged, yes. But actually *getting married*."

"Oh, Alice, that's wonderful news!" says Mum, her face breaking into a smile.

"Thank you, Mum. I know. I didn't think I was too bothered; and still, in a way, I'm not. I know it won't change our relationship, but I love the idea of being Mrs Branvall. How old-fashioned!"

"You won't be Alice Griffiths anymore," Dad says sadly.

"I will *always* be Alice Griffiths," I say. "And actually, I don't have to take Sam's name, but I feel like we're going a little off-subject here anyway!"

"Sorry, Alice," Dad says. "Your mum's right, that *is* wonderful news. You and Sam should be married, I'd love to walk you down the aisle…"

"Well, I don't know if there will be an aisle," I say. "And I'm not sure I like the idea of being 'given away' but I know, it's symbolic, and I would love you to be involved; you and Mum."

"So if there's not an aisle to walk down, what are you thinking? Underwater? Hot air balloon?"

"No!" I laugh, and end up telling them all about my dream wedding, up at the chapel. A reception at the Cross-Section, on a summer's evening while the evening slowly seeps into the night and people can dance on the decking, beneath the stars.

"That sounds lovely," Mum says. "Perfect for you and Sam. And I love the idea of both me and your dad walking you up the Island. But it sounds a bit expensive, love. Sorry to mention money. I wish it was all about romance, and love. But we're going to really struggle to pay for a wedding at the moment."

"Mum, I'm not expecting you and Dad to pay! Sam and I will sort it all out. And that's just one idea, anyway. It doesn't have to be like that. The important thing is that I'll be marrying Sam. Where that happens doesn't really matter."

11

As it turns out, it's not that simple. I return home with a long to-do list to work my way through. I have to do some research into availability and pricing for the wedding, and Sam and I really need to think about when we want to do it. Now the idea has started to take shape, it fills me with joy. And I know that in all honesty trying to pay for the chapel and private hire of the Cross-Section is probably going to be out of our league. But I'm going to find out what I can, anyway. It's OK to dream, isn't it?

The other, more pressing, thing is childcare for Ben, if I'm going to go back to work. Yes, I could come back to work at Amethi and free Mum up to concentrate on the Sail Loft, but can I find a nursery place for Ben? I settle down to make a few phone calls, hoping that Ben will stay nice and quiet. The more places I call, the more I realise that things are not going to be as straightforward as I had hoped. David was right – I should have started this way before now. There are no free spaces until January at the latest.

Still, I make appointments to visit a couple of places, and I text Suzie to see if she wants to come, too.

Our search began in high spirits. Suzie and I met up for a quick coffee then together took ourselves off up to the top edge of town, where Little Angels nursery sits.

"Hello!" Demelza, the owner, greets us with a wide smile ("No wonder she's smiling, the prices she charges," from Sam the night before while we were looking at her website, emblazoned with her grinning face). "Suzie and Alice? And these must be your two little angels."

It soon becomes apparent that she thinks Suzie and I really are 'Suzie and Alice' and that Ben and Delilah are brother and sister. "You'll find we're very open-minded here at Little Angels," she says. "We've had black children, all sorts."

I look at Suzie, a smile pinned back behind my lips. Think of Julie and how she'd respond to being branded as 'all sorts'.

"Mind you, we've never had, you know, a couple like you…"

I go to disabuse her of the misunderstanding but Suzie puts her hand on my arm, with a little shake of her head. Thus, we spend the entire tour of the place with Demelza referring to us as 'Mrs and Mrs' and smiling proudly to the staff in the various rooms as she takes us round the place.

And it is quite a place. It is expensive, as Sam identified, but it is spotlessly clean, and bright, and well-organised, with beautiful little nap areas in the baby room and the next room up, and a fantastic pre-school room, the walls covered with pictures, and a little shelf of cress eggheads sitting by the window. The children were doing some kind of dance lesson, and seemed to be having a whale of a time.

"When your two are a bit older, they're going to love it in here," Demelza beams and, as if to confirm this, Ben starts wriggling in my arms, rocking back and forth to the music.

As we leave the room, I sneak a look at Suzie and she grins at me. It was lovely to see those children looking so happy, and imagine Ben and Delilah that age. Though I wouldn't wish away this age they are now, for anything. I feel like I'll remember every little thing about Ben as a baby but Sam tells me I won't: "That space will get filled up with new stuff, all the time. It'll push out the baby knowledge. You won't remember exactly when he got his first tooth, or said his first word… all those milestones which are so important now will be replaced by new ones. Going to school, going to secondary school, exams, friendships, relationships. Break-ups," he finished with a grimace.

Sophie is still miserable about Josh. Of course she is. He and Sharon took on an important role in her life when Kate left, filling a small but vital part of the void. Now on Wednesday evenings, Sophie comes home and sits in her room, watching the kind of YouTube videos she used to when she was younger, of people playing Minecraft and Roblox. Reading books that she loved when she was ten and eleven. I suppose we ought to be grateful she has gone backwards rather than forwards, as it's not far to her being near enough a grown-up, and all the complications that brings. But she's not really into these things, and I worry for her.

I called Kate to discuss it, but she didn't seem overly concerned: "It's like a comfort blanket to her, I reckon. She's tried being a bit more grown-up and got her fingers burned so she's gone back to the things that she knew and loved before all of this. She'll be OK. I wish I could be with her, though."

"I know, I know you do. But you're right. She'll be OK. We've both been through it, in our time, right?"

I remember what Kate told me about her teenage years. Against all appearances now, with her amazingly fit, not-an-ounce-of-fat-on-her, body – and her seemingly effortless glamour – she was not a popular child, with either girls or boys. She told me she was overweight, and shy, and didn't have a boyfriend until she was sixteen. He broke her heart, going off with one of her friends.

"Oh yeah," she agreed. "And then some. I used to cry myself to sleep at night, thinking nobody would ever want me. Now I don't know if it's worse to have had a boyfriend and got dumped, than not to have had one at all."

"I don't suppose either's great," I sighed. "Doesn't it make you mad? I mean, it's completely natural to want to give this stuff a go, but it still feels like girls are pinning their sense of self-worth on whether or not some teenage boy wants to go out with them or not. It's rubbish."

"Yeah," laughed Kate, "but it's growing up, isn't it? And don't forget there are plenty of teenage boys pinning their self-worth on whether a girl wants to go out with them."

"Do you think it's the same thing?" I wondered what Ben would be like at that age. "I suppose I don't think of it like that. I just see girls and women spending so much time, effort, and money, on their appearances and I don't see men doing the same thing."

"Ah, but women don't do that just for men, do they?"

"Don't they?" I asked doubtfully.

"No, we do it for ourselves, and for each other."

"But isn't that just as bad?"

"Alice!" Kate had laughed, "You can't have it both ways. We're doing it for men, it's bad. We're doing it for women, it's bad."

I laughed too. "I just think it adds to the inequality between men and women, that we waste time thinking about what we look like while they race ahead, just about managing to shower and brush their teeth if we're lucky, getting the best jobs, the most money, and not giving a monkey's what they look like."

"I don't think it's that simple."

"No, I don't really, not for everyone. But it feels like it sometimes."

In reality, for Sam and me, I'm the main 'breadwinner' and I'm still not winning that much bread. But Amethi is a long-term prospect and it's going well. I feel relatively financially secure, although I don't have a lot to show for it in terms of ready cash at the moment and taking this time off to be with Ben is hitting us quite hard. How lucky we are to have Mum and Dad's house to live in.

Jonathan is paying rent on the cottage at Amethi but that goes into the business, of course. Julie and I are paying our wages, which are not huge, straight to Jon and to Mum, who are covering for us. It's not enough for Mum right now, she needs to be earning more. Whether or not Sam and I can afford a place for Ben at Little Angels, I am really not sure. Especially with a wedding to save for, too.

After showing us all the awards Little Angels has won, and its latest Ofsted report, Demelza runs through the pricing for Little Angels. "There's the deposit," she says, "which will be refunded to you when your child leaves to go to school." Bloody hell, that's a long time to wait. "Then there are costs of nappies, wipes, and meals when they're at that stage."

"Are those things not included?" Suzie asks.

"No." It's like Demelza has turned on Business setting. Just a few minutes ago she was playing Ring o' Roses with three little girls. Now she's itemising every little thing we might expect to pay while our babies are in her care. "We used to provide these things but they're very expensive, you know. And of course," she adds quickly, "it's all about equality here. We can't have some babies using more nappies and wipes than others, and everyone paying the same, can we?"

Again, I suppress a smile. "What if we brought our own nappies and wipes?"

"Oh no, that wouldn't do, either. I am very keen that everybody is treated *the same* here at Little Angels." She thinks she's onto something, with this lesbian couple in front of her. The equality angle is bound to swing it. "Now, let's see," she perches some glasses on her nose and wheels her chair over to the computer. "We will have two spaces coming up in the baby room soon, one in January and one in February."

Oh no. It's what I expected, but now there are two of us and only one space in January. I look at Suzie.

"Thanks Demelza," she says, "Can I book Delilah in for the January space?"

My jaw drops. I need that space more than she does; she isn't going back to work until March.

"Of course, my dear. But won't you want them both to start at the same time?" Demelza looks at me expectantly.

"Oh, I, erm, can I give you a ring, when I've spoken to my boyfriend?"

"Your…?" Demelza looks from Suzie to me, confused, her face colouring. I can tell she is desperate to ask how this all fits together but she knows she can't.

"Yes, I'll be in touch," I say. "Thank you so much for your time and for showing us around."

As we push our prams along the drive, we don't say a word then when we're safely out of sight, Suzie collapses with laughter. "Did you see her face?"

"I know," I say, smiling although really feel my nose has been put out of joint by her jumping in and taking that space. "I wonder what she's thinking of us right now?"

"But it did seem a lovely place."

"Bloody expensive, though."

"Yeah, but you get what you pay for."

"And you booked in."

"I did, didn't I? It just suddenly hit me, if it's that long to get a place, I should get my name down. I can always change my mind but I'd rather have the option."

We have lunch at Suzie's, which isn't too far from Little Angels. She and her husband Alex (and of course Delilah) live in a beautiful new-build Maisonette, with a small, sloping garden. I can see it's a far cry from the hippy commune she grew up in.

I look out of the window onto the small, neat garden. The fence at the back obscures what would be a view across town.

"It would be, if there weren't a dozen more houses like this one right behind it!" Suzie laughs. "You're so lucky, living where you do."

"I know, we really are. It's not the first time I've lived there, either."

While the babies sit on our knees and we try to eat lunch without dropping crumbs on their heads, I give Suzie a potted history of my time in Cornwall, from the first time, aged eighteen, to coming back and reuniting with Sam.

"What a story!" she says, "and how romantic, you and Sam!"

"It is, isn't it? You kind of forget the romance, don't you, when babies come along." Although, I think of that Saturday not so long ago, when Sophie was in Devon.

"Err… yeah. And before that, too." Suzie grins. "Alex isn't really the 'romantic' type. But then maybe neither am I. We've been together since uni."

"But that is romantic!"

I gently take Ben's hand away from my sandwich.

"I suppose, in its own way."

Will getting married breathe a bit more romance back into our relationship? Or just be something else to organise? We've been through a lot to get where we are, and we're shattered. All the time. But now the idea of the wedding has wedged itself in my mind and I don't think it will be easy to push it away.

After lunch, we visit Goslings – a nursery further along the road out of town. It may not have as many awards to its name as Little Angels but to me it feels better. More homely. The owner, Angie, is down-to-earth and seems to know all the kids by name. The staff also respond well to her.

There is an amazing outdoor play area, where the toddler age group are running about, a little girl squealing for joy as she zips down a slide into the waiting arms of one of the staff. There are also male members of staff, where it had been all-female at Little Angels. I like this and I am at ease immediately. Ben seems to be, too, watching it all going on from the safety of my arms.

I glance at Suzie to see if she feels the same but she doesn't look as enthusiastic. We end up in Angie's office, where she talks through pricing, rules, etc. There is a deposit at Goslings, too, but it's smaller than at Little Angels. Angie also talks about using tax credits to pay for childcare, which I think Sam and I are going to have to do. It is only when it comes to the waiting list that I'm disappointed.

"It's going to be February, I think, before a space comes up in the baby room." Angie sees my face. "I'm sorry, did you need something sooner, Alice?"

"Yes, well kind of. I've unexpectedly had to return to work sooner. February would have been perfect otherwise."

"Well, if you'd like me to put Ben on the list now I can let you know if anything comes up sooner. But no pressure. I can also give you the contact details of a couple of childminders, if you like."

"Thank you," I say, and I look at Suzie to see if she wants to put Delilah's name down now as she did at Little Angels, but she says nothing. "I will put Ben's name down, please," I say to Angie. "And if that's OK to get the childminders' details that will be brill."

"Of course," she says. "But it might be the same with the childminders, you know. There are a lot of children in this town! And a lot of working parents! But hopefully you'll find somebody. And we'll look forward to having this little one with us in February."

She smiles at Ben and he gurgles. Good, he seems to like her.

Suzie says, "Thanks for showing us round, Angie. I just need to talk it all through with my husband and I'll be back in touch."

Well, this is weird, seeing as she just jumped in at Little Angels. On the way out, I ask her why not Goslings.

"I don't know. Don't you think it's weird that some of the staff are men?"

"Err... no. Should I?"

"I'm probably being unreasonable, but I'm suspicious of blokes who want to work with little kids. Just doesn't seem right, somehow."

My jaw drops for the second time and my mind makes a hasty re-evaluation of this new friend.

"I really don't think like that. In fact, I liked that about it. It's nice for the kids to see men and women in caring roles."

"Mm, I suppose."

I can tell she's not convinced and I feel disappointed. I'd thought I'd have things in common with Suzie but today has revealed we may be less alike than I'd thought. I feel a strong pang for Julie, and when Suzie asks if I'd like to go for another coffee somewhere, I make my excuses and head home, my mood brightened slightly at the sight of the sea sparkling under a grey November sky that the sun has just begun to penetrate.

12

Sophie is already at home when I get back.

"Hi, Soph," I call but there is no answer. I pluck Ben from his pram – not long now till he can go in a proper pushchair – and he chuckles as I bound up the stairs with him, stopping as we always do for a quick look through the stairwell window. The sun's pushed all the way through now, melting the clouds like butter in a warm pan.

"Soph!" I call and Ben wriggles. "Come on, let's go and see your sister."

I knock on the door of the room which used to be mine.

"Come in," comes a small voice.

I push the door gingerly to see Sophie sitting on her bed, miserably. She looks small and forlorn.

"How was your day?" I ask gently, Ben wriggling in my arms, trying to get to his big sister. It must be so frustrating, sometimes, being a baby. Knowing what you want to say, but only being able to coo or cry. Knowing where you want to go but having no means of propelling yourself there, although Ben certainly gives it his best shot.

"It was terrible," Sophie says, and begins to cry.

"What happened?"

"Nothing, really," she wipes her nose on her sleeve, "'cept Amber tried out for netball and got on the team and so did… Annabel Fenwick."

If I never heard that name again in my life I'd be so happy.

"OK. So is that a problem? Did you want to be on the team?"

"No, course not. I didn't know Amber did, either," she says slightly scornfully of her best friend, "but she says her mum wanted her to do it. And now she's saying she likes Annabel and I shouldn't blame her for what happened with Josh."

"Oh."

"It's like, now they're on the *netball team* together, they're going to be best friends."

"Amber will always be your best friend," I say firmly, hoping I'm right. I was lucky with Julie; we never really fell out but I know it can sometimes be different. I wouldn't put Amber as the type to fall out, or be mean, though – and of course not Sophie.

"So now she's got Amber *and* Josh," Sophie wails. I wonder idly if she is due on her period but I would not voice that thought. It seems very unfeminist of me, undermining her right to feel this way about something very real.

Sitting on the edge of the bed, Ben delighted because he's somehow managed to move me towards his target, I stroke Sophie's hair. "She hasn't 'got' Amber," I say, "Amber is your friend. And she's just trying to do the right thing, because she is a nice person and she hasn't really got any reason not to. Other than sticking up for you. But if they're on the team together they probably do need to get on OK. It doesn't mean she's not your friend anymore."

"I don't see how she can be friends with her and me."

"I do. I'm sorry to say it, but I do. Annabel has obviously upset you but really it's Josh who you should be angry at. It's not like Annabel was any great friend of yours so she hasn't exactly crossed you. Josh, on the other hand, should have behaved much better. Try to look at it from Annabel's point of view, if you can. I know it's hard."

Sophie doesn't look very keen to see anything from anyone's point of view but her own.

"She is a Year 9, right?"

Sophie gives a little assent with her head. I take the chance to slide Ben over to her, knowing the comfort his little warm body can give. She does smile, and takes him from me. He is overjoyed. His masterplan has come to fruition. As his little body rocks to and fro in her arms, I continue. "So she's a bit younger than you, and Josh, and is probably really flattered that he likes her. I am sorry to put it so bluntly, Sophie, but this is where we are. And I don't want you to waste another moment of your life feeling so miserable about this. Annabel may have liked Josh for a while or she may have been flattered when he asked her out. But it was him that behaved badly, not her. Do you see what I mean?"

"I suppose," Sophie begrudges.

"I'm really cross with him, for doing this. And I think he's an idiot."

That does make Sophie smile, just a little.

"He is, Soph. For one thing, he's just lost the best girl in town. For another, he's behaved so thoughtlessly towards you that if I was Annabel Fenwick, I'd be worried. Who's to say he won't do the same to her, and then to somebody else?'

"I don't want him to go out with somebody else," Sophie has grasped exactly the wrong part of what I'm saying.

"Soph," I say firmly, "he's not worth it. I'm sad too and I know how much you loved going round to his house. I think Sharon misses you, by the way."

Sob. Why did I say that?

"But believe me," I plough on, "you are worth far more than sitting in your room, letting this ruin this time in your life. You will get over it but let's try and do it sooner than later, shall we? That's not to belittle your feelings but I am not going to sit by and watch you spend a terrible few weeks for the sake of a silly teenage boy who should have known how lucky he was. He has messed up, and he may regret it, but I am asking you now, Sophie, if he ever asks you out again, please say no."

"Do you think he'll ask me out again?"

I give up.

We end up having some fun, lying Ben on the bed and tickling him, Sophie brushing her school tie lightly across his cheek. I love watching her with him. She becomes animated, and it's clear that the feeling is mutual. In time, though, he turns restless and I can tell he wants his milk.

"You can feed him in here, if you like," Sophie says. "Here." She gets off the bed, and clears a pile of clothes from the chair under the dormer window.

How I loved this room when I first moved down to Cornwall – and the next time, too. I was eighteen; not much older than Sophie, that first time. Julie in the room next door. David downstairs. I remember coming in here for the first time and rushing to the window, sending the gull on the roof above into a flap.

David had laughed at my excitement. "It's just a little room," he'd said, semi-apologetically.

"It's perfect," I'd said, and I still think that now. Perched up at the top of the house, it can get cold in winter but David had a new heating system put in, and double glazing so that it doesn't take long to warm up. It is cosy now and I sit on the chair to let Ben feed but I want to look out of the window, into the darkness of the town on this late autumn afternoon. It won't be long before the Christmas lights are up and the place begins to bustle again with holidaymakers, but I love these quiet few weeks, when the town and its residents can all take a deep breath. Settle a little after the craziness of high season, and ready ourselves for the onslaught of Christmas and the climax of New Year, when the streets surge with people in fancy dress, ready to see out the old and welcome in the new.

"I think you're right," Sophie says to me after a while. "I know you are. About Annabel, I mean. And Josh. But what if she steals Amber, as well?'

"She hasn't stolen Josh," I gently remind her. "And Amber is your best friend. That isn't going to change. She's just a really nice person so she'll be friendly with Annabel because, really, she hasn't any reason not to."

I can see it's hard for Sophie to accept this, and I get it. I don't think I would give anything to be a teenager again. So fraught with insecurities and desperate to fit in, be accepted. Urgh.

"Look, why don't we have Amber over this weekend, eh? You two can have a pizza and movie night."

"I'm going to Mum's this weekend," she reminds me.

"Of course you are. Next week, then?"

"Yeah, that sounds good."

"Great," I smile, and Ben pulls away from me, looking up. "You are too easily distracted these days," I say, looking at Sophie. "Come on, let's leave your sister to it, shall we? You've got homework to do, Soph?"

She nods.

"OK, well you get on, and I'll go and get tea started. Tacos tonight?"

"Yes please."

I hug her before I go. "It will get easier, you know. I do

realise that's such a boring adult thing to say but it's true."

"Thank you, Alice."

I kiss the top of her head then go out onto the landing, where all is now dark. The daylight is fading quicker and earlier these days. I put the landing light on and hear the central heating pipes creaking throughout the house. Downstairs, the gentle hum of the boiler. I carry Ben with me, down the stairs. Into the lounge, shutting the blinds and curtains. Switching on the two lamps, which lend the room a different personality to its sunny summer guise.

In time, Sam returns home and when he shuts the door behind him he pulls the curtain across, ostracising the cold outdoors and sealing us into our home; our little family of four. Ben sits patiently while we eat then I take him for his bath and night-time feed, coming back downstairs when he's settled in his cot.

It seems to me that things are moving quickly and I stop for a few moments at the stairwell window, peering out into the darkness and letting the day's events wash over me. When I think of leaving Ben with anyone else, I get a slight cramp in my stomach, yet at the same time I am excited about returning to work. I felt right at Goslings, but I don't know about using a childminder. There's something about that I don't feel so comfortable with. Maybe Suzie isn't the only one with weird hang-ups.

I rub the glass where my breath has condensed, then press my nose against it. Think of Mum and Dad just up the hill. I hope they're alright.

I can hear the murmur of Sam's and Sophie's voices in the lounge. The door is ajar and there is a slight crackle behind their voices. An unmistakeable smell; the first fire of winter. I skip down the rest of the stairs, and into the lounge. There is Sam, kneeling at the hearth. He smiles when I come in and I just want to kiss him. But Sophie is sitting curled up on the settee so I return his smile then go to sit next to her. She nestles into me and I lay my head on hers. How many more years have we got when she will gladly do this? I breathe deeply, feeling the comfort that comes with the colder months moving in.

Although I know that come February I will be desperate for some sunshine and warmth once more, I will make the most of the quiet cosiness this time of year brings and appreciate it while I can.

13

At the weekend, Sophie goes up to Devon, while Sam, Ben and I spend another leisurely weekend around town, although the days have taken on a definite chill, which was not there a week or two ago.

I enjoy its freshness, as we walk along the harbour promenade, seagulls perched on the railings, watching us carefully for signs of food; little turnstones darting in and around our feet and under the benches.

"I think Ben's pretty much outgrown this thing," Sam gestures to the pram, where, sure enough, Ben is looking less than impressed, and seems to be trying to sit up.

"He can't have! They're not mean to go in pushchairs till six months!" Really, my dismay is at the fact he has already nearly outgrown his proper baby stage. How can that be?

"Yes, but he's five months, or not far off, Alice – and he's a big boy. All those things are meant as guidance, you know. And he's almost there with sitting up, unaided, isn't he? I'm sure that when they can do that they can go in a pushchair."

"How do you know so much?" I say in wonder, shocked to find tears springing to my eyes. What is wrong with me?

"Hey!" Sam laughs, putting a hand on my shoulder. "I don't, I've just done it once before."

"But you said you forget everything."

"No, I said you don't remember all those little details that you think you will. Like when they roll onto their tummy for the first time. When it happens it's like the greatest thing ever but they don't stop growing and developing. I don't remember when any of that happened for Soph. They've all been pushed out by newer things. And now she's so grown-up…"

It's his turn to look miserable.

"She is, Sam, I know. But she's also still so young. And she needs you, now more than ever."

"That's it!" Sam says. "When they're babies they're totally dependent on you, for feeding, changing, being put down for sleeps, all of that. It is emotional, of course, but it's also physical. As they get older, they learn to feed themselves, clothe themselves, have showers when you can persuade them to, and then stay up far later than they should. They detach themselves in that way. But emotionally, they need us more than ever."

"Sophie will be OK," I say.

"I know. I know she will. But when I look at Ben and look at Soph – it's only fourteen years since she was like this," he reaches into the pram and strokes Ben's cheek, to Ben's joy. "Now she's… she's already had her heart broken. And she's had to choose between living here with us or moving to Devon with Kate. I sometimes wonder if she made the right choice. I look at you and Ben and yes, he loves me, but he's like a part of you, you're a part of him."

I had no idea Sam felt like this. "Well, I guess that's just biology," I say. "I've carried him literally inside my body for nine months. You can't get closer than that. And look, Sophie chose to stay here. She wants to be with you."

"But she misses Kate, doesn't she? So much. I feel like she's being torn in two between the both of us. And it was her friends as much as me, wasn't it? The deciding factor, I mean. And now that little…"

"Sam!" I laugh. "You said it had to come to an end sometime."

"Yes, I did, and it did. Unless Sophie wants to tie herself to some local boy and never go anywhere or do anything."

"I don't think it has to be like that…" I protest.

"Whose side are you on?" Sam asks, but he's smiling. "But I didn't realise just how deeply she'd be hurt by it all. And I can't help wondering if the hurt is coming from somewhere else as well, from being apart from Kate."

"Oh." We walk on, turning up one of the steep side streets, where we are sheltered from the breeze off the sea. In fact, with the sun somehow managing to slice into this narrow slip of road and warming our faces, it feels almost like spring.

It's hard work pushing a pram up the slope, though. Sam offers to take a turn.

"No thanks, it'll do me good!" I puff. "The hills in this town are like a proper work-out, especially as Ben's getting bigger every day."

We don't speak for a while then I come back to what Sam was saying. "Sophie absolutely adores you, you know."

"I do know," he sends his smile sidewards to me, "but I don't know if I'm enough. You're great, too. You know more about… *being a girl*," he pulls a face. "You also had the benefit of a proper mum growing up."

"Karen's a proper…" I begin to protest but Sam laughs.

"You see, you couldn't finish that sentence! Mum is Mum. And I'm glad she's back here, most of the time, but Janie and I didn't have the kind of mum you did. Your mum put you first, it's obvious. Our mum put herself first, and we came second if we were lucky, or third if there was a bloke on the scene."

"Ouch," I say.

"Yep. It seemed normal enough, until I went to Luke's house or another mate's, saw what their mums were like. Realised what I was missing."

"But Karen's…" Again, I can't find the words. Karen is… what? Well, since she came back to Cornwall, she has changed. To some extent. She is a doting grandmother, to Sophie as well as Ben, and keen to help when she can, when it suits her. Sam and she had very stern words before Ben was born, and I was sure she was going to scoot back to Spain but, to be fair, she has stayed put. Even finding her own place to live, and getting work as a cleaner of holiday lets. And she helped us furnish Ben's bedroom. She sometimes has Sophie over to stay at hers, too.

"She's Mum! There are reasons why she is how she is, no doubt," Sam says. "Her mum wasn't amazing, either, and her dad was a great man in many ways but he wasn't around much. Too busy working, in the pub, or out with the lifeboat boys. I don't think Mum saw much of him."

"I was going to say, you're forgetting how important dads are," I lean into Sam, kiss his shoulder. "You are amazing. You and Sophie have so much in common and don't forget Kate wasn't always the most stable person. When she was single, when it was just her and Soph in that flat…"

"True," Sam muses, "but she did always, *always* put Sophie first. And she didn't disappear off for three years to get a degree, did she? I did that. Remember what that did to Sophie."

It's hard to forget. It nearly meant the end of our relationship, as it became clear that Sophie couldn't bear to share her dad in the little time he did have back home in Cornwall. Which was completely understandable. I don't answer this now. I am thinking it through, wondering where this is all going, if it is going anywhere.

We walk on, along the flatter street, with its row of terraced fishermen's cottages, one with a plaque proclaiming itself to be the place where a famous 'artist and mariner' lived. In the summer, these streets are often a nightmare to walk along, with a steady flow – and sometimes full-on traffic jams – of people trying to find a car park that actually has spaces. Red-faced drivers, sweaty passengers, all desperate to park up, get out and enjoy a share of everything this beautiful town has to offer.

I appreciate the quiet now, with the occasional fellow pedestrian to greet. Sam takes the pram from me, without a word, and I walk freely for a while. Taking in long, slow breaths of the luxuriously sea-clean air. Ben is asleep now and we slow our pace, taking our time, each lost in our own thoughts.

***

"Alice! Sam! We weren't expecting you! I'll just tell your dad," Mum seems slightly fraught, I think, and I feel bad that we turned up with no notice. Our walk had just taken us this way and with Ben awake now we'd decided to pop in and say hello. "Phil!" Mum calls and we hear some muttering from behind the heavy office door.

"What…?" His head appears. "Oh, Alice! Sam! We weren't expecting you!" A smile flicks onto his face.

"No, Mum said! Sorry for just turning up unannounced."

"Oh, that's OK, how's my little man…" Dad is over by the pram quick as a flash and Ben gurgles with pleasure to see this silly man who has a tendency to bounce him high into the air and hold him over his face, not yet put off by Ben's new dribbling habit.

"May I…?" asks Dad.

"Be my guest," Sam and I say at the same time.

"Oh you two, you're like twins," Mum says.

"I hope not, I'm pretty sure that's illegal," says Sam.

"Oh, you know what I mean! I'm really glad you've come to see us, we could do with the change of faces, couldn't we, Phil?"

"Oh?"

"Yes, just me and your dad here this weekend."

"Really? No guests?" *Obviously not, Alice, you idiot.* But I've never known the Sail Loft to be open and completely free of holidaymakers, even at this time of year.

"No," Mum says, unconvincingly brightly. "Shall I put the kettle on?"

"That would be great."

"We might as well go and sit in the dining room," Dad says, "it's not like we'll be in anybody's way."

Something's not right here. I look at Sam, who raises his eyebrows at me. We follow Dad through.

"What's going on, Dad? Is everything OK?" I ask gently.

"Oh yes," he smiles at Ben, "everything's just great." This last word had an edge to it.

"So, no guests this weekend? Is that just a blip?"

"If it is, it's a long one," Dad says grimly but he lifts Ben into the air, making him laugh with glee.

I feel a little panic inside. I knew they shouldn't have done this. It's too much. And Mum's health… she can't afford to have so much stress. Bea always says people take on businesses like these believing they're a ticket to a life by the sea. Leisurely, and relaxed. No more days stuck in the office. "People don't see what hard work it is," she's said to me more than once. "Look at me. I was in my early thirties when I took this on. Just divorced. I didn't have a social life for years. It was just me and the Sail Loft. Which was what I needed then, I guess. But still, I didn't meet anybody else, not really, till I met Bob, and he was on the other side of the bloody Atlantic."

"Are you struggling?" I ask Dad gently.

"I wouldn't say that… oh, who am I kidding? I would definitely say that. I think Mum said to you that people don't want to come now Bea's not here. At least, that's how it feels. She had her regulars, who have apparently all seized upon this as a chance to try new things; new places."

"Oh, Dad. What about locally? I know Bea worked with some of the other smaller hotels, and I did when I was here, so we could send business each other's way."

"They don't want to know," says Dad.

"Really?" That surprises me.

"It's like they closed ranks, when Bea left. We're not local, are we?"

"Well, neither are half of them! Have you been to any of those networking events I mentioned?"

"No, not yet," Mum says, coming in with a tray. "We haven't had a chance."

"But they're really important," I say, slightly exasperated. "That's where you keep those local links going. You need to make time for them."

"We will," she says, but I'm not convinced.

"Well, I'm going to be back at Amethi as soon as I can," I say. "You need to be here now, Mum. You and Dad need to make some plans. You can do this, I know you can."

They both look at each other, doubtfully.

"Of course you can! I suppose you couldn't really expect to take this on and for it to run smoothly immediately. It's a big undertaking. I will sort out some childcare for Ben, until he can start at Goslings, and then you will be free to make this work, Mum. And one of you can come with me to the next networking meeting, OK? I can introduce you. It'll be fun." Again, the dubious expressions. I feel annoyed. Sa, wisely, is staying well out of it, looking intently at the newspaper. "You're going to have to do it. If you want to make this work, you need to do everything you can. Remember," I say, warming to my subject and also aware that I am beginning to lecture my own parents, "we were talking about you making the Sail Loft *yours*. Put your own stamp on it. At the moment it is just as Bea left it, and it worked for her, and it reflects who she is. Maybe you need to think about what you want it to be."

"I would love to redecorate," Dad says.

"But that would be expensive," Mum says. "I don't think we'd be able to do that."

"No, maybe not yet. But there must be a few things you can do. And maybe you two need more living space as well." I have been thinking this for a while, feeling guilty to have their big, beautiful house while they are confined to the owners' apartment at the Sail Loft. It was fine for Bea, as a single person. Not so much for Mum and Dad who, besides there being two of them, are used to something bigger, with a garden to relax in, which they didn't have to share with anyone. Now, the living rooms downstairs are for guests as well – when there are any – and the outdoor spaces, too. Meanwhile, Sam, Sophie, Ben and I have the run of their three-storey townhouse, complete with private garden. We are paying them rent, of course, but still it doesn't seem right.

I move the conversation on, knowing they need to talk about this between themselves and I'm also too excited by this next topic to leave it any longer.

"What time of year do you think's best to get married?" I ask, nonchalantly. Sam looks up, smiles at me.

"You're really doing it?" Mum asks, clapping her hands.

"Well, yes, we are engaged, Mum," I say. "And we did talk about it last time I was here."

"Oh, I know, but I thought that was just…"

"Just what?" I ask, half-amused. "An overactive imagination?"

"No! I know you've been thinking about it. But you two have got such a lot on your plates."

I look across at Dad, who is smiling quietly.

"What do you think, Dad?"

"I think May is the perfect month to get married," he smiles at Mum.

"Oh, you!" she says. "Your dad's such a romantic. Still, I'd say Sam's the same."

"What do you think, Sam? How does May sound to you?" I ask.

"I'd marry you any time, Alice, you know that."

"See?" Mum says, "That's proved my point. It's the men who are the romantics in this family. We're more practical, aren't we, Alice?"

"I like to think I'm quite romantic, too!" I protest.

"And that's why, when I mentioned it to you, you said it would be 'nice'," Sam grins.

"I did, didn't I? Well, it would be nice." I correct myself, "It *will* be nice."

"That sounds smashing, Alice. And Sam. Something to really look forward to," Dad says.

"Better get planning, then!" I say, and a little thrill runs through me. I may not be the biggest romantic but I one hundred per cent believe in love. Having spent ten years apart from Sam and never forgetting him, I know this is it. He's the man for me.

I'll never forget the year Julie and Luke got married, and Martin and David, and Bea and Bob – and Stefan and April. I wanted that for myself. For me and Sam, but I never thought we'd even get back together. Against maybe not all odds, but certainly some odds, here we are. It is something to celebrate and if not now, then when?

We leave the Sail Loft with my mind whirring; ideas for the wedding, and for helping Mum and Dad, fluttering about like butterflies. I will keep a lid on them for now, until I've had a chance to think them through and conduct some investigations.

14

On Saturday evening, we're so tired that once we've got Ben off we slide into bed too, under the covers, and far away into a deep, deep sleep. When Sunday morning comes, it's 5.37am and I realise Ben hasn't woken me during the night. Or did he? I scan my memory, wondering if I was just so tired and half-asleep that I can't quite remember what happened. But no, I have no recollection of being woken up.

Panic.

Is he OK? Why didn't he wake? I sit up cautiously, Listen in the dark, quiet house. All I can hear, though, is Sam.

I ease myself out of bed and I pad across the room, out of the door to Ben's doorway, increasingly scared of what I might find when I get to my baby's cot. But no, there he is, fast asleep in his favoured position of what I like to call 'backwards frog' – on his back with his little arms above his head and his legs bent outwards.

Relief!

Although I hadn't felt that there was something wrong. It was just that 'what if' feeling – and I've become used to being woken every night, often more than once. I'm amazed I didn't wake myself anyway.

But, I realise as I make my quiet way back to bed, this means that Sam and I have had hours, and hours, of luxurious, uninterrupted sleep. I slip in under the duvet, as close to Sam's warmth as I can without disturbing him. He mumbles a little and shifts around so he's curled next to me. Laying a hand on him, I smile to myself. What shall I do? It's Sunday morning, I've just had the most sleep I've had in one night ever – or at least for this last year.

What I don't want to do is disturb either of these sleeping beauties. If I was sensible, I'd go back to sleep myself, but I think I am too wide awake now. I would dearly love the indulgence of an uninterrupted cup of tea in bed, but it is almost guaranteed that if I try to go downstairs, it will wake one or both of them.

So is this it? I wonder, trying to ignore my bladder's cries for attention. I do not want to leave the safety of this bed and these moments of succulent darkness and silence. Is this where Ben sleeps through the night, where I reclaim those lost hours? I don't want to count my chickens but the fact he has done it once is cause for celebration.

I lie still and warm, and I listen to Sam's breathing. Outside the window, the other side of those thick curtains, there might be a vague grey November light seeping into the sky; soon, if not just yet. And aside from early-morning joggers and dog-walkers, the next ones up will be the gulls. I love their waking cries as they take to the skies for the day, lifting up over the rooftops and swirling around above the town.

My mind flits to Mum and Dad. Are they awake? Worrying? I hope not. And I hope I can help them, soon. Ease some of their troubles.

What time is it where Luke and Julie are? It's late morning, it's got to be. I wonder idly what they're doing today.

And then… the wedding. My wedding. I smile, at the thought of it. Imagine a beautiful spring day. Sam on the Island, flanked by Luke, and perhaps Christian. A small gathering of family and friends. Sophie holding Ben. How big he will be by then? Nearly one! Julie, next to her… holding her own baby? I know I shouldn't think like that but why not be positive for her?

Then I reel my thoughts back in, stop my imagination running away with itself, though it can't hurt to dream. Instead, I try to concentrate on the here and now. Be in the moment. It seems a long time since I have told myself that; a lesson I learned from Lizzie. It's a good thing to do. I close my eyes, relax each part of my body in turn. I almost feel like I could fall asleep…

Snuffle, snuffle, murmur, in the dark, sleepy house.

Ah. Here he comes.

Murmur, murmur. The sound of wriggling.

Sam is still asleep. I ease myself back out of bed, try to get to Ben before he wakes Sam…

"Waaahhhh!"

Just as I get to the cot. Ben is trying to push himself up, to focus his eyes on me in the dark. His cry is short-lived, now he knows I am close. He's like the Predator. I can dimly make out his shape and I reach down to pluck him from his cot. He is warm and solid in my arms. And though I was enjoying my few moments' respite, in truth I'm just so happy to be reunited with him, as daft as that may sound. To know that he is safe.

Back to bed we go and I give him his first feed of the day. Next to us, Sam mumbles something, turns over, and is fast asleep once more. I lean back against the headboard and listen to the sounds of the town waking up.

***

Following the success of Ben sleeping through, I am jubilant, although also, strangely, more tired than ever. It seems as though, now I have let sleep in, I only need more. It's addictive.

But while Ben has his morning nap, and Sam is out on his bike, I sit down and start to jot down some ideas for Mum and Dad, and the Sail Loft. I don't want to interfere, or take over, but it feels to me that they are floundering, and I suppose I am in the fortunate position of having worked there, managed the place, before. It would be silly not to make use of that knowledge and experience.

I drink a cup of decaf tea and eat a warm cinnamon bun while I make notes, getting sticky fingerprints on my pencil and the paper. I give up and eat the bun first, then wash my hands, then get back to work. Which is another issue. Getting back to work. How do I do this, without a place at nursery? And is it unfair to Ben, anyway, just shoving him into nursery when he's so little?

I'm well aware that once these days are over, I won't be getting them back. Yet, I have a slight thrill at the thought of Amethi. And, guiltily, at the thought of some time to myself. Even if it will be spent working. I smile when I think back to my idealised vision of working with my baby by my side. How had I ever thought that might be possible? As if I'd get a moment's peace to concentrate on anything.

I push those thoughts to the side for now. I am meant to be thinking about the Sail Loft. And I think I've got a great idea. I smile to myself, hopeful that I will be able to help my parents and in some small way repay all the help they've given me throughout my life.

Sam arrives, sweaty and elated from his ride, striding in through the patio door while Ben is in his bouncer and I'm in the kitchen making leek and potato soup.

"Hello, you!" he kisses Ben.

"And hello you," he kisses me.

"Hello," I turn and kiss him tentatively. "Sorry, no sweaty men in the kitchen, it's unhygienic. Julie would blow her top if she could see this."

"But Julie's not here, is she?" he smiles and kisses me a little more.

"Sam, Ben is watching."

We both turn and look at our son, presently engaged with trying to ram a whole rubber bunny into his mouth.

"Doesn't look too bothered," says Sam. "But I'll leave you alone. I need a shower anyway."

"You're in a good mood," I observe.

"Well, yeah – after that amazing night's sleep and a proper good bike ride, I feel pretty good. And… I've had an idea."

"Oh yeah?"

"Yes! I will look after Ben. I'll take the shared parental leave. I mean, I'll have to speak to Tony about it, but we're quiet at the moment. I reckon I could do it, till February, when this little monkey can go to nursery."

The thought had never even crossed my mind. Why had I not thought of this?

"Don't you have to give eight weeks' notice?"

"I don't know," Sam says, a look of doubt passing across his face. "Hope not. Let me speak to Tony tomorrow and see what I can do."

Well, that really would be amazing. I kiss him, and hug him tightly.

"Hey, what about the hygiene?"

"Ah, it's only soup for me and you, anyway."

"Reckon he'd be up for a bit of it?" Sam looks towards Ben.

"Oh, no, you're meant to wait till six months…"

"I'm sure Soph was smaller. They change these things all the time, don't they? Anyway, he's a greedy little bugger, it might do him good – and give you a break, too."

I ponder this while Sam showers. Ben does watch us incredibly closely when we're eating. He's worse than a gull. And if he's sitting on my knee while I eat, he has been known to try and intercept my fork/piece of cake on its way to my mouth.

When the soup is done, I find the plastic bowls I've already bought and tucked away, and I put a little soup into one. Then I find a rubber spoon, and sterilise it. Is that what I'm meant to do? Surely people don't sterilise everything every time their child eats. I am just not quite sure of what I'm doing. I take the baby book from the shelf – this is something I do want to read about – and lift Ben out of his bouncer, then take him and the book through to the lounge.

"I think he's still a bit too young, you know," I say to Sam, when he comes back down, smelling delightful after his shower. His hair is still damp, the curls more pronounced than when it's dry. "I think people used to do it at four months but now they're saying six. And apparently we should be doing this baby-led weaning, letting him pick up and eat his own food."

"No worries," says Sam. "I am sure they'll change it again. We're going to have to get him taking the bottle, though, if I'm going to be looking after him the next couple of months. Why don't you have some soup then get out for the afternoon? Give us a chance to have a go at getting used to the bottle."

"Really?" I want to leap at the opportunity, but also don't want to seem too keen.

"Yes!" Sam laughs. "Could be a long afternoon, but

we'll get through it won't we, mate?"

Ben beams at Sam.

"See?" Sam looks at me. I decide to seize the moment, before he changes his mind.

***

I gulped down my soup, pulled my coat, scarf and boots on, and resisted the temptation to tell Sam where everything is... it's his home too, and Ben's his son. He already knows.

I have a strange feeling in my stomach, and I can't tell if it is nerves, excitement, or guilt.

It's silly, though, isn't it? Sam has been out this morning, and it was no big deal. I suppose it's because over these few months, Ben has been with me, almost all of the time. I feel that full responsibility for him. What will it feel like, handing that over to Sam day after day, assuming he is able to get parental leave?

It fits with my ideals of shared parenting, and equality, but if I am honest it also feels a bit uncomfortable, just a little, the thought of handing over my role as primary caregiver. What if Ben loves me less? Loves Sam more? More than me, I mean. The thoughts roll around my head like marbles while I walk towards the harbour in the thin November sunshine, pushing my hands deep into my pockets and trying to keep warm.

15

I end up retracing the walk that Sam and I did with Ben yesterday, although I add in a little stroll on the beach; so much easier without a pram to try and navigate across the sand, or even a heavy baby strapped to my chest.

I keep my boots on as I can't quite face the idea of cold, wet feet today. But I stride across and down to the shoreline, hoping that the recent waterproofing I did has worked, or else I will have cold, wet feet inside cold, wet boots, with no chance of drying or warming up. I stop for a moment, look out across the sea; while its turquoise colour holds under the clear winter sky, I can well imagine its icy depths and I shiver as I imagine walking into it now; plunging headfirst as I like to do in warmer months. But being close to it, my eyes scanning the waves, drinking in the sight of this endless stretch of water, makes me feel alive.

I hope Sam and Ben are getting on OK and I feel an almost physical yearning to be back with Ben, in particular, and a guilt that I am out on my own, but I shut it down.

I am allowed to do this, I tell myself. I am allowed some time for me, and if Sam is serious about doing this parental leave thing then the sooner he and Ben get used to being together more, the better.

I walk all the way to the end of the beach, looking up the face of the slippery, slimy-looking rocks there; a trickle of water running down them, dripping into the rockpools. At the top is the coastal path. It would be a beautiful day to walk that path but today I have other things to attend to and so I turn, retrace my steps part of the way, then head past the Beach Bar, waving hello to Andrew, and up the steps to the steep road which will take me towards the Sail Loft.

***

"Alice!" From his seat in the sunshine of the dining room, where he has the paper spread out in front of him, Dad has already spied me. "Twice in one weekend, to what do we owe this honour? And where's Ben?" he asks as an afterthought.

"With Sam. At home. I've been out for a walk," I say, almost proudly.

"Oh, lovely. It's a beautiful day. Bit cold, though – that's why I'm in here. Plus, my paper would blow away out there."

I smile. "Is Mum in?"

"Yes, she's about somewhere. I'll get the kettle on and give her a shout. Here," he pushes a chair towards me with his foot, and digs the magazine out from under the sports section. "Have a read of this if you like."

I do like, and I sit there while Dad goes off in search of Mum, the sun streaming through the windows and my skin beginning to feel the post-outdoors burn; the after-effects of cold air, the wind off the sea, and the sun. It feels like my cheeks are glowing. I unwrap the scarf from around my neck and I idly turn the pages of the magazine, soaking in the peace of this place. It is such a beautiful building, the Sail Loft. Standing proudly at the top of the hill, privileged with its views across all sides of the town and the glistening sea.

I look at the ridiculous fashion pages, where people of all ages and sizes don't mind looking ridiculous, and flick through the memories of working here. My first day. I was so nervous. I was eighteen. I was intimidated (unnecessarily so) by Bea, and by the guests. But I had already been charmed by the town itself, and David, and Julie's and my little rooms at the top of his house. I knew I would have to push myself through the awkwardness and lack of confidence, and that is what I did.

There are certain guests who stick in my mind as well; the first people I served, the Crockers, were lovely. They were a little older than my parents but they had a really nice way about them and were so kind – in stark contrast to a pair of, for want of a better word because I don't think there is one, spinster sisters, who were never satisfied with anything. The Willoughbys. They gave me a hard time over the heat of the water in the teapot, and the lack of cold breakfast options. Also, as I recall, the eggs being too runny, and the cutlery not being shiny enough. Thankfully, the Crockers would sneak me secretive sympathetic smiles, Mr Crocker even daring an eye-roll, which possibly saved me from running out and never coming back. It's a good job I didn't give up and run away.

I hear my parents' voices, and my Dad heading to the kitchen, while Mum comes in. I stand to hug her.

"It's so lovely to see you again, Alice, are you OK? Where's Ben?"

"With Sam!" I laugh. "In fact, I have some news about that."

"Oh?" Mum looks expectant, then worried.

"Yes, oh, I'll tell Dad in a minute. Sam wants to look after Ben properly, I mean on parental leave from work, until Ben can start at nursery."

"Does he really?" Mum asks in wonder. "Well, isn't that wonderful? Things are so much better these days, though I dare say they could still be improved. But is this just so that you can start back at Amethi? I don't want you rushing through your maternity leave for my sake. I won't hear of it."

"No, it's not just that." Although it kind of is. "Look, hang on for Dad, and we can talk it all through."

Dad soon appears, bringing tea and biscuits for three.

"Sam's going to look after Ben, Phil," Mum says.

"I thought he already was," Dad looks confused.

"No, so Alice can go back to work."

"What about his job?"

"He can take parental leave, Dad," I say. "Or we hope he can. He needs to clear it with his boss and also get all the paperwork in order, but he is positive he might be able to arrange it to start in the next week or two. Which means," I continue before either of my parents has a chance to interject, "that Mum can come back here, full-time."

My parents look at each other and I can't quite read their expressions. "This is a good thing, isn't it?" I ask.

"Oh, yes, Alice, it is. It's just, me and your dad have been talking, trying to work out what to do about this place…"

"OK." This doesn't sound good.

"We don't know if we've made the right decision, at all." Mum is close to tears.

"Oh, Mum."

"What do we know about running a hotel, for goodness' sake?"

"Well, more now than you did a year ago," I offer, not convinced my answer is that helpful.

"But, it's too much. I think it's just too much. We both

do, don't we, Phil?" Mum looks at Dad.

"I don't know," he says, looking at me as if I've got the answer.

"Be honest, this is Alice we're talking to," Mum tells him. "We're under a lot of strain, love," she says. "And Stefan got his job. He's going to be leaving us."

"OK." I need a moment to let all this work its way through my mind. I put my hand on Mum's and squeeze gently. "Alright," I say. "Stef's going. And Stef is good. But Stef also costs money. So without his wages, that gives you a bit of extra cash to play with. And that is something I wanted to talk to you about, but I don't know now if you're going to like this idea at all."

"Go on," says Dad.

"Well, you know we were talking about how the Sail Loft still feels like Bea's Sail Loft. And how you feel like you're losing people because they were loyal to Bea. I really do think if you're going to make it work, you need to make it *your* Sail Loft. I know you must feel stressed, and I completely understand why you might feel you've done the wrong thing, taking this place on. But it couldn't just be plain sailing, really, could it? It's a huge undertaking. Plus, Mum, you've been covering for me at Amethi so you haven't been able to throw yourself into this."

Both my parents are looking at me and I can see Dad wants to say something.

"Just hang on a second, Dad, sorry. I was going to say, I think if you want this to work then you both need to be in it, a hundred percent. And you've only been here for a few months. Don't give up, not just yet, not unless you really hate it and you don't want to try and make it work."

"We… we don't hate it, do we, Sue?" Dad asks tentatively.

"No," I recognise Mum's pulling-herself-together look. "No, we don't. Of course we don't. But it's the living space, too. We're on top of each other, all the time. And if we come downstairs either there are guests here, so there's no space for us, or there are no guests, and far too much space. I don't know which one is worse."

"That was the other thing I wanted to say," I take a deep breath. This isn't really what I want but it has to be said. "I don't know about your finances, but I think if you are going to make a go of it here, you need to do some work on the place, and part of that should be losing one of the upper rooms, maybe even two, and extending your living area. You can't stay cooped up in those rooms you've got at the moment. You need to actually be able to enjoy being here, or what's the point? And you could also think about refurbishing, and relaunching. And yes," I cut Dad off at the pass before he can speak, "I know this is going to cost even more money. I have some great contacts who might be able to help and who I know won't rip you off, but it will still cost. I think you need to consider selling the house."

16

Once the words are out, I can hardly believe I'd said them. And I know I should have told Sam what I'd be suggesting to Mum and Dad but I'd only half-formed that idea at home. It was the walk on the beach that really clarified things for me. They can't keep a huge house on, which they can't even live in, and stay cooped up in the current owners' accommodation, feeling miserable and stressed. What would be the point in that? They have made this decision to run the Sail Loft, and not had anywhere near enough time to find out if it's for them.

I have been thinking also of the kind of things they might do to change the business a little. We could possibly link up the Sail Loft with Amethi; guests could come to the yoga sessions or maybe even the writing courses, if that would work. It might. It might not.

But what I do know is that they need to either go for it now, or cut and run. And the second option seems an awful shame.

They both look at each other. Then back at me.

"I can't believe you've said that, Alice," says Dad. "I know how much you love that house."

"Well, yes, I do, but a house is a house. And there are plenty more houses," I say glibly, in the back of my mind well aware that we might struggle to find the right place and that, whatever we do find, it won't be anything like where we live now.

"I think we should be honest, Phil," Mum says, and looks at me. "We have talked about this, Alice. We've had to.

We need to look at all our options. But we're not going to see you and Sam and Sophie and Ben out on the street."

"It won't come to that!" I laugh, hopefully. "We can rent somewhere. I mean, we're renting from you, anyway."

"You couldn't move back to Amethi?" Dad asks.

"No, it's too small, the cottage. I can't see Sophie wanting to share with Ben, somehow."

"No!" Mum laughs. "But even if we sold the house, I'm nervous about putting any more money into this business. What if it all goes down the drain?"

"I don't know," I admit. "And I know it's a risk. I suppose you need to work out if you really want to do this. Run the Sail Loft, I mean. And if you do, then I guess the risk is worth taking. If not, perhaps you don't need to sell the house at all but this place instead."

"And move back to the house…" Mum says thoughtfully.

Whatever they decide, I know we have to leave the house. It's sad but it's more than fair. We've been so lucky to have lived there at all.

"We won't get back what we paid for this," says Dad, "with the books as they are."

"You just need to think it all through. There is a lot to consider. It might be worth making contact with some of the other local hotels; there are a couple of really nice people who I think will be happy to talk to you about their experiences. But you need to network," I say scoldingly, irritating myself for sounding like I think I can tell them what to do.

"Maybe," Mum says doubtfully.

"I think you have to, Mum. Both of you have worked for bigger companies before but now it's just you two, or it will be when Stef goes. And it's a completely new thing. There are the Bluebell and the Regent, who we," I say 'we' as if I still work here, "normally link up with, if we're full or they are – sending guests each other's way. Those kind of things are important. And Janet and Steve have been running the Bluebell for years. And they're lovely. I'm sure they'd be happy to discuss any problems you're experiencing. Look, I won't go on about it anymore. I know it's a lot to think about. And I'm sorry if I sound like I'm lecturing you – again. But I really want this to work for you! Or else you should sell up and move on, and enjoy life."

"We appreciate it, Alice," Dad says, but I feel uncomfortable, like I've overstepped a boundary – the daughter telling the parents what to do.

I stay a little longer, moving the conversation on to more neutral territory, and Mum exclaims over Ben sleeping through.

"Yeah, but I'm not counting my chickens just yet," I say.

"Isn't it sheep, you're meant to count sheep if you can't sleep," says Dad.

"Very good, Dad," I grin. I'm pleased they both seem relaxed and not too annoyed that I came in and started bossing them about.

When I leave, I hug them both and I look around the entrance hall.

"I love this place," I say.

"We know, Alice," Mum smiles.

"But if it's not for you, then you need to do the right thing."

Mum hugs me again. "Thank you, Alice."

As I step outside, I stop on the top step for a moment, to admire the familiar view. When I was eighteen I'd normally hurry off down these steps, barely taking in my surroundings. I'd be too busy thinking of a nice little afternoon nap before a night out or, later in the summer, a date with Sam.

When I came back here and began to work at the Sail Loft a second time, I saw things more clearly. Appreciated the beauty of this amazing town, where all the streets lead down to the heart of the place; the harbour. Three beaches of fine, almost-white, sand. Wild, open sea to one side and the beginning of the estuary on the other. Behind the town, unseen from here, is farmland and moors. Ancient standing stones and forgotten tin mines. And of course, Amethi.

I breathe deeply then trot down the steps, aware that Mum and Dad might be able to see me still standing there. I'm ready for home, anyway; that invisible, fine silk-like cord pulling me back to the place I belong. But it's not the place; it's the people. I just hope Sam will remember that when I tell him I suggested that my parents need to sell our home.

17

"Hello!" I call when I get back but all is quiet in the house. I wonder if they've gone out for a walk and I feel disappointed as I've spent the short walk back looking forward to seeing them. Needing their physical warmth and presence. And needing to tell Sam what I've just been talking about with Mum and Dad.

But no, the pram is tucked under the stairs. I push open the door to the lounge and there they both are, on the settee. Sam lying on his back. Ben lying on Sam's chest. Sam opens an eye, then another. He looks tired.

I smile. Whisper, "Everything OK?"

He nods almost imperceptibly. I know that feeling, of desperately not wanting to disturb Ben.

"I'll put the kettle on," I mouth.

He smiles, looking tired.

I go through to the kitchen and Sam joins me. "I managed to put him into his pram, and he's still asleep!"

"How's it been?"

"I'm not going to lie to you, Alice, Ben was not very happy that you'd gone out."

"Oh," I try to hide my pleasure at hearing this.

"I can see you smirking. Yes, he loves you best and most. And he does not like bottles. They are not an adequate substitute, apparently."

"Oh no."

"But… we persevered. Or I did. Ben was having none of it. How is it possible for somebody so small to cry for so long? And so loud?"

"I'm sorry, Sam."

"It's fine!" He puts his hand on my waist, kisses me. "Because he did, eventually, take the bottle, and this felt like my finest achievement, ever."

"That is brilliant," I say. "Really brilliant. Hopefully he'll do it again."

"He'll have to, when I'm looking after him, or he'll go hungry."

"Don't say that," I say, experiencing a physical ache at the thought of this.

"As if I'd let that happen! Look, Alice, if the worst comes to the worst I can bring him up to you at Amethi and you can feed him."

"I suppose…"

"I promise you, I will do everything I can to look after him as well as you've been doing."

Oh no. I'm crying. What is wrong with me?

"Hey," Sam puts his arms all the way round me and pulls me towards him. "It's going to be weird. I get it. And you don't have to do it, we'll find another way."

"I do have to, Sam. I do. Mum needs to be at the Sail Loft. Stef's got a new job."

"Has he?"

"Yeah, but I think it's a good thing. I've had a really good chat with Mum and Dad about it all and…"

I am steeling myself to tell him that we might need to look for a new home, when Sam's phone starts vibrating. He glances quickly at his smartwatch. "It's Kate. I'd better get this." He kisses me on the head. "We'll continue this conversation in a minute, OK?"

"OK."

I move quietly past still-sleeping Ben in his pram. He looks so big in there now. Going into the lounge, I sit with my knees up, cuddling a cushion to me. I will be so sad not to be able to come to this place anymore. It's been a part of my life for a long time now. Though I suppose for ten years of that time, I had no idea I'd be back here.

Integral to the fabric of the town, this house feels like it is part of everything. If it were to disappear, the street would be like a mouth with a missing tooth. I have always wanted to find out more about its history; who has lived here over the two or three centuries of its existence.

David says he has always wanted to do this, too. "Maybe the house has a long history of occupants who have always wanted to find out more about it but been too lazy to do so."

Now, it feels too late. *It's just a house*, I tell myself. And it is. But it holds a lot of my own personal history, for future people not to find out about.

I hear Sam's voice in the next room, though I can't make out any words. I hope he won't mind that I've suggested Mum and Dad sell this place. They have to. It's ridiculous to try and keep it when the Sail Loft is not doing well, and while they are crammed into the tiny owners' accommodation.

I should start looking at other places to rent. At least at this time of year it may be easier. Though there is a marked difference between the holiday rentals and residential rentals, in pricing and availability.

I hear Sam say bye to Kate, and tiptoe past the pram. I can't believe Ben is still asleep! Maybe this really is the start of him becoming more settled. Perhaps we will have another uninterrupted night. But I don't want to assume anything, or take anything for granted. I gird myself, ready to tell Sam about the house. I may as well just say it.

He looks serious.

"That was Kate," he says, though I already know. "Sophie's on her way back. Apparently, she's been talking to Kate about moving to Devon."

***

Of course, after that bombshell I can't just tell Sam I've encouraged Mum and Dad to sell the house from under our feet.

"Really?" Perhaps I am not as surprised as I should be, having given so much thought to Sophie and Kate's relationship lately – and knowing how unhappy Sophie has been.

"Yeah." Sam's mouth is a grim line. "I could kill Josh."

"Why? Is that why she wants to move?"

"Yes, well, no." He sits. Sighs. "That's part of it, Kate says. She also said Sophie's been talking about how much she misses her. I know she does. I know she must. But I hoped I'd... we'd... be enough."

"Oh Sam," I put my arm around him and he leans into me. "You are enough."

He emits a short, mirthless laugh.

"You are," I insist. "It's not about that. It's not about you. It's about Kate." I am reminded of Josh's words, breaking up with Sophie. *It's not you, it's me.* It's not Sam, it's Kate. "And it probably is partly about Josh, too. But that will pass. And maybe when Sophie has got over it a bit better, she might see things differently. But she might not. She is in a very tricky position."

"I know. I was amazed she ever decided to stay with me in the first place. It's always been her and Kate. And I'm not even her biological dad."

"You can stop that talk right now. We all know that

140

doesn't make a blind bit of difference to anything. You are Sophie's dad, it's as simple as that. You don't want her to hear you saying you're not her biological dad, do you? As if it makes any difference."

"No." Sam rubs his eyes. "Oh, I feel tired all of a sudden."

I pull him further towards me, and he moves his legs onto the settee, settles his head on me. Ben starts crying.

"Bloody hell…"

"I'll get him," I say, and I kiss Sam on the head. I gently move and he curls up on the seat. "Just give me half an hour or so and I'll sort myself out," he says.

"No problem."

Ben is wriggling around in his pram, pulling himself up, or trying to.

"Hello," I smile but am rewarded with an angry, hungry cry. "Come on," I lift him up and out.

Ben relaxes against me. We make our way upstairs, stopping at the stairwell window, where I sit Ben on the sill so he can look out. We watch a gull pass close by, and a sparrow on the roof of the shed in next door's garden. The sky is low and grey now, settling itself over the town like a blanket. It feels like the place is ours for now; it belongs firmly to those people who live here. While the vast blue skies of summer open it up for tourists from far and wide, now the nights are coming earlier, and the weather closing in, it's like drawstrings being pulled gently in, securing us in place, keeping us safe.

I take Ben up to his room to change him and think about what it will be like, moving to a new house. Will he realise he is in a different place? I am sure he's old enough now to know that, but I don't suppose it will make much difference to him, as long as he has me and Sam.

I don't like the thought of leaving here. I would live in this house for the rest of my life if I could. But I've always known it can't last forever. And I much prefer it to Mum and Dad struggling on. I have some more ideas to share with them; things I think I'd do, if the Sail Loft were mine, but they have enough to think about for now.

With Ben changed, I settle in the easy chair to feed him, listening to the familiar sounds which characterise this house. The boiler firing up and the heating coming on, the comfortable creaking of the pipes warming up. Somebody's footsteps ringing against the walls outside as they walk down the street. A gull, on a rooftop close by. All so normal to me. Where will we go next? I don't suppose we'll be able to live anywhere near as close to town as this.

Sophie flits into my mind. Does she really want to move to Devon? Leave her friends? Leave her dad, and me, and Ben? Be with her mum. Yes. I can see she might want that. If she does move, I think idly, then I suppose we would fit back into our cottage at Amethi. After all, Julie will be back soon and Jonathan's been on about leaving Cornwall. He probably won't want to stay in that cottage when he's not working there anymore.

Too much, too soon. I can't seem to stop my mind getting ahead of itself like this, sometimes. And really, I hope Sophie stays with us. Of course I do. I decide I won't tell Sam today, about the house. I'll leave him be for now and he can make sure he's got his head straight before Sophie is back. He has enough to worry about and I think he could do with the rest.

18

As I drive to Amethi, my tummy is full of butterflies. It's so strange, really – it's not like I've been away from the place entirely while I have been on maternity leave. In fact, I bet I've been up here at least once or twice a week. It's just such a beautiful place to come to. But today, this is it. I am back.

And while it made my stomach ache just a little to leave Sam and Ben – both in their pyjamas still, I might add – as soon as I was in the little red car and on the road, I was filled with excitement. Which is not to say that I won't miss these last few months, when work has been almost the last thing on my mind.

There have been so many lasts. Last time at the Wednesday morning baby and toddler group. Given how much I didn't want to go in the first place, as I walked down the hill to it last Wednesday I realised how much I had come to enjoy, and rely on, this weekly event. And how much Ben has grown and developed since our first time there. He's keen to move now, though I think he is still some way off. But he can sit up, usually leaning on me but he really is strong enough now to do this unaided. He will spend most of the time stuffing one toy then another in his mouth, and we'll sit in a circle with some of the other mums and babies.

I asked Sam if he'd be taking Ben along. "I probably will," he said, which surprised me – and made me feel even more like I'd be missing out. But if I am as committed to the principle of equality as much as I say, Sam needs to be able to do these things. And I will just have to learn to cope with the feeling of missing out.

Another last was having all The Mums and babies/toddlers round. Suzie talks excitedly about Delilah starting at Little Angels in January – and her having some time to herself. "I don't start work for another five weeks after that. What will I do with myself?"

We others pretend not to feel envious. I've revised my opinion of Suzie even further since our day looking at nurseries and I don't think I'll be keeping in touch with her once we're back at work. We don't have a lot in common and I hate her derisory comments about other mums not in our little group, or about 'emmets' (holiday-makers), or foreigners. While I'd have thought her upbringing would have made her quite open-minded, it seems to have done quite the opposite. Maybe it's her own way of rebelling.

Miriam is already back at her job, part-time, Esther with Miriam's mother-in-law. She has Fridays off.

"That sounds lovely," I said dreamily.

"It is, to be honest," she said. "It's a day for me and Es before Tom's back from work for the weekend. It feels like a real chance to enjoy a little bit more time with her."

It does sound nice. But then I'm lucky that Sam is going to be with Ben and, hard as it is, I'm glad that he will get to experience some of the special times I've shared with our little boy. Plus, I remind myself, Amethi needs me, and the Sail Loft needs Mum. This is about more than just me.

As I drive through the shield of trees, which are bare now and make striking shapes against the winter sky, I feel a sigh escape me. *I am home*, I think. Unbidden, that thought surprises me. I did used to love living here. I think of the happy time I spent living in the cottage here. The peace, the seclusion. But it is not right by the sea. And I do want to be by the sea, if I possibly can be. There's nothing like stepping out of your front door into the fresh, salt-soaked air, whatever the weather.

Nevertheless, as I arrive in the car park, I am flushed by a warm feeling of belonging. And I have the luxury of a full day to myself here, catching up on everything. Sitting in my office, drinking coffee, reading emails, letters, reviewing plans… all uninterrupted, except perhaps for the odd phone call. It seems like bliss.

As the day unfolds, every now and then I experience a little twinge, as if I've forgotten something, or something is missing, and I have to remind myself that it's OK, that Sam has Ben. And as I haven't heard anything from him yet I am going to assume that everything is alright with them.

At lunchtime, there's a knock on the door.

"Welcome back, Alice!" Jonathan presents me with lunch. Avocado and poached egg on granary bread. A glass of pineapple juice. A piece of cake.

"That looks amazing!" I stand to take the tray from him then give him a hug. "Thank you so much. I have a slightly dry sandwich and an apple in my bag. I think I'll give the sandwich to the birds."

"Enjoy," he smiles. "It's good to have you back."

"I could get used to this."

"Yeah, well I'm not planning on making a habit of it."

"Where's yours?"

"I'll have something with Janie in a bit."

"Oh, that sounds nice. Is she working? Maybe I can come and see her a little later."

"Of course, she'd love to see you. Yeah, she's just finishing some project at the moment, then having a break till New Year. She was on about spending some time with Sam and Ben."

The words drop like pebbles into my mind. Just for a moment, I feel it again. That sense of missing out. Of missing them. Missing Ben. "That's a great idea," I say, though. And it is. Sam will love spending time with his sister. "And I guess we need to talk about the future, at some point. With Julie coming back in February."

"Yeah," he says reluctantly. "I don't really want to think about it. I have not a clue what to do, yet. But right now I need to get back to the kitchen. I'm making an afternoon tea for the Hunters – Mrs Hunter doesn't know. It's for her and her mum. I think Mr Hunter just wants to escape for a while." Jonathan grins, displaying those beautifully straight white teeth I am so envious of.

"Ha! Probably. We'll need to finalise everything for winter solstice, too. Not long now."

"No, this year seems to have gone extremely fast in many ways. But when I think back to last Christmas and how miserable I was, I can't believe how much has changed."

"It is pretty amazing, what can happen in a year."

Last Christmas, I was pregnant but could never have imagined just what motherhood would be like. And Jonathan was on the verge of leaving Cornwall. Then Janie turned up, and something clicked between the two of them. And when Julie and Luke left for India, Jonathan agreed to take her role on here, to cover for her while she was away. It was a swift about-turn but now it's approaching Julie's return, I wonder what Jonathan will do next. At the back of my mind I again turn over the idea of claiming back the cottage, but that could only be if Sam wants to, and of course if Sophie really does leave us to go to Devon.

I still can't believe that will actually happen but she has talked to Sam about it and explained how unhappy she's been and how she thinks she might just like a fresh start. "It's not just Josh. Or Amber and Annabel being friends. Or any of that. I do… miss Mum. And it's not that I don't love you, Dad. Or Alice, or Ben. I can't explain it."

"I understand, Soph." Sam brushed the top of her head with his lips. "I promise I do. Kate's your mum. It's always been you two. You can't expect to just be able to turn that off, just like that."

I could see he was trying to be straight-backed and strong. Sensible. Understanding. I wanted to hug him. I wanted to beg Sophie to stay. But I can't do that. And Sam is trying so hard to do things right. I have to support him. As things stand, nothing is settled.

Sophie is having next week off school, visiting Devon, looking at schools. If it's going to happen, it seems it is going to happen fast. Kate is talking about the new year. But she's not being tactless, or gloating. She's just trying to get things sorted so that Sophie has as little disruption as possible, and as much time to get used to her new school before the really hard work of GCSEs begins.

I can't imagine life without Sophie, so god knows how Sam feels. I have to keep reminding myself that this must be how Kate felt, when she left for Devon. But deep down I also feel slightly aggrieved that it was her decision to leave Cornwall – hers and Isaac's – and now we will be paying the price.

"But I left, to go to Wales, didn't I, Alice?" Sam said when I voiced this feeling. "I did what I wanted to do. And Kate never did. She was the one who put so many things on hold for Sophie."

"I know," I sighed.

"So I guess what will be will be," Sam leaned his head softly on mine.

"And we'll still see Sophie," I said, with an effort to sound bright.

"Course we will."

"But it won't be the same." The brightness faded.

"No."

***

My first day back passes quickly but I make time in the afternoon to do a little wedding research. I can't help myself. I've had it in mind for what I imagined as this first long, luxurious day alone. In reality, I find I only have half an hour, but that's better than nothing.

Although I'd always imagined I would like to have the ceremony at the Island chapel, now when I imagine it, I think of how busy it can be there. And how Sam and I know an awful lot of people around town. It makes me think we might be very self-conscious, and I'm warming to the idea of something much more private.

There's a farm not far from town, where they hold private ceremonies and have a small private beach as well. Now, that sounds perfect. But predictably it's very expensive. Then there's one of the beach cafés in town, but again I'd feel a bit like we were on show. I know I need to do this with Sam, really, but I can dream, can't I?

When five o'clock swings around, I feel like I have accomplished very little. I am a bit more up-to-speed on what's been happening here, and I can tell Mum has done such a great job keeping things going. I hope now she can turn that same attention to the Sail Loft and she and Dad can make a success of it – and be happy there.

148

In the run-up to coming back to Amethi I was busy doing a bit of work on my parents' behalf; linking them up with Janet and Steve at the Bluebell, and Karen at the Regent. I went with Mum and Dad to the meeting, which seemed to go well, although Dad was nervous to begin with.

"My name's Phil and I run an independent hotel," he joked. Mum sent a look my way.

Miriam's husband, Tom, is a builder, and he's been to see Mum and Dad, to discuss options for extending their accommodation. And I have a half-idea to suggest Sarah to them, to help with interior design. I'm just nervous about this because although I really like her as a friend, I have no idea what her work is like. I would hate to recommend her and for my parents to be unhappy with her. Or, likewise, for her to not want to work with my parents. It's a hard position to be in as my natural instinct is to pair people up and help people out but I know sometimes it's better to step back and let them work things out themselves. I find the idea of refurbishing the Sail Loft very exciting. But that is not for me to be excited about. It's for Mum and Dad. So for the time being I will leave well enough alone.

It's completely dark as I leave the office and I realise how unaccustomed I've become to this type of darkness. There are no streetlights out here and because the holiday lets have their curtains drawn, there is very little light emitting from them. I see the windows of my old cottage glowing, and I'm tempted to knock on the door and say bye to Janie but I could see how busy she was when I dropped in earlier. She doesn't really need her sort-of-sister-in-law coming and interrupting her again.

Besides which, I want to get back to my boys. In fact, I

feel an almost physical force pulling me back to them.

As I crunch across the gravel towards the car park, I hear something behind me. It makes me jump. I turn and there, stopped dead in its tracks as if it's pretending to be a statue, is a dog. I stop still, too. I don't know this dog. What if it's aggressive? We eye each other, for a moment, then the dog sort of curls in on itself, as if trying to make itself smaller.

"Hello," I say softly. It gives a very small, unsure, wag of its tail.

"Hello," I say again, more enthusiastically, and the dog creeps towards me. I tentatively put the back of my hand out for it to smell, which it does. Then I reach out and stroke the animal's back. I can feel its bones. I guess it's maybe come from a nearby farm. Hopefully it will find its way back. I give it a good fuss then say, "I have to go now."

As I walk to the car, the dog is behind me. I stop, stroke it again. "You have to go home, too," I laugh.

When I get in the car, the dog stops on the gravel and before I drive off into the darkness I look in my rear-view mirror. I can just make out the shape of the dog, lit up by the rear lights of the car. Just sitting, and watching. With apparently no intention of going anywhere.

19

I ask Jon about the dog the next morning, while I'm getting coffee in preparation for a call with Julie.

"Oh, yeah. It was here a few weeks ago... I gave it some scraps. It looked so skinny! I haven't seen it for a while, though."

"And you've no idea where it belongs?"

"No, I'm guessing one of the farms. Maybe it doesn't get fed enough, that's why it's turning up here."

"Probably!" I think of the feel of its bones right below its skin; that's how it felt to me. I never had a dog, growing up – in fact, always felt quite scared of them. But then I met Julie, and her family had Buster; a dog of unknown lineage who was the nicest, most affectionate animal you could ever imagine. He completely changed how I felt, and I remember going on at Mum to get me a dog of my own...

"Please? Please. I haven't got any brothers or sisters. A dog would be like a sibling to me."

"We can't, Alice, I'm sorry. I'm out most days, and so is your dad. Who'd look after the dog while we're at work and you're at school?"

"It would be OK. Loads of people do it."

"But I don't think it would be fair on the dog, do you? It would need letting out, and feeding... and company. Can you imagine being locked in a house for hours on end? Without any way to get out or get a drink if you ran out? I'm sorry, love, it's just not possible."

We had compromised on a rabbit; a big, lolloping creature called Quentin. And sponsorship of a Dogs Trust dog called Tito. To give Quentin his due, he did his best to fill the dog-shaped hole in my heart. He would follow me around the garden, and would even run after a ball, though stopped short of actually doing anything other than sniffing it. He also loved attention, sitting on my knee while I watched TV, and hopping round our feet at dinner time. During the day, he could be in the run in the garden, and I'd say he had a pretty happy time of it. I was devastated when he died, which was early in the year that I first came down to Cornwall.

Now I find my mind returning to a familiar fantasy; this dog might need me, and we could adopt him, Ben could grow up with him… I cut it short. We already have enough to think about, with Sophie and with Ben, and possibly having to find a new home.

I did, finally, broach that subject with Sam last night. I didn't feel like I could leave it any longer. Once Ben was down, and Sophie upstairs chatting to her mates, we sat, together, on the settee. The fire was going and the TV was off. It was a rare chance for some peace.

"How did your first day go then, Daddy Daycare?"

"I'll have you know that's a very sexist attitude, actually, seeing as he's my son. You always say how you hate it when dads looking after children is referred to as babysitting."

He was right. I do. "Sorry," I grinned. "Did you have a good day?"

"We did. It was nice. We played here for a bit then went for a walk. Came back for lunch. He had a nap, I watched TV. He woke up..."

Hearing Sam say those words, I had a little twinge of missing out. Wishing I could have it both ways. I was also aware that put like that, looking after a baby does sound incredibly easy. Maybe it's understandable how people who have never done it – including many fathers – don't get just how exhausting and all-consuming it is.

"How about your day?" Sam put his arm around my shoulders.

"It was good. I feel like I've only got to the tip of the iceberg, with catching up, I mean. But it was nice to be back. Though I missed Ben. Oh, and there was a dog…"

I described the dog to him.

"Don't tell me, you want to adopt it!"

"No," I said quickly, defensively.

Sam just laughed. He seemed happy and relaxed. I decided to bite the bullet.

"I've got to tell you something, Sam, which I should have told you before now."

"Oh?" He looked intrigued, not worried, which is something I love about him. If he introduced a subject to me like that, I would probably think the worst.

"Yeah, it's about this place."

"This place, our home?"

"Yeah… our home." I sighed. "It's possible Mum and Dad are going to have to sell it."

"Alright. I can understand that. You said it's not going so well at the Sail Loft."

"Exactly." I had looked at him, unable to believe that he was just taking it in his stride like that. "But I kind of suggested it to them," I confessed.

"Well, I don't blame you, to be honest. They can't be keeping this place on, can they? Not if they want to make the business work. I guess they want somewhere a bit bigger for themselves, as well."

"Sam, how is it possible that you are so bloody brilliant?"

"Dunno," he smiled. "Just comes naturally."

"I'd been worrying about telling you! Especially with what's going on with Sophie."

His face had fallen then. "Yeah, well that's a different matter. We can find somewhere else to live. We can't find another Soph. And I wouldn't want to."

We had both fallen silent. I watched the flames flickering in the fireplace, and I leaned against Sam. "I'm so sorry."

"Yeah, me too. I'm going to miss her, like you wouldn't believe."

"She's definitely going, then?"

"I don't know. She says she hasn't made her mind up yet but I think she's trying to soften the blow for me. And Kate's right, that if she does it's better to do it sooner. From an education point of view. So we won't need to look for a three-bed," he laughed bitterly.

"Yes we will," I said. "Of course we will. Sophie will be coming to stay with us and we'll always have a room for her."

"Alice," Sam kissed me, "how is it possible that you are so bloody brilliant?"

"Dunno. Just comes naturally."

So that's where we are now. Sophie will most likely be moving to Devon, and we are most likely to be moving to… who knows where? I know that really, despite that momentarily appealing idea of us moving back to Amethi, we need to find somewhere new. We do need to have a room for Sophie. And it should be her room; not a guest room. I have become very used to her living with us, and it's a strange feeling as she's not my daughter, but I do feel maternal towards her. I also feel like she's a much younger sister. And a friend.

I've spoken to Kate numerous times, and she's been

154

worried about Sam. I've tried to reassure her. "He is disappointed, of course. And yes, 'disappointed' doesn't really cover it, but this is a difficult situation and he understands. I know Sophie's been heartbroken about Josh but I don't think really that she's ever got over being apart from you. She kind of filled time with things like visits to Karen, and to Josh's house, but I don't think any of it has really made up for the fact that she's missing you."

"I feel terrible, for putting her in this position."

"Well, don't. It's difficult. Really difficult. You could have just told her that she had to come to Devon with you. Plenty of people move to new places. But you tried to do the right thing in giving her the choice. It was great that she could have her say. And she's given it a go but you've won out." I meant that in a kind way but it sounded wrong.

"It's not a competition, Alice. I never meant it to be. I just…"

"It's OK," I said. "That's not what I meant. I just mean, she doesn't want to be without you. And she's looking forward to being with you, and Isaac and Jacob. I think it's an adventure to her. Maybe she wasn't ready for it before but I think she is now. And she will always know it's been her decision, and that you and Sam are there to support her, no matter what. I reckon that's pretty cool."

"Thank you, Alice. That's a lovely thing to say."

"I mean it. And I will miss Sophie, a lot. But I bet you can't wait to have her back with you."

"I can't. I really can't."

I do feel for Sam, and I know it isn't going to be easy for him, but it's nice to know Sophie and Kate are so happy.

Karen, on the other hand, is spitting chips. "She's taking my granddaughter!"

"No, she's not. *Sophie* has decided to be with her mum."

And anyway, I thought, being a mum surely trumps being a grandmother, in most situations. Certainly in this one, where Karen was nowhere to be seen for the first thirteen years of Sophie's life.

"You say that…"

"Because it's true. Sophie has decided this. Kate and Sam gave her the choice, when Kate was moving, and Sophie tried staying here without her mum, but it hasn't worked out."

I have become fond of Karen, and her heart is (usually) in the right place but I couldn't help thinking how she left Sam, when he was sixteen. Tripped off to Spain with Janie, who is quite a lot younger than Sam. I don't know how much of a choice Karen gave Sam in the matter.

We were sitting in the lounge, Karen with Ben on her knee. She smiled at him. "You're not going to leave Grandma, are you, my little cherub?"

"He's not going anywhere," I had smiled. "Not till he's thirty."

"I'll be dead by then," Karen said, but she was smiling, too.

"Don't say that, Mum!" Sam was sitting next to her. It's nice seeing them together these days. They are generally quite relaxed together, and I can see similarities between them. They share the same way of moving their hands when they talk, and their foreheads crumple in a similar way when they're deep in thought. I am not sure Sam is ready for such comparisons with his mum, though.

I might speak to Karen, see if she knows of any places we could rent, although I feel like the moment I do she'll have found somewhere and signed the papers before we've even had a chance to see it.

For now, though, back to work. Winter has set in good and proper today and I have the heater on in my office, which makes the windows steam up but ensures I am warm and toasty. It won't be long before we have our second winter solstice yoga retreat. I am really looking forward to it, remembering how fantastic last year's was.

Lizzie has once again taken the reins in terms of organising it all. This year, she wants the Christmas tree up before the event: "We should have done it last year, really. The tree isn't just a Christian thing, you know. They were decorated as part of solstice celebrations by the ancient Egyptians."

"I didn't know that."

"No, well, I've been reading a bit more about it, and the Romans did it, too. They had pine trees in their goddess groves and on the eve of the solstice the priests would cut down a tree to decorate for the temple celebrations. In the UK, people used to bring trees indoors as a place for wood spirits to keep warm during the winter months."

"I didn't know all that."

"No, I was aware of some of it, but I think we should definitely make the tree part of our celebrations. And what do you think about a tree in the communal space, too? We could give each person an ornament to hang on it, on the first night, and they can take them back home at the end of the week."

"It all sounds fantastic, Lizzie, as long as we're keeping to budget."

"Yep, all within the week's budget, as long as you're OK getting the main tree, like last year."

"Of course. I think Mum's already ordered it anyway. I'll speak to the farm about getting an indoor tree, too. Let me know what size you want."

"I will. I can't wait for this, you know, Alice. It was a real highlight for me, last year."

"For me, too." I think back to standing outside, with Sam and Sophie, and Julie. She was much more into the whole thing than I'd thought she would be. We all cast wishes into the fire and I think I know what hers was. I know her greatest wish was to become a mum, and as far as I know it still is. I will miss her this year.

But I can imagine having Ben up here, watching the fire. Last year, he was a minuscule being, tucked safely away inside me. Now, he's already outgrown the three-to-six-months clothes and he's raring to get moving. And eating. I can feel it in him, this restlessness, and drive. What will he be like in another twelve months?

For Christmas, we are fully booked, again. Jonathan has offered to prepare full-on Christmas dinners, ready to cook, with careful instructions for the guests. He has been in touch with them all, to confirm their requirements, and has had everything ordered for weeks. Until now, we have left people to their own devices for much of Christmas week, partly because Julie and I wanted some time to enjoy ourselves, and partly because we thought people would like their own space at Christmas time. Jonathan has other ideas, though.

"I think it's an extra draw for people. And isn't that the whole point of Amethi? It's not like other self-catering places. We go above and beyond here, and you've said more than once that it's the little touches people love."

"You make perfect sense," I'd smiled.

It's hard to believe this is the same Jonathan who I remember failing to get the first Christmas menu at the Sail Loft sorted. I'd had to ask Julie to do it. And the time he bunked off work with a hangover and because he'd slept with Lydia, who was a waitress at the Sail Loft. The two of them went on to become a couple, eventually. She went on to break his heart.

With Lizzie taking control of the solstice week, and Jonathan covering catering, I feel well supported and in a great position to do some planning for next year. But I can't do it without Julie, hence today's video call.

With coffee in hand, I lean back in my chair, watch the call signal on the screen, then a little bit of flickering, and there she is.

"Julie!" I exclaim, delighted as I always am to see my friend's face. "I miss you."

"I miss you too, loser."

"Ha. Takes one to know one."

Not the most professional way to begin a business call but it works for us.

"How are you?" she asks. "How's life without Ben?"

"It's not life, it's just daytimes. And I miss him."

"I bet."

"But Sam's loving it."

"That's so cool. So good his work let him do this."

"I know, but I must admit I feel a bit jealous sometimes, I did enjoy those months at home."

"You're with our baby now! Amethi. God, I miss that place."

"Do you?" I feel elated at this idea. I think I harbour fears that Julie isn't going to want to come home.

"Of course I do! Every day. I think a year here might be more than enough for me. I don't know about Luke, though. He's so into it. I don't think he wants to come back to his normal life. Travelling to London. Staying away. Working long hours. Don't worry," she grins, her smile lighting up the screen. "We've got some plans. And now you and I need to make plans."

She waves a notebook at me. Over the last few months, Julie definitely seems to have become more business-like, but I think it comes from having to conduct all these types of conversations over the internet. We need to keep focused.

"Let's do it!" I say, and I sip my coffee, letting its heat flood through me as I chat with my best friend, and business partner, about the coming year. We confirm four yoga retreats and two writing courses, on dates we had already pencilled in. It's very gratifying to see that there is barely a week otherwise when we don't already have at least one booking.

"It's going well, isn't it?" Julie smiles.

"It is. And it's going to be even better when you're back here."

"I can't wait."

"And is everything OK? Have you got any news? I mean, of course, are you still trying to get pregnant?"

What I want her to say is that no, she is no longer trying, because she already is pregnant. She looks slightly uncomfortable, though.

"No, not really… well, it's a bit difficult right now. I hope things are going to change next year."

"I hope so, Julie."

I hate asking her. I don't want her to think that now I am a mum everything revolves around having a baby (though it kind of has to). I just know how painful she was finding it, trying and failing to get pregnant. It is certainly a harder subject to broach over a video call than in person. The last thing I want is for our friendship to change due to our different situations.

160

"Anyway, let's not worry about that now," she says cheerfully and I follow her lead.

"It's a cold day today, Julie. Hang on a sec, I'll show you the view." I lean forward to rub away the condensation from the window. "No way!"

"What?"

"There's a dog outside."

"A dog?"

"Yeah. It was here last night, as well. It's pretty skinny. I don't know if you can see it, if I just…" I disconnect my laptop and turn it so the camera is pointing outside. "Can you see it?"

"No, but it's nice to see the place. Makes me miss it more."

"We miss you too," I say, turning the laptop back to face me.

"And I'm really going to miss Christmas there."

"We'll have to have another one, when you're back."

"Great idea. Anyway, how's the wedding planning going? You'd better not be getting married before we're back!"

"As if. We haven't got very far with it, anyway. There's so much to do. And a wedding is going to cost so much."

"I know, they're really expensive. Although, they don't have to be. Maybe you should do it at Amethi!"

"Can you imagine?"

"Why not? It's a perfect place for a wedding."

"Hmm." We've spoken before about getting a licence for Amethi but I don't know; I like the way things are. And there's something about the idea of hosting weddings that makes me feel uncomfortable. Some people have very strong, set ideas about how they want their wedding to be. Imagine the stress.

"Look, I'd better get on for now." Julie smiles. "Give my love to Sam and Ben and Soph, will you?"

"Of course. Give my love to Luke."

"And keep an eye on that dog!"

"I will."

When the call is over, I go straight downstairs and push open the door. There it is, the dog, sniffing the hedge by the wildflower meadow. I click my tongue and it looks round, unsure of itself. I crouch, hold my hand out. Very nervously, the dog moves towards me. My thighs are beginning to ache, but I don't want to move and startle the animal.

It seems an age, but it does finally come to me and immediately falls onto its back in a classic submission pose. I move onto my knees, relieved not to have all the pressure on my thighs any longer, and I rub the dog's belly. It's a girl, I can see now from her teats, which make me think she may have had a litter, though I am no expert.

"Hello, girl," I say softly, and she wags her tail, tries to lick my hand. "Where have you come from?"

I hear the kitchen door open and the dog jumps but I keep my hand firmly on her and she stays put.

Jonathan comes out. "She's back again, then?" He crouches next to me and gives her a rub. "Shall I get her something to eat?"

"I think so, yes please. And some water?"

"Sure."

She twists onto her feet as soon as she sees the bowls, gulping down the food then much of the water, her hot pink tongue splashing it all around. The she nudges the bowl to see if any scraps of food have got underneath it.

"She's starving," I say.

"It looks like it," agrees Jonathan.

"Do you think she belongs to anybody?"

"I've no idea. She should be micro-chipped, shouldn't she? I guess we could take her to the vets."

"I might do that, if she's still around tomorrow. Oh but maybe I should take her today…"

"It's your call."

It's hard to know what to do for the best. There is work to be done. And I need to be home at a reasonable time, but I now feel a responsibility towards this dog. I decide to leave it till tomorrow. If she's still here, I will take her and hopefully find out where she's come from.

I give her a rub on the back. "Good girl," I say.

"Think she likes you," says Jonathan.

"She'll like you more, you're the one who feeds her."

"I don't know. She's gazing at you like Ben does."

I'm touched by Jonathan noticing this detail. "Well, I'm definitely not that. I'd better get back to work." I stand up, my legs easing as I do so, and turn to go back inside. Jonathan does the same.

I get my head down but I can't shake the thought of the dog from my mind and every now and then I check out of the window. Every time, she is still there.

20

When I left to go home, there was no sign of her. Maybe she just goes from house to house round here – though they are few and far between – to get a meal at each one. Judging by her skinny ribs, though, I suspect not.

"Don't tell me, you really do want us to adopt her?" Sam says jokingly. I am feeding Ben, just before our tea is ready.

"Well…"

"Really?" He raises his eyebrows. "You think we should get a dog, when we might not have a home for much longer?"

"Sometimes I think things happen and you have to go with them."

"Are you turning into Lizzie?"

"No!" I laugh. "But if that dog keeps turning up, and she doesn't seem to look any better than she does now, I think it's my responsibility to find out who she belongs to, if she belongs to anyone."

"OK, well I wouldn't argue with that. It's going to get even colder next week, according to the forecast. It's not right for her to be living outside on her own in the cold."

Aha. A slight chink in his armour. There is no way that animal-lover Sam will be able to let this dog be alone, hungry and homeless.

"I tell you what," I say, "if she's there tomorrow, why don't you and Ben come and see her? I'd like your opinion. I know some of these farm dogs can be lean but this one seems far too thin, I think."

In reality, I don't suppose getting a dog now is the

greatest of ideas. And we don't know the first thing about this one. I'd never put Ben's safety at risk, of course. But she has turned up, out of nowhere, and it feels like there is a reason for that.

It's strange, only having a short time with Ben in the morning and the evening. His face beams when he sees me but I can't help worrying that the smile will diminish over time, as I spend less time with him and Sam becomes his main playmate and care-giver.

"It won't," Sarah assures me, "and I am so jealous of you getting to go out and do a normal day's work! The twins are a nightmare at the moment. Rory's taken to climbing on the windowsill. Ethan keeps trying to eat everything. I've got a little bit of work writing for the magazine but by the time evening comes around, I am shattered. I'm still glad of the work, though."

"I was going to talk to you about that, actually," I say. I have had the go-ahead from Mum and Dad to put them in touch with Sarah – on the proviso that there is no guarantee they will employ her. I explain the situation now.

"Oh Alice, thank you! That sounds amazing. But I get it; your parents can't employ me out of sympathy, or charity, or whatever. I'd love to see the place, though."

I haven't yet told her that they are selling the house. It feels like it's giving too much away about my parents' financial situation. Although I really don't think Sarah would take advantage of anything like this, I have not known her a very long time.

"I hope you get on," I smile. "I'm sure you will. But it's as much up to you, as to whether you want to do the work, as to whether they want you to do it."

"I don't think there'll be anything to worry about there," Sarah said and I could hear her smile down the phone – taking me back once again to the World of Stationery sales training: the 'sound' of a smile on a phone call. It's about the only thing I can remember now but I do think it's true. "You get back to Ben and Sam now."

"I will."

I give Ben his bath after tea. I am keen to do it every night, now I don't get all that time with him during the day. And I want to do his bedtimes, too. He is really enjoying books now. Generally just whacking one up and down on our mattress while I read to him, but still. It's nice he has an interest.

We sit on the chair in his room and I read him *My Zoo* by Rod Campbell. It's a touchy-feely book, though Ben is not really old enough to appreciate this yet and just pulls his hand away when I gently try to guide it towards the lion's mane, to stroke it. One step at a time, I think.

Although full of energy, even after his lavender-scented 'bedtime bath' oil, he soon becomes tired and crotchety. I feed him, and he becomes sleepy, but he no longer falls asleep on me as he used to. I can now, usually, tiptoe across to his cot with him and put him in, just still slightly awake. It's a careful balance, though. Any sudden movement and those eyes and that mouth will be wide open with disgust at me leaving him alone in his bed.

Tonight, I manage it, and as I leave the room I say a silent prayer that he will sleep through. It has only happened once since that first time so we are definitely not out of the woods yet.

Downstairs, Sam is on the laptop. "Thought I'd have a look at that school Sophie might be going to, in Devon.

Looks good," he grudgingly admits.

"Oh, Sam." I sit next to him, so grateful for the comfy cushions of the settee. It turns out I'm shattered.

Sophie is at Amber's house tonight. I'm glad; I didn't want them falling out because of *Annabel Fenwick* – and if Sophie is going to Devon, she should still try to hang on to her friendship with Amber. It's a special one.

"I thought we might look at what's out there to rent, too," he says.

"There's no rush." I feel like I just want to go to bed, though I know of course that this is important. "Mum and Dad haven't got this place on the market yet."

"Yeah, but when they do, how long d'you reckon it'll take to sell? Not long," Sam says gruffly.

"I'm sorry, Sam."

"What for?" He turns to me, looking genuinely surprised.

"I feel like this is my fault; the house thing, I mean."

"Of course it's not. Your mum and dad have got to do what they've got to do."

"But I suggested they sell the place…"

"Don't you think that must have crossed their minds already?"

"I suppose…"

"Anyway, it's not the end of the world. And without Sophie this place is going to be far too big for us."

"But we still need a room for her," I remind him.

"We do," he sighs.

"Look, leave it for tonight, eh? I don't know about you but I'm worn out. Maybe we could just go and sit in the garden for a short while. I know it's cold but it's a beautiful clear night out there. We could take a hot drink out, sit a while, then go to bed."

"That does sound nice," he says.

"Not exactly wild," I admit laughingly.

"No," Sam kisses me, "but wild's over-rated."

Outside, the white-painted walls glow in the light from the windows. I shiver at the cold, even wrapped as I am in my coat, hat and gloves.

"Is this a bit weird?" Sam asks, putting a couple of cushions on the bench as a barrier between the cold seat and our legs.

"Maybe," I admit. "But it's so nice out here. And I'm going to miss this little garden. And the sound of the sea."

"We might still have that," Sam says, but realistically we both know we're more likely to be living up and out of the heart of town. Most of the places here are holiday lets rather than residential, or extortionately expensive.

We both go quiet for a while. Sam sits, and I place myself next to him, trying to relax my shoulders against the cold. I look up. See the stars. In the cold winter night they seem somehow more sharply in focus than in the haze of balmy summer nights.

I do feel sad about leaving this house, but I hope that wherever we go next we will be just as happy. I am sure we can be, once we become used to Sophie being with Kate. Maybe being in a different place will help with that. Her absence might not be quite so pronounced, as it would be here. We will just have to take each day at a time.

I sip my hot chocolate, clutching the baby monitor in my other hand, tucked inside my pocket. I don't like Ben being in there and us being out here but I know nothing can happen to him, and we'll hear him if he wakes. I just want to make sure I am always there for him, when he needs me. But it is nice, to be outside in the cold night air. Sam and I lean against each other, companionably, not really talking.

My mind flits to the dog, hoping she is OK now. And to Mum and Dad, in the Sail Loft. Half the rooms are full this week, which is not bad for this time of year. They will make things work, I am sure of it.

And behind the sound of the occasional car or breathless voices of people climbing the steep steps behind the row of gardens, I can just hear the sea. Its constant murmur as the waves move in and out, in and out, like breath.

"So this dog…" says Sam.

"Yes?"

"You want her?"

"Oh… I… I don't know."

"I think you do."

"I would love a dog, one day…" I admit.

"Me too. We did have one, when I was little. Gordon."

"Gordon? The dog?"

"Yep!" he laughed. "Didn't seem weird then. I remember him dying, I was about ten. It broke my heart."

"I didn't know about Gordon."

"No, I suppose I haven't thought of him that much lately. I did love having about, though; somebody to play with. Janie's so much younger than me, it was just me and Gordon a lot of the time, when I was little."

"Aahhhh." It strikes a chord with me, this. I suppose Sam was an only child for the first few years of his life. I have been an only child all my life; the difference being that Mum and Dad always showed a huge interest in me and my friends, too. Trying to make sure I always had company, and things to do. I know Karen very much left Sam to his own devices, a lot of the time.

"OK. I'm coming to see this dog, tomorrow. Me and

Ben. Tell me when's a good time."

"If you can, that would be great." I don't want to overplay my hand. But I don't want to put any pressure on him. And we still know nothing about this dog. We certainly couldn't just bring her into our home.

"We'll have to find a place to live that'll allow pets," Sam says thoughtfully, as though he's already made his mind up.

"One step at a time, eh?" I say, but inside I'm jumping for joy.

***

When I bump along the drive to Amethi the following morning, I am already looking for her. I can't quite get this little dog out of my head. So much so that leaving Sam and Ben was not as hard this morning as it has been the last couple of days. Still, I felt my stomach contract a little as I walked away from my little boy. Maybe that will happen every day, till he leaves home. Even beyond that. Who knows? When I reach the car park, being a creature of habit, I take my regular spot.

Mr Hunter, he of the surprise afternoon tea, emerges round the corner.

"Morning!" he beams. "I'm off to the bakery."

"The bakery?"

"Yes, the one up at the crossroads. It's a little walk but I feel like I then deserve the pastries I bring back."

"That makes sense," I smile. "How was the afternoon tea?"

"I made myself scarce, to be honest. Took the opportunity for a beer in town. But I believe Jonathan is a very popular chap around here. He did an excellent job."

"I'm very glad to hear it. Enjoy your walk."

As I round the corner, and the place opens up before me, I look around, and there she is. Sniffing the gravel outside the Mowhay.

"Hello!" I say, and she looks up, comes trotting over. I feel like I've gained her trust already and that feels like quite a compliment. I crouch, and she licks my hand, pushes her nose into me. "Hang on," I laugh, putting a hand to the ground to steady myself.

As I kneel down, the cold sharpness of the stones pushing through my jeans, Janie comes around the corner.

"She's been waiting for you, I think. She's not as friendly with me. I guess I'm not much of a dog person. Plus, my allergies, you know…"

"I didn't know you were allergic."

"Oh yeah, to loads of things. Dogs and cats, particularly. Goes with my pasty IT-geek image though, doesn't it?" she grins and I see Sam's smile on her face.

"True. So I guess you're not going to be taking her in?"

"Er… no. Are you thinking about it? Does Sam know?"

"Yeah, in fact I think he's pushing for it."

"Well, he did love Gordon. Though I was quite little when Gordon died. I remember Sam going on about him, and he had about ten pictures of him in his room."

"Why have I never heard of Gordon before?"

"I don't know. Mum never let us have any more pets, she said because of my allergies but I think she couldn't be bothered, really. The allergies were a great get-out for her."

"I only ever had a rabbit. Quentin."

"Quentin!" Janie exclaims. "A rabbit called Quentin?"

"A dog called Gordon?"

"Yeah, fair enough. I can see why you and Sam get on

so well. Right, I'm off for a jog, before I get to work. Jon'll be up and about soon, I expect. I'll leave you and your new BFF to it."

"I'd better get to work, too," I say, as much to the dog as to Janie. "Don't go anywhere, though. Sit," I try.

The dog sits. I am impressed, although that does make me worry she must have a home. Somebody has obviously trained her. "Lie down." She does. "Good girl." She wags her tail and licks her nose.

I am not sure what kind of dog she is. She has brown eyes and white and brown fur. Long, skinny legs with quite big paws. "Stay there," I tell her, and she does. I unlock the door and go through to the kitchen, getting a bowl of water for her. Have we got any meat? I wonder. I look in the fridge and see a foil package. I unfold a corner to reveal what looks like turkey or chicken. Bingo.

Using a knife and fork – I really can't stand touching meat, which I know might be a problem if I am going to look after a dog – I put some slices on a plate and then rewrap the parcel and take the bowl and plate outside. The dog is at the door, waiting, and dances in circles around me as I move away from the building and onto the gravel.

"Wait," I say, and she stops still. "You are so good!" I place the plate and the bowl onto the gravel and the dog is straight over, gobbling down the meat.

"Hey! That had better not be my turkey!"

I turn. Jonathan is heading our way. The dog doesn't pay him any attention, until she's swallowed the last mouthful.

"Erm… no. What turkey?" I smile and turn to the dog. "We didn't see any turkey, did we?"

"Sure. I believe you, thousands wouldn't. So looks like you've managed to win her affection via her stomach?"

"Seems that way. It's one of the things we've got in common."

"I don't think she went anywhere last night, you know. I did come out to look for her, though I don't know what I'd have done with her. Janie's allergic."

"Yeah, she said. She's looking very well, though. Off for a run, as well Why aren't you joining her?"

"I don't need exercise to keep this manly physique."

"You say that now, but you're approaching thirty. All those years of carefree snacking and drinking will hit you, if you don't look after yourself."

"Thanks, something else to look forward to. I'll take my chances."

"Don't say I didn't warn you. Right, I really had better get some work done now. But Sam said he was going to come up and see the dog today, and bring Ben, of course."

"Are you thinking of keeping her?"

"I don't know. She might already have a home. She's very well behaved."

"She is," Jon muses. "Weird, isn't it?"

"Very," I agree. I pat the dog then head inside. Jon follows me, but goes into the kitchen while I head upstairs. The dog stays just outside the doorway.

"Good girl," I tell her, and try to stop myself thinking she looks sad at being left alone. I will tell Sam to get up here and meet her, and we'll take it from there. And I mustn't get too excited, she almost certainly already has a home.

"Hello!" Sam says, handing Ben to me as if he's a parcel, while the dog slinks cautiously over. "Who are you, then?"

He crouches, and the dog moves closer. He holds out his hand, gently, and she sniffs at it.

"She's very well trained," I say, trying to stake some kind

of claim. *I saw her first.* "She can sit, lie down and stay."

"I bet you can, can't you, you clever girl?"

I have never seen Sam like this. I like it, but it's quite funny, too. She gives in, and falls onto her back for a fuss. He rubs her tummy and looks at me. "Any more idea where she's come from?"

"No, none. But she must be from somewhere, and she is clearly used to being outdoors. She won't step foot over the threshold."

"But it's too cold for you out here, isn't it?" Sam says to her in a voice I've never heard him use, even with our son.

I wish Ben was old enough that I could roll my eyes at him. Instead, I enjoy an extra cuddle, wrapped up and cosy as he is in his blue pram suit. "Daddy's a softy, isn't he?" I say.

"She's so lovely," Sam looks up at me and I think I can see what he would have been like as a boy. I almost expect him to ask, *Can we keep her? Pleeease?*

"She is," I smile. "And Jon reckons she was here all night. I think we need to get her to the vets to see if she's been chipped and needs to be returned home."

"I suppose," Sam says, disappointed. "But we don't know what she's like in the car. And I don't really fancy taking her and Ben at the same time. Also, we have no idea what she'd be like with him."

"Tell you what, why don't you take her to see Ron? I'm sure he'll fit you in if he can. I'll have Ben here while you're gone."

"Are you sure? It's only day three of you being back here, it feels a bit wrong to already be handing him back to you!"

"It's fine, as long as it's only a short time. Go on, see if she'll go with you."

"I wish we knew her name," he says. "Come on, girl.

Come with me." He holds his hand out, walks a couple of steps. She follows.

"I can't believe it! I thought she liked me," I say.

"I'm sure she does. I just have a natural way with animals, though," Sam grins.

"You're on the same wavelength. Look, I'll come with you to the car to get Ben's bag, and make sure she's OK travelling with you."

Good as gold, once I've retrieved Ben's bag, the dog jumps into the boot of the car. She curls up on the floor.

"She's too good," I say. "She must belong to somebody."

"Then why's she hanging around here?"

"I don't know."

As Sam drives away, there is no sign of the dog in the boot. Presumably she's stayed lying down. I hope she's not plotting to savage Sam as soon as they're out of sight.

"Come on," I say to Ben. "Let's get into the warm, shall we?"

We go into my office, and I settle Ben on my knee while I scroll through emails. He wants to hold the mouse, though, and eventually I give up, opting to take him for a walk around the grounds instead. We stop in the bird hide for a feed and I try to ignore the cold as I watch the winter birdlife on the feeders. Blue tits, coal tits, sparrows and chaffinches, and a couple of pheasants hanging around on the ground, pecking up anything the smaller birds have discarded. It's nice to spend some time just sitting, and enjoying one of the special places tucked away at Amethi. I will always cherish the days I spent with Ben in his first few months but I am happy to be back, and excited to think it's not too long now till Julie's return.

As ever, though, there is much to do and with the solstice fast approaching, I need to make sure we're ready to make it as good as it was last year. I also need to think about a Christmas present for Sam, and a dog bed and lead, and… I am getting carried away, I know.

The chances are, Sam will be coming back with an empty car, the dog heading home to a worried and thankful owner. But now that door to dog-ownership has been opened, it feels like it will be very hard to close it again.

21

I may have been expecting it but I am still disappointed when Sam returns with no dog.

"They traced the owner," he says, "who's been worrying about the dog. Apparently, she's been gone for a week this time but it's not unusual for her to take herself off for a walk. She belongs to an older man, lives in a farmworker's cottage not far from Zennor. They had some walkers through, dogs off lead, which scared her and she ran off."

"Poor thing," I say, "but I wonder why she didn't go back home?" I think of her thin frame. That couldn't have happened in the space of a week, surely?

"Poor old chap as well, I think. Ron spoke to him, said the dog's his only companion."

"Oh. Well, I don't suppose I can feel too bad that they're being reunited, then."

"No, that's it. Ron said he's going to give her a good once-over then take her home at the end of his shift today."

Ron is a friend of Karen's. A jovial bachelor – is that word just as bad as 'spinster'? – and a really nice bloke. He's been at the vets in town since he graduated and now he's the main partner there. He's also heavily involved with the RNLI. In fact, it's usually him I have to thank for rekindling the idea in Sam's head, sidling up to him if they meet in the pub and reminding Sam what a great man his grandad was. It's nice of him to do this, though. "That's good; he'll make sure she's OK."

"Yeah, and then get her home, where she belongs."

"Oh well, it was a nice day-dream."

"Yes, it was. And you know, once we've moved into our new place, we can think again about it."

"I suppose." I'm disappointed. I'd got my hopes up. I must be mad, though. We've got a baby, for goodness' sake, and I've only just gone back to work. Plus, we need to find a new place to live. Why do I want to add to our responsibilities, right now? I just really liked that dog. And I think of the way she wouldn't set foot inside – and again, those skinny ribs. I wouldn't treat her like that. I'd feed her up, bring her into the warmth, she'd be part of our family, part of our home. But she's not my dog, and maybe that man really loves her, really needs her.

I look from Ben to Sam, and back again. I know we're going to be without Sophie soon, most likely, but still we are so lucky to have each other. I can't begrudge a lonely old man his dog.

"One possible bright spot," says Sam, as we eat chilli together – provided by Jonathan, watched by Ben – "is that Ron says he might know of a place we can rent. It should be empty at the end of January."

"Really? Where is it? How big is it?"

"One thing at a time!" Sam laughs. "Ron thinks it's a three-bed but he's going to check. And it's on the road out of town. So a bit of a walk up to it but he did say it's got a big garden, and views of the sea, on the estuary side. Through some trees, he said, but still views. I'm quite excited, actually."

"It does sound good," I put in hopefully.

"Ron said he'll find out more and let me know. He was also," Sam raises an eyebrow, pushing his fork into the fluffy rice and chilli, "asking about Mum."

"Oh yeah?"

"Yeah. What she's doing these days. Where she's working. If she's still single." He raises an eyebrow. "Apparently, he never sees her at the pub anymore."

"Really?"

"Yes."

"Well, that is interesting."

We may not have got the dog as we'd have liked but perhaps there was more to this seemingly chance encounter than may have first appeared.

***

Now it's all-systems-go with preparing for the solstice yoga week. The self-catering guests left this morning and now, Saturday afternoon, I'm working with Cindy, our housekeeper, to make sure all the accommodation is set up and ready for our yogis.

"It's been quite a hard time," I tell her, as we parachute a sheet between us, pulling it tight before folding it in under the mattress. It's a bright winter's day outside and the sunshine is lighting up the room, illuminating the dancing dust that's been unsettled by our activities. "Sam is in pieces at the thought of Sophie going, though he's trying not to show her, or me for that matter. I feel a bit bad working this weekend, actually, but he and Soph and Ben are going to do some fun things together. And she's staying with us till the day after Boxing Day but then Sam's taking her to Devon."

"Poor Sam," says Cindy. "It must feel like a kick in the teeth."

"I don't think he's taking it like that," I feel defensive, on Sam's behalf and Sophie's; their relationship is as strong as ever. "He knows it's been tough for Sophie and Kate, and

I really think that Sophie has just missed her mum more than she thought she might. She's always lived with her, apart from the last year or so."

"Poor girl," Cindy sighs. "Life is tough sometimes."

"It is, but she'll be OK. And she seemed to really like that school in Devon – and said that the girl who showed her round is really nice. She's very brave, choosing to start somewhere new."

"Well, she's a great girl," Cindy says.

"She is," I agree, and we move on to the next room.

Back in the kitchen, Jon is going through his menus. Checking the guest list and dietary requirements – mostly vegetarian; some vegan; some gluten-free – against all his plans.

"Hi," he smiles.

"Hello, how's it going?"

"OK! It's looking good. I think I've got everything covered. I hope so."

"You will have, I'm sure of it."

"I'm glad you've got faith in me."

"Of course! Now, are you going to be doing any of the yoga?"

"Not my scene, really."

"You might be surprised."

"Yeah... Nah, I can't see it, somehow. Are you doing it?"

"I'll do bits, when I can. It was a bit easier when we lived here, as I could come and go from the sessions in the evenings as well. Oh, and I didn't have a small child depending on me."

"Sam can look after him, though. And won't he be asleep in the evenings?"

"He should be, that's true, but I kind of need to be about

to feed him." Is it my imagination or has Jonathan just blushed at the thought of breastfeeding? "And also, Sam could do with a break. It's hard work, you know, looking after a baby all day."

"I like to think Sam's waiting for you with your pipe and slippers, when you get back from a long day at the office."

"I'd like to think that, too... the slippers, at least. Generally, it's mayhem when I get back. It's crazy, you know, how one very small person can turn the lives of two much bigger people upside down."

"I don't think I can imagine it," muses Jonathan.

"Honestly, I thought I could, but until we had Ben I had no idea. I think it is impossible to imagine. Maybe you'll find out for yourself one day..." I chance a cheeky suggestion.

"Maybe." He smiles. "But not yet. I need to talk to you, about the cottage, and what we do when Julie gets back."

"We do need to talk about that. How about we get through this week then have a sit down and maybe try to get Julie on video call, too? It's hard to talk about it without her. But I think I can say that in terms of the cottage, if you want to carry on renting it, you can. Julie and Luke have already got a house, of course, and Sam and I are going to be looking for somewhere with three beds."

"You're looking for somewhere new?"

"Yeah, sorry, I haven't filled you in on everything that's been going on, have I?"

"No. Janie mentioned Sophie's moving up to Kate's but why does that mean you're moving house?"

"I tell you what, if you've got some coffee on the go, and a few moments to spare, I'll tell you all."

***

I go home on Saturday afternoon, happy that all is in order for the coming week. Sam, Sophie and Ben are out when I get there. This gives me a chance to tidy up and make the place nice for an evening in together. We won't have many more of these before Sophie goes up to Kate's.

Her leaving isn't all about us, either; she has friends she is going to miss and next weekend, once the school term is over, Sam's taking her and Amber and a couple of the other girls to Penzance to watch a film and go for a meal.

"I won't watch the film, I'll take some work with me."

"Are you sure, you don't want to watch with the girls?"

"No way!" Sophie had exclaimed. "Dad can't come in. It'd be so weird."

She seems happier now that she has a plan, though I know she is nervous about her new school, and new life in Devon. Matilda, the girl who showed her round, has been texting her, which has really helped.

Tonight, at Sophie's request, we are having takeaway pizza, and watching *Mary Poppins Returns* – a film she would never choose to watch with her mates. I'm looking forward to seeing it. And after an hour or so of the house to myself, I'm starting to feel very keen to have my family back home. I'm excited when I hear the key in the door.

"Hello?" I call, and go through to the hallway.

In come three smiling, rosy-cheeked people. I kiss each in turn, taking Ben from Sam's arms, and dancing him around so he laughs. "Good day?"

"The best!" says Sophie. "We went to Sennen, and it was so cold on the beach, I don't think Ben liked it much, did you Benny? So we went to the café and then back to town to the arcade."

"I have literally not a penny left," Sam grins. "But it was worth it."

"Good," I say. "I wish I'd been with you."

"Everything alright at Amethi?"

"Yeah, great. Can't wait for this course. You will all come to the Solstice Eve thing, won't you?"

"Of course."

"Can Amber come? She loved it last year. And her mum and dad?"

"I'm sure that will be fine," I tell Sophie. "Now, I suspect I already know which pizzas you're having but just confirm I'm right as usual, and I'll order them. And you can get the film set up."

"I'll get the pizzas sorted," Sam says. "I think Ben's been looking forward to seeing you."

"You mean he wants milk?"

"Well… yeah. He's had his bottle a couple of hours ago but I think he'll be wanting more. And," he looks slightly shamefaced, "I gave him some yoghurt today."

"Yoghurt? Really?"

"Yeah. He loved it!" Sam smiles but he's looking at me as if I need to approve this. "I mean, I know he's not on solids yet but seriously, he couldn't take his eyes off Sophie, eating, could he Soph? And he tried to get her spoon."

Sophie, busy on her phone, laughs. "No, I videoed it, look."

I look. "A highchair, too?" Two firsts in one afternoon, and I was there for neither of them.

"Yeah, the woman brought one over for him, and he seemed to like it, didn't you mate?" Sam kisses Ben on the head. Ben is by now wriggling around, trying to work his way down.

"Alright, alright!" I laugh. "Come on, Soph. I've got the fire going. Let's go through, shall we? Sam, can you add extra chillies to my pizza, please? I feel like a bit of heat."

Sam sends me a look over Sophie's head. It makes me smile. I go into the lounge and settle Ben in then I watch Sophie. She is curled up on one of the chairs, intent on her phone. I think as I often do how it seems such a short time since the day she managed to soak me with seawater from her rockpooling bucket. And it is, really – just over five years. But look at all that's happened in that time. And look how much she has grown up.

"I'm going to miss you, Sophie."

She looks up. "I'll miss you, too."

"But you're doing the right thing, I think. And you know Sam and I, and Ben, are here, whenever you need us. And we're already looking forward to your first visit back."

"I feel guilty."

"You mustn't. You have nothing to feel guilty about."

"I know. But Dad…"

"You dad understands. Don't worry."

"I hope so."

Sam comes in then, with a Coke Zero for Sophie, a ginger beer for me, and a beer for himself. "Pizzas ordered, where's this film, then?"

"Oh yeah… the film." Sophie gets it set up, while I feed Ben, and think about the things he's done today. His first taste of yoghurt, and his first sit in a highchair. Neither is that monumental but I feel sad that I missed them. This is a feeling I am going to have to get used to. I just need to remember that it doesn't mean anything, in the great scheme of things. He will always be my little boy, just like Sophie will always be Sam's little girl.

22

Sophie's room is almost all packed up. In fact, she and Sam took quite a lot of her stuff up to Kate's a couple of weeks back.

"What's it like up in Devon, now?" I whispered, so as not to wake Ben up. Sam and I were in bed, the night they got back. We had all four of us been up to visit, last winter – Sam, Sophie and I, and Ben in my belly – and it is a beautiful place, but the house itself was in need of some work. I still shiver when I think of how cold our bedroom was.

"It's almost unrecognisable, when you're inside," Sam said. "Seems like Kate's got quite a talent for interior design."

"She could have helped at the Sail Loft."

"Why? Is it not working out with Sarah?"

"Oh no, it's not that. I think it's going really well, actually. Mum and Dad seem happy, and Sarah says she's having a great time. Her mum couldn't have the twins the other day so Dad entertained them while Sarah and Mum were making some plans."

"I can imagine they ran him ragged," laughed Sam.

"Yep, I'd say that pretty much covers it, by the sound of things."

Mum and Dad have instructed the estate agents, to put this house on the market in January. "One last Christmas there, before everything changes again, and without having to worry about nosy buggers coming for a look round and disrupting the peace," said Dad.

In truth, the changes have begun already. I feel really sad about Sophie going and although Sam is putting a brave face on it, I know how much he is going to miss her. And now, with Sophie's room down to the bare essentials, it feels like a step has already been taken towards us leaving as well. Once New Year has swung round, I think we need to go best foot forward, accept we're going, and get on with things.

Sam and I have been to see the house which Ron put us on to. It is beautiful, and in a great place, up at the top of the town, not all that far from where Julie and Luke's house is. I hadn't thought we would have the chance to live somewhere like that, and we are trying to work out if we can stretch our budget just a little. The only thing is, we're pushed for cash as it is. And it feels like our dream of a wedding is going out of the window, fast.

Ron, meanwhile, has asked Sam about Karen again. He's gone as far as asking Sam for advice on asking her out.

"I dunno, she's my mum," Sam had said, with a mock-shiver, when he was telling me about it.

"He should just ask her out! Or should he? Do we want to risk our relationship with the best vet in town; say Karen chews him up and spits him out?"

"As I said, Alice, *she's my mum*. The image you paint is not a pleasant one."

"Sorry," I laughed.

I think through this on my drive to Amethi. My stomach doing little leaps and not just because of the red car's suspension. Today is the start of solstice week. And I have realised that as much as I love normal weeks here, the thought of these special event weeks – and this one in particular – really gets me excited.

I'm pleased to see that Lizzie's car is already parked up. She is sitting inside it but when she sees me approaching she gets out, ready as ever with her huge smile, and a hug for me.

"You are looking well, Alice," she beams. "You'd never think you gave birth only a few months ago."

"Thank you, Lizzie. Flattery will get you everywhere."

"I mean it. You look… glowing."

"The last time anybody said that to me, I was pregnant. Let's hope that's not the case this time!"

Lizzie gives me a look but I laugh and head across the gravelled car park and around the side of the building. I couldn't have asked for a more beautiful morning. On the drive up, I could see the perfect winter sea behind me, the sun hanging low above the horizon in the watercolour sky. It won't be climbing a whole lot higher all day. Up at Amethi, I'm filled with love for this time of year – the best part of winter, in my opinion. The trees hold a host of noisy jackdaws, and a gang of unruly sparrows twitter in the hedgerow by the wildflower meadows. A pair of blackbirds skitter across the hard, cold ground as we approach, seeking shelter in one of the nearby trees.

"What a beautiful day," I say.

"It's perfect," Lizzie agrees.

We have a hot drink to start: coffee for me – and I am treating myself to a full-on caffeinated one – and tea from some of Lizzie's home-grown herbs for her.

"That does smell nice," I say.

"Try one later, if you like. It's the midwinter blend, like I had last year."

"Oh yeah, that was lovely," I remember.

"I've been growing loads more herbs this year, to make

more tea. And I wanted to make sure we have enough for all of us this week, not just on Solstice Eve."

"Thank you, Lizzie. Maybe you should think about selling some of your teas. Not here," I hastily add, "or at least not now. I guess there will be all sorts of legal things to think about. In fact, we should make that clear to the guests – that this is homemade tea…"

"You worry too much, Alice," Lizzie smiles.

I say nothing. That may be so but I also take responsibility, along with Julie, for the health and safety for our guests. I am sure the tea is fine, but I have to think all these things through.

We go into the Mowhay and I put on the heaters, although there is a part of me that wants to open the doors to the day.

"I'll go and get the mats," Lizzie says.

"OK. I might just pop up and check emails and all that."

"Great. See you shortly."

The office is so cold. Even with the heater on it takes a while to warm up and I wrap my fingers around my mug while I wait. The laptop is also slow this morning.

I scroll through my emails, pleased to see most of it is festive junk and there are no cancellations for this week. Lizzie is very keen to get the balance right, including in terms of numbers. There will be twelve people, as we can fit that many comfortably in the space available. It is also important that the accommodation doesn't get too cramped. Often, guests at these events come alone, and may have to share with somebody they haven't met before. Something else I need to be very careful about – trying to make sure everyone has a bathroom of their own, and are in same-sex pairings.

There's an email from Julie, which I open keenly.

Hi Alice,

I was just thinking about you and Amethi, and the solstice week. I hope it goes even better than last year.

Christmas in India is promising to be amazing. Apparently, there are places where they put clay pots on roofs of houses, with burning oil, to show Jesus is the light of the world. And there's midnight mass, with a huge feast after. I don't suppose I'll be going to church but then again, it seems like an experience, I should maybe give it a go.

The solstice celebrations here won't be until January, so I will be thinking of you all this week and wishing I could be there.

See you soon, my friend.

Lots of love from Julie and Luke xxxxx

I send a quick reply back:

Hi BFF,

I wish you could be here, too. It seems such a short time now, since last year's solstice. I hope this one goes just as well.

You should definitely get to church for midnight mass, if only for the amazing feast afterwards. It could be research for work, when you get back here. Although I am sure you've been sampling plenty of food since you've been there. I wish I could try some. I'd love to see you there. Spend a day together. I try to imagine all the things you

tell me about, and your pictures are brilliant, but to actually be there in person would be something else. And just to give you a huge hug. I miss you like you wouldn't believe, and Ben is looking forward to meeting you.

Loads of love from Alice and Sam and Sophie and Ben xxxx

***

In the afternoon, the guests arrive, all within the space of two hours. Lizzie and I greet them, and I show them to their accommodation. Jonathan is busy in the kitchen but I make sure each person pops their head around the door to say hello as well.

"First Night feast!" Jonathan grins, the kitchen air filled with the warming scent of spices. "North Indian curry."

My mouth waters, and my stomach rumbles. "Make sure you save some for me."

"Won't you be joining us, Alice?" Christina, who has been on a couple of our yoga retreats now, asks.

"I'm afraid not. I have to get home to my little boy."

"Of course! Is he at nursery?"

"No, Sam's on shared parental leave," I say proudly.

"Oh, that is marvellous. Your turn next," she says cheekily to Jonathan, who waves a spatula at us.

"Don't you start!"

I raise my eyebrows at him. Christina and I take the chance to escape.

"He's gorgeous!" she breathes when we get outside. "If I was thirty years younger…"

"You wouldn't be the first person to make that observation," I smile. Luckily, Janie seems as laidback as

Sam about these things and seems to find it amusing how many smiles and furtive glances Jonathan receives from some of our female, and occasionally male, guests. "Now come on, let's get you to your room, you can settle in for a while before we meet again at five. Then I'm going to have to leave pretty sharpish."

The tree was delivered in the morning by the same less-than-cheerful driver as last year, though he did look like he recognised me. Maybe his expression had softened by a degree. Perhaps in ninety years' time it will have become a smile. "You want an indoor one, too?"

"Yes, please. That was the plan."

"S'on there, but under them," he gestured to a pile of three or four netted trees. "I'll drop it on my way back."

"Alright," I said. "Thanks."

With no further words, he headed back into his cab.

Jonathan, Lizzie and I, sweating and panting with the effort, dragged the huge tree round to its place, in prime position to be seen from as many parts of Amethi as possible. Janie, spotting our struggle, came out to help as well. Still, it took quite some time.

"You know you should grow a tree, instead?" Lizzie said.

"I have been thinking that. But I'd miss out on the lovely chats with the friendly driver. I suppose I'd just have to get used to it," I say.

"Tell you what, after Christmas, come with me to my mate's nursery. He'll have something for you. Should have thought of it before," says Lizzie. "And the smaller one, for indoors."

"Alright, I will."

Now, the tree is ready for decorating. Jonathan and I have strung the lights around it, and he and Janie are busy hanging up the many outdoor baubles which we bought last year. I would have liked to do it, too, but have so much going on. Plus, I realised, the day we did this last year was the day they met. It's quite romantic, I think, them doing this together now.

At 5pm, I am in the Mowhay, ready to greet the guests, many of whom are already settled on seats. My internal body clock is telling me I should be going home. I wait until all twelve are present and correct, plus Lizzie, and Jon, and I give a short introductory welcome.

"Thank you so much for coming, to what promises to be a fantastic week. This is our second winter solstice yoga retreat and I know a couple of you were here for the last one." There are a couple of small smiles and murmurs at this. "Unfortunately, I no longer live on site, so I won't be here quite as much as last year. I also have a baby to get back to these days!"

"And a husband?" one of the men quips.

"A boyfriend," I correct. "Yes, I do need to get back to him, too. And both of them will be here on Solstice Eve, along with my stepdaughter. In the meantime, I will be around the place as much as possible but I will leave you in the very capable hands of Lizzie, and Jon our brilliant chef. You all have my number, so if I'm not here and you need me, please make sure you use it. This week is all about you."

I smile, at the small smattering of applause. Then I bow out and walk through the cold early evening to the car park. The drive home is illuminated by the moon, and as the sea and the town swing into view I feel my heart leap with happiness and excitement, at all that I have now, and all that is to come.

23

Last year, Solstice Eve was on a Thursday. Sam had work the following day and Sophie had school, but we were living at Amethi at that time so they could come and go as they pleased. This year, it is the last day of the school term and Sophie's last day at school. It's going to be emotional.

I spend the day in the office, reviewing the figures for the year and compiling information for our accountant. I can't get hold of Julie, which is annoying, as I want to double-check a couple of things, but I phone Mum instead.

"Hi Alice!" She sounds more cheerful than she has for some time.

"You sound happy."

"I am. We're having a good week, your father and me. And Sarah. She is a marvel. And we've had a last-minute booking for Christmas so we're full. And you know we've been booked up for New Year for ages. I know we still have a long way to go, but it's given me a real lift."

"I'm really pleased, Mum. It's going to be a different Christmas for you this year."

"It is, but I think it will be lots of fun. Plus, we get to see our grandson's Christmas. Life feels good."

"It is, Mum. It is." I feel relieved to hear her like this and realise how long it's been since I last heard her sound less than stressed. "Now, I have some boring questions for you, as I'm getting the quarterly figures together. Have you got a moment?"

"Of course."

We go through the questions I've got. "Thank you, Mum,

that's really helped. It's a shame you're not still working up here, or that we never got a chance to work together."

"I know, although… maybe better to stick to mother-and-daughter stuff as much as possible, eh?"

"Probably!" I laugh. "See you tonight?"

"I'm not sure, I don't know if it's your dad's kind of thing. And we're very tired, to be honest."

"Alright, well no pressure, but you'd be very welcome."

"Thanks, darling. I'd better go."

Tonight, I am not going home after work. Sam, Sophie and Ben are coming up here, instead, to join the feast that Jonathan's prepared. He's borrowed Julie's menu from last year, starting with spiced pumpkin soup, topped with roasted pumpkin seeds and accompanied by home-baked bread. For the main course, butternut squash pizza with roasted vegetable salad. He has swapped last year's less-than-popular warm brussels sprout salad for sweet potato wedges. I've seen the huge pans of them, coated in oil and spices, ready to sizzle in the ovens. The smells emanating from the kitchen have wafted into the office throughout the afternoon, making my mouth water. To drink, rum-spiced egg nog or a rum and ginger cocktail.

When my little family arrive, it's clear that Sophie has been crying. I go straight to her, sending Ben a smile which I don't think he appreciates, and put my arms around her. "How was it?"

"It was… I'm so…" she bursts into tears and I hold her to me.

"Shh," I say, "don't worry. You can tell me in a bit."

Sam smiles sadly at me. It's a really tough time for him, and for all of us. I am going to miss Sophie so much. I wonder if Ben will; if he is old enough to. I suspect not. I think even if something were to happen to me, he'd miss me extraordinarily for a short time but would get used to life without me. I shiver at the thought.

"Come on," I say, "let's go and see the tree." I take Sophie's hand and lead her out of the car park, Sam and Ben following on.

"He's going to jump out of my arms if I don't give him to you," Sam laughs.

I turn to see Ben straining forwards. "OK, you little wriggler," I squeeze Sophie's hand and somehow manage to put it in one of Sam's whilst also taking the solid warmth of Ben from him. Ben laughs with satisfaction. "Yep, got what you want now, I hope you're satisfied," I say to him. "We'll have a proper chat later, Soph, I promise."

As it is, within ten minutes Amber and her parents arrive. "Sorry we're early," her mum says, "but Amber wanted to spend as much time with Sophie as possible."

"That's fine," I smile, watching the two girls gravitate towards each other. Amber has a gift bag, which she hands to Sophie.

"Amber!" Sophie squeals as she peers inside. "How many things?!"

"She's been buying them for weeks, ever since she knew you were going, Sophie. She's going to miss you. We all are," says Amber's dad.

I feel a lump in my throat.

"We've already booked onto a course up in Devon, though, in the Easter holidays, and Amber's going to stay in the house with Sophie."

"And you'll be back every other weekend," I remind Sophie. "Amber, you're very welcome to come and stay over with us when Sophie's back."

"Every weekend?" asks Sophie excitedly.

"We'll see," Sam says. "There will be family things, too. But I can't see any reason that you won't get to see Amber at least for a little while, whenever you're with us."

The girls look like they don't know whether to be pleased or disappointed by this. They scurry off into the communal area, and Sophie begins unwrapping her presents, emitting little exclamations and hugging Amber at each one.

"Let's get a drink," I say to Sam, and Amber's parents. Ben is entranced by all that is going on; the lights on the tree, and all the different people. He looks over my shoulder at it all as we go into the warmth of the communal area, which is bustling with this week's course participants and full of good humour, some of it possibly spurred on by the warming winter cocktails.

The evening follows much the same pattern as last year, with dinner followed by readings from Vanessa and Rosie, who lead our writing courses and have become part of the family up at Amethi. After this, Lizzie lights the fire outside. Jonathan, who has worked throughout the dinner, comes to this, accompanied by Janie. She gives Sophie an enormous hug and whispers something to her niece that makes her smile.

I seem to remember that last year it had rained all day but this had died off for the evening. This year, the perfectly clear winter's day is followed by a perfectly clear winter's night.

"It's the solstice," Lizzie smiles knowingly.

I let her off, even though I can't believe that every solstice eve is as lovely as this one.

Sophie and Amber have sparklers at the ready, and the flames start to grow in confidence as they taste the wood of the fire built by Lizzie, Sam lights the sparklers for the girls and they laugh with delight, in a way that they would not normally allow themselves to do. They seem younger, returned to their pre-teen days for a short time. I see Amber's parents looking at them and my breath catches, for a moment. Sophie going feels like the end of a particular era, of the girls' youth. It feels sad and beautiful at the same time.

Ben is very tired now, his head resting on my shoulder. My arms are tired, too. I hope that tonight isn't going to mess up our carefully engineered routine for his bedtime, but I can't miss out on this.

Lizzie bangs a spoon against her tin cup. "Quiet, please, ladies and gents, just for a little while. I wanted to thank you all for coming. It has been another wonderful, unforgettable week. As those of you who were here last year will remember, in the morning we will celebrate the return of the light. I have it on good authority that the beautiful weather will hold overnight and I will of course keep the fire burning."

"You're staying up all night, Lizzie?" Med, one of the course participants, asks.

"Yes. Always do," she smiles.

"I might keep you company. If that's OK," he says.

I glance quickly at Sam, who returns my look. I'm not imagining it, then. It seems Lizzie has an admirer.

Lizzie smiles at Med in apparent agreeance, then continues, "Tonight, we give thanks for this last year, and the wonderful feast we have enjoyed—" she breaks off so people can give Jonathan a little round of applause "— and as always, the most wonderful welcoming atmosphere of this very special place, Amethi." I smile, trying to accept my applause graciously. It is easier somehow, being centre of attention in the dark. "Any of you are welcome to join me by the fire tonight," Lizzie continues. I am sure Med is hoping nobody else will. "But if you prefer the comfort and warmth of your beds, I don't blame you. Please be back here in the morning for 6:00am. I will talk you through the celebration of the returning of the light, welcoming in the spirits of the east, south, west and north as the sun begins to rise. Make sure you wrap up warm!"

Just as last year, there are murmurs of excitement around the fire. I've got to hand it to Lizzie, she knows how to create an atmosphere.

I glance at Sophie and Amber – who is staying with us tonight. They say they will come back with us for the morning celebration. I say we'll see what time they actually get to sleep tonight. I know I am going to have to be up extra early, to make sure Ben is fed and ready. But I wouldn't miss it for the world.

"Now, I want to sing you a solstice song."

I hide my smile as Lizzie produces a tambourine from within her poncho. I am expecting it, though I still have no idea where she keeps it under there, or why she doesn't sound like a one-man-band everywhere she walks. We are all quiet, though, watching her, a breeze ruffling clothes and hair, and skimming across our faces. Lizzie begins to sing, the same song as last year, keeping time with her tambourine. She closes her eyes and we watch her, listening as she sings about the green man; the holly king, giving way to the mighty oak king. Two brothers, who each govern half of the year.

When the song is over, there is quiet for a beat or two, then a round of applause for Lizzie, who opens her eyes, smiling.

"We'd better go," I say to Sam. I thank Lizzie, and Jonathan. Sophie gives Janie a huge hug.

"See you in the morning!" Janie says.

"Yes, we'll be here, I promise."

"See you tomorrow, Janie," I kiss Sam's sister on the cheek.

With Sam carrying a now-sleeping Ben, we cross the gravel, and walk to the car. Sam manages to slot Ben into his seat then Sophie and Amber squeeze next to him onto the back seat, muffled giggles as they try to find their seatbelts. When Sam gets into the car, I stand for a moment, looking around in the darkness. There is a murmuring of voices from where we have just come, where the celebrations are still continuing, but other than that all is quiet. I hear an owl call from the trees. Another calls in answer. Above, the sky has remained clear and I can see the sliver of moon amongst the stars, which appear to be randomly scattered but I wonder if there is more order to it all than first appears.

Head tipped back, I spin round slowly, getting a 360° tour. But Sam has started the car now and I know we need to get the youngsters home, not least Ben. I need to find a way to get him into his cot without him waking. And I hope his nappy's clean. These thoughts somewhat take the edge off my stargazing wonder but still, I smile into the darkness as I get into the car, feeling that Lizzie is right. This is a very special place.

In the early morning, I'm impressed. Not only has Ben slept through, but the girls are up. As I tiptoe across to the cot in the darkness, I can hear their voices. Although, does that mean they actually haven't been to sleep at all?

Reluctantly, I gently wake Ben. I can't believe I am cutting into his precious sleep, and risking undoing all the good that has come lately, but needs must. I lift my sleepy baby into my arms and bring him across to the bed, where

Sam sleeps on. In the dim light from the clock on my bedside table, I feed Ben, who has become expert and takes far less time than he used to, then I wake Sam. He holds Ben while I dress, then call up to the girls.

"We're all ready!" Sophie cries in a delighted voice.

"Have you actually had any sleep?"

"Yes!" she calls, and she and Amber break into peals of laughter. I roll my eyes and grin.

I take Ben while Sam gets ready then, nibbling croissants, we walk back up to the car, through the very quiet and sleepy streets, just the odd light on here and there. I shiver as I get into the cold car and the engine sounds too loud against the stillness of the early morning but we head up and out of town, the car soon heating up, the sky behind us perhaps just beginning to lighten, the sea still a dark, unknowable mass beneath it.

At Amethi, everybody is already present and correct, many brandishing steaming mugs, of Lizzie's solstice tea.

"Would you like some?" she asks and Sam and I say yes but the girls aren't sure. "Bog-standard tea for you two, I think," laughs Lizzie.

I go with her ostensibly to help get drinks, but I do have an ulterior motive. "So… Med…" I say, leaning on the table while she pours hot water into the girls' cups.

"Yes?" she smiles sweetly.

"Seemed quite keen to spend the night with you… by the fire, I mean."

"Yes, he did, didn't he?"

"So…"

"So?"

"You're giving nothing away, are you?"

"Nothing to give away, Alice."

She smiles sweetly and turns to go outside, leaving me to follow with Sam's and my mugs.

At the fireside, in the dark, Lizzie guides the way she did last year, asking me to say a few words, which include a huge thank you to her. There is a short round of applause and a whoop, I think from Med. Then Lizzie steps up.

"I can assure you all, it is my pleasure. Now, as the light begins to seep back into the world, let's begin. This is the longest night of the year. Now is the time to celebrate the return of the light. To gather with friends and welcome back the sun…"

It feels familiar now, this ceremony, though I have only seen it once before. The invitation to the spirits to join us. The incense to cleanse the space. Lizzie walks round the fire. She stops when she comes full circle. "Look up!" says Lizzie. "It is time to greet the spirits."

I glance at Sophie and Amber. They look very serious, standing close next to each other. I feel sure their friendship will not be broken by distance.

We follow much the same order as the previous year, following Lizzie's directions to turn and show respect to the spirits of the east, south, west and north.

We do as we are told. A breeze swishes around us, ruffling the branches of the tree, making the lights dance. Lizzie lights a small red candle and holds it out, towards Sophie. Slightly unsure, Sophie glances at Sam, who gives her a small nod. She takes the candle. Lizzie explains that the colour red represents the root chakra. She follows this with an orange candle, representing the sacral chakra, which she gives to Med. Sexuality. I send a knowing glance her way but she doesn't look at me, of course. Yellow, she gives to Sam, representing the solar plexus. Green, she passes to Janie. Christina is given the blue candle for communication and creativity, and me the purple candle: the third eye; inner wisdom and extra sensory perception. I like that idea. Lizzie keeps hold of the final candle, which is white, and represents spirituality and consciousness. "And now, we stand together to face the sunrise. We open our hearts and let the light grow within us."

We turn and, just as last year I see that to the east the sky is lighter. I picture the sun rising over the horizon, filling the new day with light. I am aware of the birds in the surrounding trees and bushes, calling to each other, seeming to sing for the sheer joy of a new day.

Then Lizzie hands out paper and pencils, instructing us to each write down a wish to cast into the fire. "The paper will shrivel and burn but the meaning of your words will be carried up into the air, rising higher, towards the light."

This year, I know exactly what to write. The same as last year. *Happiness.*

It covers all eventualities, and I extend that wish to all. Not just happiness for me. It's a big ask, I realise, but still it's what I wish for.

All around me, people are either writing, thinking, or already folding their pieces of paper. Jonathan is chewing the end of his pencil, deep in thought. I catch his eye and he smiles. Then he writes. Next to him, Janie yawns and leans against his arm.

We stay quiet while each person steps forward with their wish. I wonder about all these people who have come to stay here; spent money to come here and put their faith in us to provide an unforgettable week.

I hope that is has been unforgettable for the right reasons, and that each of our guests will return home at peace and full of positivity.

One by one, we all cast our wishes to the flames and feel the atmosphere grow deeper, somehow, while all around us the day is taking shape. The fire takes each person's words, burning the paper and freeing the wish.

In time, Lizzie takes the lead again. We thank the spirits for their help, turning from north to west to south to east, stopping for a moment in each position to express our gratitude.

We are still for a moment and I close my eyes, aware of the sun lighting my eyelids, and the breeze passing my face. Then I feel a hand on my shoulder and hear a very quiet, "Alice." Whispered into my ear.

I turn abruptly, still somehow managing to stay quiet. I know this voice, you see. I turn, and am met by two strong, familiar arms and two laughing eyes.

"Shh," she mouths, because around us everybody is still, quiet, and thoughtful. It takes all my will not to exclaim out loud.

"Julie!" I whisper and I fall into her embrace, utterly overcome with emotion.

24

I can't believe it. I simply can't believe it.

"You must have written my name down as your wish," she grins, when we're back at home.

"How did you know?"

"So obvious. What else do you get the woman who has everything?"

There had been tears when we'd first been reunited. I had snuck away from the fire with her, Lizzie opening one knowing eye and sending a small smile our way.

Sam had followed us to the communal area, with Ben in his sling, and expertly detached himself, handing Ben to me so I could introduce him to Julie.

"Oh my god," she said quietly. "Ben. At last."

Ben, cool and collected, looked past her, holding his arms out to Sam.

"Hey!" I said, and turned him round so he could see me, and smile, then back again to Julie. It made him laugh so I did it again.

"Hi Ben," Julie said. "It's so good to meet you."

"Sorry, he's quite tired. It was a late night last night and an early start this morning."

"Well that's OK," she held out her hand and Ben put his on it, grabbing her finger. "What a strong grip. Isn't that one of those things people say to babies?"

"It is!" I laughed. "Along with, 'Doesn't he look exactly like his dad?' That's not at all annoying."

"You just get annoyed when Mum says it," Sam smiled.

"Well, it does feel a little primeval, like she's trying to

stake some kind of claim to him. There are two sides to Ben's family, you know."

"Alright, you two. I haven't come back to hear you bickering!"

"So why have you come back?" I asked with genuine curiosity.

"I just couldn't get used to the idea of missing Christmas here," she admitted.

"Ahh, really?"

"Yep, and I feel bad. But it was Luke's Christmas present to me. He knew how much I wanted to be back home. Though he's stayed over there, to help with some Christmas celebrations at a Christian orphanage. I should have done that but…" She held out her hands. "I've struggled, to be honest. I love it. And I love the kids. But there's no place like home."

"So, you're back for good?" I asked hopefully.

"No, till New Year, but then it's only another month or two and I will be back properly. We both will be."

"I can't tell you how happy I am to see you, Julie."

"Why not?"

"It's a state secret."

There were tears in my eyes and she reached out to hug me again, Ben in between us, I suspect distinctly unimpressed.

Now we're back at the house and I'm filling her in on all that's been happening.

"So this place is going?" she asks sadly.

"Yep. Mum and Dad are putting it on the market in January."

"It's so sad. Such a beautiful house. So many memories."

"I know. But I keep telling myself, it's just a house. And

it is. It's the people in it that matter."

"Speaking of which, Sam said it would be alright if I stayed with you guys, in the room next to Soph's? My old room."

"Sam knew about this?! Bloody hell. How did I not know there was something fishy going on?"

"We've been working very hard to keep things secret. Let's just say it's a good job this one can't talk." Ben is now sitting happily on Julie's lap, playing with her bangles.

Sam and Sophie are out. They took Amber back home then were going on somewhere for a bike ride. I'm not expecting them back all day. Which means I have a full, delicious day with my baby and my best friend.

"So what shall we do, today, I mean?"

"Shall we not just sit and chill? If Ben's alright with that, of course. I'm shattered from the travelling and you must be worn out after the solstice celebrations."

"I am pretty tired. I think maybe we should take this one out for a walk later, in his pram I mean. Or maybe he's ready for a pushchair. This could be his first go in his pushchair! Sorry, that must sound weird, being excited by that."

"Not at all," Julie smiles. "It's so great seeing you as a mum, you're just as I expected you to be."

"Is that a good thing?"

"Definitely." Tears glisten in her eyes. I have to ask.

"So you and Luke… what's going on with you and, you know, getting pregnant?"

"It's not happening, Alice. I think we have to accept that it isn't going to. I know, I know, some people try for years and it eventually works, but we can't assume that will happen and anyway, what about those years while it isn't working? Does life just become about that, and do we become bitter and disappointed by everything?"

"Hmm. No. I don't think that sounds like you."

"So we have a plan," she brightens. "And it's slightly unusual, although not as unusual as you might think. We're going to adopt."

"Are you, really?" I think of David and Martin, and how it hasn't been easy, but what a fantastic thing it is.

"Yes, but we're adopting from India, not here."

"Wow," I take this in for a moment.

"It's not been an easy decision – and it's not like a fix-all solution. I am still trying to deal with the fact that I probably won't have a baby of my own. I should say *we* won't have a baby of *our* own. And I'd love to. I'd love to be pregnant, to know how it feels; even to give birth. I want all of that, so much. But I also know those are things which don't last forever and once they're gone you are left with a baby and that's the important part of all this." She kisses Ben on his head. "The baby."

"Wow," I say again. "And you're right. You know, I think, that I really enjoyed being pregnant – most of the time – and I wish you could have that experience, too. And I get what you're saying. It's not as if choosing to adopt can be a magical solution that makes everything right.'

"No."

"But... how brilliant. Is it not really complicated, though, adopting from overseas?" I squeeze Julie's hand.

She smiles. "There is quite a long process to follow, but it might only take a year. And we're well along that road anyway. I'm sorry not to have told you before, but I just really wanted to tell you in person."

"That is quite alright!" I laugh. "Especially as it means I get to see you sooner than I would have done. So will you have the baby when you come back in February?"

"No, I don't think so. And I don't know for sure it will be a baby, but there is a good chance it will be."

"Isn't it amazing, thinking that your child might already be out there, just waiting for you?"

"Yes, and in the meantime, what's it going through? Julie's mouth sets in a hard line. "Honestly, Alice, you wouldn't believe some of the things I've seen. But it's the same here, isn't it? The weak and vulnerable are preyed on, in ways that are unseen by most of us carrying on our happy, healthy lives. India is an incredible place, with incredible people. I love it. But I don't want to stay there, and neither does Luke. But we do both want to continue helping in some way. And we've had to think very long and hard about whether this is the right thing; adopting a child away from its home country. For me, it doesn't matter. I don't think that where you are born has to have any bearing on where you go on to live. It's one world, right? But I can see that other people will have plenty to say about it."

"If anyone can let what other people have to say wash over them, it's you, my friend. And I agree. I know we need to be sensitive to things, and I know how much people take the piss out of celebs like Madonna, for their adoptions, but really, if you can bring a child into your life and give him or her a happy life, as long as you haven't stolen them from their parents, I don't see that there's a problem."

"I had no doubt you'd understand. I might need your support, sometimes, especially at those cut-throat mother and baby groups you've been talking about!"

"Oh yeah, they do get pretty nasty! But I'm back at work now. I won't be going to any groups anymore. And... won't you be back at work, too?"

"That was the other thing I wanted to talk to you about.'

I can tell this is going to be quite a conversation, so I suggest that we wrap up warm and give Ben's new buggy a whirl. It's funny trying to get him into it, and he looks fairly surprised at the whole thing, but I can see he's enjoying being upright, and once we get it out of the door he can see where he's going. He sits very still at first, clearly not quite sure what's going on, but after a few metres and a couple of little bumps that set him giggling, he's grinning away.

We walk down the hill, towards the town, and follow the route along the harbour promenade, taking a sharp left up the steep streets, pushing the buggy in a near-vertical line, or so it feels to me. I check on Ben. He's happy as can be and becomes very animated at the sight of a seagull tucking into somebody's dropped chips.

Through the little warren of streets, approaching the surf beach. We haven't spoken much till now.

"So what's the plan, then? With work?" I ask.

"I don't know. That is really another important reason I'm back now," Julie looks at me. "I need to talk it through with you. Come up with a plan. I have no intention of backing out of Amethi," she says. "Let's get that straight right now. But when the baby, or child, comes home with us, it is going to impact on work. So I don't know what you think about this, but one solution I've come up with is that we keep Jonathan on, as the chef, at least for a while. If he wants to." I'm not sure I have ever heard my friend sound so hesitant. "And I work with you on management issues, so it's still the two of us running the place. Only I don't have to do the chef hours I was doing before. I don't know. What do you think, Alice?"

She looks at me, concern written across her face.

"Wow, well, erm, it's a bit of a surprise. Though it makes

sense, given your situation. And, financially, I guess it will work as it does now…? We'll have to work it out. I'm taking a wage again, and so is Jon, of course. How would it work financially, for you?"

"We'll have to have a proper look at it all," she says. "But this would be the same, if I was pregnant. And if you get pregnant again. We are going to have to find ways to work through these times."

"You're right," I say. "How did we never see this coming? Two women in their early thirties, starting a full-on business like Amethi. Were we mad?"

"No!" Julie laughs. "Not at all. We will work it out. There will be a way. I know we couldn't get your mum to help again but if we needed to we could find somebody else. And it might be a bit tight financially but we'd manage."

"You would," I say ruefully. "Sorry, I don't mean it like that! But Luke's business is doing well, isn't it? We're pretty strapped, though, and now we have to find somewhere new to rent, plus pay nursery fees, we're going to be stretched pretty far. So I don't think another baby is on the cards for us for some time! Or our wedding, come to that."

"Oh I'm sorry, Alice. We'll make this right, though, I promise. And financially, this should only impact me, not you. And Jon and Janie still pay rent for the cottage, so hopefully we'll get through this financially pretty well."

"Yeah, we'll be OK. And now Sophie's going, though I wish she wasn't, we will probably save some money on food and stuff – though Sam's going to be sending some support to Kate.'

"Wow. I suppose he has to, doesn't he?"

"I don't know. I think he would have to, yes, but he and Kate have always sorted this out between them."

"Feels like we're proper grown-ups now, eh?" Julie links her arm through mine and we emerge onto the beach road. It's not too windy today but still, there's a stiff breeze and I pull Ben's rain cover down over him, to save sand blowing in his eyes. He looks perplexed.

"Anyway," Julie says, "what about this wedding of yours?"

"I don't know," I feel really disappointed as I say this. "I would love to, and Sam too. I've even got pricing and availability for venues and I had next May in mind, or the one after perhaps. But realistically, how can we think about getting married, right now? Mum and Dad can't foot the bill, not that I'd expect them to. We've got to find a new place to live, and everywhere is so expensive. No, I think it's going to have to wait a while longer."

We walk the length of the road, past the café, warm lights glowing in the windows, inviting us in. We resist. The clouds hang thick and grey and low today, above the sea. The clear sky of the solstice morning already forgotten.

I look at the vast expanse of the beach, dotted with dog-walkers and the occasional couple or family. The sea is, as always, populated with the ever-watchful surfers. Sometimes it feels like they live there, on their boards. Condemned to a life awaiting that one perfect wave that never comes.

"Come on," I say to Julie. "Let's go to the Sail Loft. Surprise Mum and Dad. They'll be so happy to see you. And yes, we will work it all out. We'll find a way. I promise."

25

On Christmas Eve, I work during the morning, ensuring all our guests have what they need for the big day, and processing bookings for the new year. I speak to Shona, girlfriend of the lovely Paul Winters (don't tell Sam I called him that), with whom I had a brief, unsuccessful fling. I say unsuccessful but it actually resulted in Julie and me finding Amethi so perhaps it wasn't all bad.

Paul has become a friend since then; Shona, too. She has helped us with PR since the 'Tony incident' and is working on getting us some more magazine features but I have to say, right now Amethi is doing pretty well off its own back. What I really want to ask about is the Sail Loft.

"How are you, Alice?" Her soft Scottish accent is warm and friendly. "It's lovely to hear from you. How's the little one?"

"Ben is just great thank you, Shona."

"And business is good?"

"Busy as ever," I say, "and I've got an interview lined up in the new year, with *Kernow Life*."

"That's fantastic. It's got excellent circulation figures, you know, and not just locally. There's a lot of international readers. People all over the world want a bit of Cornwall. Ask Paul. Wherever he has a meeting he says somebody will have been there, and fallen in love with the place."

"I was going to ask if you might be able to help another local business, Shona… or at least how much it might cost if you did." I go on to explain my parents' situation.

"That lovely hotel where you used to work? I'm sure we can do something for them. In fact, I've just taken somebody on. It might be perfect to break her in gently. And I could charge less then, too. But don't worry, she's really good. I'll make sure your mum and dad get what they need."

"That would be brilliant. Thanks so much, Shona. Let me just speak to Mum and Dad first, and I'll pass on your number if that's OK."

"Of course it is, Alice. And hopefully we might pop in to see you over Christmas and New Year. We'll be at Paul's for the duration."

My mind turned wistfully to Paul's amazing beachside house. If only Sam and I could afford somewhere like that… I can dream, can't I?

Better than a beachside house, though, is the fact that Julie is with me, and we're sharing our little cosy office once more. I can't help wondering what the future looks like, but if there's anything I've learned these last few years, it's to be adaptable. Accept that nothing stays the same forever. And if it did, it would be boring.

"It's like old times, Alice," Julie says, as if reading my mind. "I'm so happy to be here. I mean, I'll miss Luke over Christmas but he's dead busy over there. It's just so good to be with you."

"It's bloody brilliant," I agree. "I've missed you so much while you've been gone."

"Not half as much as I've missed you. But I feel like – now I'm going to sound like Lizzie – I feel like India was meant to be." She smooths her dark, glossy hair thoughtfully, her eyes momentarily sad. "I mean, we went out there heartbroken that things were looking ropey for us, in terms of getting pregnant, I mean. Now, we'll be coming back, if not with a baby, then knowing we're hopefully going to be parents soon."

"It's so cool, what you're doing."

"It's not, really. I think it's probably quite selfish of us. But I'm done with wrestling my morals about it all. There are so many children there who need homes. So many abandoned girls," she sighs. "Such a beautiful country, and beautiful people, but I'll never get my head round it."

"It's not selfish. You've found a solution to something which is no fault of your own. And the solution is going to benefit not only you but the child you bring home."

Julie can't help smiling at those words. "I know. And I do believe it's true, that it doesn't matter what country you're born in, and we're all just humans, but there's still a part of me which feels like we're just privileged tourists coming in and taking what we want from India. Then happily trotting back to our nice big house in England."

"It's Imperialist guilt!" I laugh, knowing as well as Julie does that it's highly possible her own ancestors were slaves. I don't think she has any apology to make for the British Empire. "Look, Julie," I continue, "you and Luke are going to be amazing parents for a very lucky child."

"I hope you're right, Alice. I really do."

She swivels back to her computer screen and I watch her for a moment. I am sure she's crying. But I'm not going to make a big deal of it. She may not have pregnancy, or post-pregnancy, hormones but she's got a lot of other emotions to deal with.

We break off at lunchtime, and head down to the communal area. Jonathan is waiting for us, with Janie, the two of them sitting on a seat by the window, holding hands and talking earnestly. On the dining table is an assortment of warm and cold snacks: vegetable samosas and onion bhajis; freshly fried crisp poppadoms; home-made mango chutney and raita; three-bean salad with feta cheese; sweet potato pakoras with sour cream dip. There are plates of mince pies decorated with a little A for Amethi, and a fat, glistening fruitcake, all laid out beside champagne flutes and ice buckets containing bottles of prosecco.

"Jonathan, you've outdone yourself!" I exclaim. This had been his idea; a little pre-Christmas gathering for all our guests.

"I don't know about that." He looks almost embarrassed at the praise. A far cry from the cocky young chef who first came to work with me at the Sail Loft.

"You have, Jon, it all looks so good," Julie says. "Happy Christmas, mate." She goes to the table, pours four glasses of prosecco, and hands them round, keeping one for herself. "Cheers. Merry Christmas."

"Merry Christmas," we echo, and I think that a cold glass of wine has never tasted so good. What a year. I sit back, to relax for just a moment, but as soon as I do, the first of our guests appear. The Wenlocks; a very jovial family from Julie's and my neck of the woods: mum, dad, three kids, and grandad. I suspect that the dad and grandad have already had a drink or two.

"Look at this!" Mrs Wenlock exclaims. "We're not going to need Christmas dinner after all."

Jonathan stands, smiling his best smile. "I hope you enjoy it. Let me get you a drink."

Julie and I share a quick, silent look. Janie sits quietly, shy in her role as chef's girlfriend. Very much Sam's sister, she is not one for the limelight and her job being a very clever and talented IT professional suits her well. She works in the spare bedroom of the cottage – the room which Sophie and I decorated – at a small desk, the window overlooking the courtyard area, face glowing in the light of the computer screen. In this way, she is hugely different from her brother, whose passion is for nature, and the outdoors. But they share the same smile and the same nicely understated manner. Both very different from their mum.

"Stick around as long as you want to," I say quietly to her. "You are very welcome. But also don't feel any pressure to be here."

"Thank you, Alice," she smiles. "I might just drink this and slip away."

"You do whatever you like. You can take it with you if you want."

I might also like to slip away quietly but that's not what this job is about. Instead, I stand, and greet the other guests, who come thick and fast now. There is only one party who have opted out, which is of course fine. The others mingle and chat and make merry. They won't be going anywhere this afternoon, by car at least – but there are plenty of walks around these parts, and for once Christmas Eve actually feels Christmassy. We awoke to a really cold morning, the air on the street infiltrated by a low-lying mist which had crept up from the sea.

Up here at Amethi, it is colder still, and crisper. The mist had made it this far, wreathing the fields. It has lifted now, revealing sparse, short vegetation and the occasional pheasant or two, picking their way through the undergrowth. The bird feeders are popular, with sparrows, finches and blue tits; fat wood pigeons hanging around below to take advantage of any spillages.

I can see a robin sitting on one of the outdoor tables. It

would make the perfect Christmas card picture and I want to take a photo, but I am on duty. There is something so right about Julie being here, too; like a balance has been struck once more. But Jonathan is a very welcome addition and he's agreed on principle to stay on here as chef ("Maybe I can talk to you about some ideas I've had") so all seems well with the world.

I'd love to have set up a time-lapse camera, focused on the table, showing the piled-high platters and deep-filled dishes gradually empty themselves onto people's plates; into people's mouths. Soon, there are just crumbs and the odd pakora left, alongside a number of empty bottles. Somebody has turned the radio on, and we all find ourselves singing along to Christmas hits. As we painfully strain to make East 17's *Stay Another Day* sound sincere and emotional, I am filled with joy (quite the opposite effect that Tony Mortimer had in mind) and love for the people around me; particularly Julie and Jonathan, and Janie, who I am really happy to see has stayed and is chatting to Mrs Wenlock. The three Js. I raise my glass to Julie, who smiles and mirrors my gesture. I hope that she has much happiness to come.

I think of the first Christmas I arranged at the Sail Loft; the choir on Christmas Eve. Maybe that's something we can do here next year. And who knows where we will all be then; what changes a further year will have brought.

By mid-afternoon, we have managed to shepherd the guests out and we all work together to clear everything up. Jonathan and Janie come to wave Julie and me off. I've only had one glass of prosecco as I'm driving, but Julie has had certainly her fair share, if not somebody else's as well.

"It's so great to see you again, guys," she slurs out of the car window.

"You too, Julie!" Jonathan has his arm round Janie's shoulder and I am reminded for a moment of my parents, waving me off on my way to university.

"Happy Christmas!" I call, and we are off in the little red car, bumping along the drive, emerging through the shield of trees into the outside world. Heading towards a festive town, twinkling with Christmas lights. Streets packed with last-minute shoppers. Children eager to hang up stockings, thinking maybe they will go to bed early tonight, to make Christmas come quicker. That will be Ben in years to come. I smile to myself at the wonder of it all.

26

Christmas Day. When I open my eyes, it hits me: it actually is slightly bright behind those curtains; a slim sliver of daylight glowing around their edges. What time is it?

It's 7.43. *What?*

I leap out of bed, shocking Sam, but head straight to Ben's room. Relief. He is breathing deeply, little arms bent and hands up above his head, as if he's being held at gunpoint. I can't believe this. I sneak back to bed.

Sam mumbles, "What time is it?"

"It's quarter to eight. Ben's still asleep! His Christmas present to us."

I kiss Sam and snuggle into his warmth. Who knows how long this will last? I'm determined to make the most of it while it does.

"Happy Christmas," he says into my hair.

"Happy Christmas."

Snuffle, snuffle. A tiny snore. A murmur. He's awake. I am up and out of bed again in a flash, Sam complaining as I'm letting the cold in to our warm, cosy bed.

"Hello, little one. Happy Christmas," I say to Ben, who is holding his arms out to me. He smiles, pleased with himself, as I reach down to get him.

His first Christmas. It makes me feel quite emotional and I'm embarrassed to find a lump in my throat.

"Are you OK?" Sam asks as I come back in. He sits up, puts the bedside light on dim setting.

"Oh, yes. I'm OK. More than OK. I'm so happy."

"Me too," he smiles. "Well, except Soph…"

"I know," I say as I climb carefully back into bed for a second time, wrapping the duvet carefully round myself and holding Ben to me. "I know. I'm sorry."

"Hey, nothing to be sorry for. It's OK. I've got used to the idea. And I think she's made the right decision, in a way. Being with Kate, I mean. Those two have been through a lot together."

"I suppose they have."

"We all have!" he laughs. "God, remember that year…"

"Don't!" I say, recalling all too easily the night just after Christmas, when Sophie had gone missing. I'd sat at the window of this very room, for hours, just keeping watch. Thinking it was all my fault. A situation filled with such emotion I'm sure it's left an etching of itself like a ghost in the room. "Urgh."

"Sorry," Sam smiles. "I didn't mean to make you feel bad. It's just one thing which has happened to us all; between us all. But we came through it, and we'll come through this just the same."

"You are pretty great," I say.

"You're not so bad yourself," he kisses my shoulder. "Now, I'm going to have a shower and get downstairs to make coffee while you're feeding him. Then you can bring him down and have a shower yourself."

"That sounds pretty amazing."

"I'll give Soph till nine then if she's not up I'll shake her out of her bed! Can't waste a moment of Christmas Day."

As it happens, Sophie is already up. And she comes into our room while Sam's in the shower, holding a stocking stuffed full of gifts.

"Can I open this in here?"

"Of course you can." I free a hand and pat the bed.

"Come and sit down. Want to wait for your dad? He won't be long."

"Yeah, I think I will," she says.

"Great. Here, find some Christmas music, will you, please?" I hand her my phone.

Soon enough, we have Carols from King's ringing out and when Sam emerges from the en suite – I managed to shout through to him that Sophie is here so he's got his dressing gown on – he pulls on some boxer shorts, jeans and a jumper, then gets back under the cover.

"Hey! You said you were making coffee!"

"I was, but Sophie wasn't here then."

"Alright," I say, "I tell you what, you look after Ben and I'll make the coffee. Soph, get under the covers and you can open your presents."

"Can I hold Ben first?" she asks.

"Of course!"

Before I leave the room, I take a look at the three of them, cosy in bed. I don't think it will be long before Sophie will shy away in disgust at the thought of getting under the covers of our bed. Or sitting under a duvet with her dad. This time next year, I think, she will have changed again, an awful lot. She will be nearly sixteen.

Lizzie would say, be in the moment, and I've come to realise how right she is. We have no option anyway, and it would be wrong to waste moments like this.

***

Downstairs, Julie is in the lounge, on a video chat with Luke. She is preparing the fire while she talks.

"Happy Christmas!" I say from the doorway. She turns and smiles. "Happy Christmas, Luke," I call.

"Hey, Alice. Happy Christmas. I miss you guys."

"We miss you, too. But you're doing a great thing. I hope you have a brilliant day. Can't wait to see you in the new year."

"You too, Alice. Give Sammie a manly slap on the back from me, please."

"Of course. And I am sure he'll send a proper blokey handshake right back to you."

It's nice to see Luke's face grinning away on screen. I really can't wait for him to be back with us. I don't want Julie to leave again but at least this time I know it's going to be only another month or two.

I leave them to it and move through to the kitchen. While the kettle boils, I look out of the back door to see our resident seagull sitting on the wall. I open the door, gently, and he raises his wings in a momentary flutter of panic, but quickly settles again.

"Merry Christmas," I say to him but he just looks at me like I'm stupid. It's cold outside, but I wanted that blast of air. The sounds and smells of the seaside town.

The church bells are ringing and other gulls have taken to the skies, others calling from rooftops. What a place to be for Christmas morning! I breathe deeply, in and out, until I hear the kettle click.

Semi-reluctantly, I close the door on the outside world, turn my attention back to the Christmas household. Julie, Sam, Sophie, Ben and me. That is how we are starting the day. Then Karen is coming for a light lunch, before she goes to Amethi to spend the rest of the day with Jonathan and Janie.

We are planning a little walk round town, then up to the Sail Loft to see Mum and Dad, who will no doubt be shattered after Christmas lunch. I dropped some presents off yesterday, hiding them under the desk in the office. Not that I think any of their guests would steal them but, when you run and live in a hotel, you are essentially inviting strangers into your home. You do have to remember that, because people can surprise you, and not always in a good way. I will never forget that nastiness with Tony, who came to stay at Amethi. That was a terrible time. But we are through it now. Even so, I'm glad that we live separately to work these days, especially now we have Ben.

This is something we still have not settled, though; where are we going to live next? The place Ron told us about is really nice, but it's expensive.

"If we take it, we'll be waving our wedding goodbye, for another ten years," Sam sighed.

"Don't worry about that," I said. "It's not important. Well, it is. Of course it is. I'd love to marry you. But we both know that we're together, and now we have Ben as well as Sophie. A wedding would be lovely but most important is keeping our family safe and well, with somewhere to live, and enough food to eat."

"I know," Sam had put his arm round me. "But when I proposed… it was so romantic. I want us to be romantic. I don't want us to get totally swamped by the demands of life; earning a living, cooking, cleaning. It's going to get even more complicated when Sophie's away. I want time for us. You and me. Alice and Sam."

"We will make sure there is always that time," I kissed him. "Married or not. And the wedding will come. But it's OK, I promise. Everything is OK."

"I guess it feels like things are a bit transient, with Soph coming to us from Kate, and Kate going, and now Soph going. And us having to leave this house. I know it has to happen. And it's not our house. But will we ever get to a point when things just settle for a while?"

"I don't know," I admitted. "But maybe that would be boring. Perhaps it's not so bad to accept the changes occurring and go with them. I know, the main thing is Sophie going. That is worse than us not getting married, or having to find a new house. But we'll make it work. We'll find a way."

My words echo what I said to Julie, on our walk that day. *We'll find a way.* We'll have to. It's that or give up, and we're not going to do that.

"Thank you, Alice, I don't know what I'd do without you."

"And I don't know what I'd do without you. We keep each other going, and we always will. That is far more important than a wedding."

***

Three days after Christmas, Julie leaves to see her Mum for a few days before her return to India. We both cry a little.

"But you'll be back soon," I say, to reassure myself as much as her.

"I will," she agrees. We hug tightly.

"Keep me up-to-date," I say, "about everything."

"I will," she says again.

The day after that, Sophie leaves, too. Sam packs his car with all her stuff, trundling up and down the hill – I am sure he just wants something to do; a way to expend his energy – while we three others sit in the lounge together. Sophie is very quiet.

"Are you OK?" I ask.

"Yes," she sniffles. Then, "No. I don't want to go, Alice.

I don't want to leave. What if I'm making a huge mistake? I'm going to miss you and Dad and Ben and Amber…"

"We are going to miss you, too. So much. But it will be OK. And you'll be with your mum, and Isaac, and Jacob. Can't get away from those little brothers!" I try to make light of the situation, and she does give a small smile. "Sophie," I say gently, "whatever you do, and wherever you are, we are always going to be here for you. And you won't have made a huge mistake in what you're doing. But you will need to give yourself plenty of time, to settle in, and get used to the new place, and new school, and new friends. I don't suppose it will all happen immediately but you are a lovely, really fun person, and people will want to be friends with you. And you know how much your mum is looking forward to you being with her again. You must be looking forward to that. And that's OK. That's good, in fact. It isn't going to upset me, or your dad."

"Are you sure?"

"Yes, Sophie. I promise. It's a hard decision you've had to make, and you tried staying here without Kate, which was really brave. But you'll always have a place here, and you'll always have us, and Amber, and your other friends. At least you can see them at weekends."

"And Amber can come for sleepovers?"

"Of course! When you're back in Cornwall, you'll be home, just like always. It won't be this house for much longer, but wherever we are there will be a room for you and you can treat it just as if you were with us all the time."

I sound braver than I feel, and when Sophie does go, and it's just Ben and me in the quiet of the house, I sit and cry for quite some time. I may be all for accepting change, and life being boring if it stayed the same forever but it doesn't mean it's easy.

27

Before I lived here, I used to imagine that every year I would be out and about on New Year's Eve, soaking up the atmosphere of the town-wide annual fancy dress party. In fact, most years I've stayed away – sometimes because of work; sometimes just because I don't feel like it. This year, neither Sam or I feel like partying and besides, we have Ben. I don't think he'd want to be out in the dark and cold, with 30,000 lunatics – I mean, 'revellers' - dressed as Deadpool and Donald Trump on the wild.

I do actually love New Year's Eve here. I love the fancy dress and the way that the town fills with so many people, many of whom have had at least one too many, yet there is minimal trouble. Still, I am happy to be in tonight and just listen to the sound of happy, excited voices and loud footsteps pass by the window. Curtains drawn, they can't see us, and we can't see them, but I can well imagine the scene out there.

Sam has not really been anywhere since Sophie left; he's stayed at home, coming to terms with it. When he returned from taking her to Devon, he was as sad as I've ever seen him. He kisses me and Ben, and goes through to the kitchen to make us cups of tea, then he sinks onto the seat next to me and just sits quietly. Ben, blissfully unaware, is waving a rattle wildly about, until he clonks himself on the head with it. All is still for a moment as he ponders what has just happened, then his face scrunches up and he starts to cry.

I lift him for a cuddle and it's as if his crying has allowed me to do the same. I let quiet tears form, rolling one-by-one onto my cheeks. I glance at Sam but his eyes are dry. His face tells the story.

When he'd dropped Sophie off, Kate and Isaac had lunch ready and waiting for the two of them. Sam told me this later, in bed. He said Kate was on edge but clearly so happy and excited to have her daughter back with her, while Isaac kept talking too much, and casting guilty glances Sam's way. Sophie was quiet, and contemplative, while Jacob – a good few months older than Ben – was unmoved in his highchair, interested only in getting as much food into his mouth as he possibly could.

After lunch, Sam and Isaac unloaded the car. With one bag left to go, Sophie came to find Sam, in tears.

"What if I've done the wrong thing, Dad? I feel sick. I don't want you to go. I want to come back with you."

It sounds like Sam said much the same to her as I did. "Look, Sophie. You're bound to feel like this. It's a big change. You know you feel sick when you're nervous or anxious. Just give it time. Nothing has to be forever, if you don't want it to be, but you'll surprise yourself, I'm sure you will." He had hugged her tightly. "And I will miss you, so much, but don't you ever go feeling bad for me, because I only want you to be happy. Just remember it might take a bit of time. Don't expect things to be perfect straight away."

"Oh Dad," Sophie had sobbed.

As Sam tells the story, I feel so sorry for her. She went through the process of saying goodbye to her mum, not a year ago, and now she's having to do the same with her dad – although she does now have her Mum back. But what a situation; stretched and split between two parents.

Sam had unloaded the last bag, deciding it was better to go, and let Sophie begin her new life as soon as possible.

"Without me," he said glumly.

"Sam," I put my arms around him, "she will never be without you. No matter where either of you are." But I know what he means.

So, come New Year's Eve, just a nice night in is fine for us. We have a Chinese takeaway, ordering far too much; not yet used to ordering for two, instead of our usual three. Sitting at the dining room table to eat it, we hear some premature fireworks. It's only 8.30.

"Might as well go out to see them," Sam says. "Reckon we'll be in bed for the midnight ones."

He's right. With a stomach full of delicious but heavy food, and a couple of glasses of wine in me, I am already yawning. We step out into the garden, shivering in the night air, although the day has been unseasonably warm. Now, though, the sky is clear, allowing all the cold of winter in. There is a huge *CRACK* and some cheers as an explosion of colour lights the sky, swiftly followed by another. Gold, green, blue, red and white sparks fill the air, again and again. High-pitched squeals as each fireworks launches into the air, heading for its moment of glory, exploding into colour before plummeting to earth, an empty shell.

Sam stands behind me, his arms around my waist. I settle into him. When all the noise and light is done, we stay awhile in unspoken agreement. There is music coming from the direction of the harbour, the sound of people traipsing down the steps behind the garden wall, and occasional shouting from nearby streets. Celebrating the coming of a new year, or the end of an old one?

"It's been a good year," I say, "mostly. Certainly an unforgettable one."

"I feel like every year's been unforgettable, since you've come back, Alice. That sounds cheesy – and I do mean it in that way, but also, I feel like life was always pretty quiet. Pretty much the same, year in, year out. Then you came back and everything changed. Think about it, what's happened in these last few years. You came back. Luke's mum died. We got together. I passed my exams, went to Wales. Then that night Sophie disappeared."

"Don't remind me," I interject but Sam just kisses the back of my head, squeezes me reassuringly, and continues.

"Then it was that year when I was back, and everybody got married. You and Julie started your own business. I came back, Kate went to Devon, you got pregnant, we had Ben… and that's not even half of it."

"If you put it like that," I turn to kiss him, "I guess it has been pretty eventful."

He kisses me back, his skin cold against mine. I close my eyes, enjoy the moment's quiet amid the noise and excitement of the town. I rest my head against Sam's shoulder, feeling his familiar body pressed to mine. Turning my head slightly, I look up to the sky, and the stars, and the near-full moon, which seems further away tonight, keeping its distance but ever watchful.

"No wonder I'm so bloody tired," Sam says. "How about we tidy up, get the house nice for the morning, and just say goodnight to this year?"

"Sounds like the perfect plan." Hand-in-hand we go in, separating to perform our now well-practised tidy-up, putting anything we can save in the fridge; rinsing plastic and foil for the recycling; a cork in the wine bottle, the glasses washed, dried and put away. Very soon it's as though we have never been here, and I like Sam's thinking. Knowing that we start the new year with a clean and tidy house. Begin as we mean to go on.

***

After a leisurely breakfast, I decide to go to Amethi, and check that everything is OK there, and that our guests enjoyed their New Year's Eve. As has happened previous years, some of the households have pooled together to share transport to and from the town.

Judging by the quiet of the place, they have either not made it back, or they're all still asleep. Hopefully the latter.

Then the silence is broken, by some familiar-sounding paws on gravel.

"Hey!" I say, as the dog appears round the corner, her whole body wagging, as if just her tail would not be enough, in apparent ecstasy to see me. "What are you doing here, you naughty girl?"

I crouch to stroke her and she pushes herself into me.

"Are we going to have to get you home again?" I ask. "Here, let's get you some water, shall we?"

As I cross the gravel, the door of the cottage opens and Jonathan emerges, wearing just baggy tracksuit bottoms and a t-shirt, outlining his strong physique.

"Happy new year, Alice! I thought I heard your car." He grins. "She still here, then?"

"Yes…" The dog is behind me, following my every step. "So she hasn't just got here?"

"No, she appeared last night, while the fireworks were going at midnight. Amazing how loud they are all the way up here. I suppose there were others in the village, too. But she wasn't a happy girl, probably scared by all the noise."

"You poor thing," I say, crouching again. She pushes her nose into my hand. "Everything else OK up here?"

"You talking to me, or the dog? It was fine. Brian brought the minibus, got everyone here and back, as far as I'm aware. We were still up, watching a film, and I peered out to count everybody back in. I think it was the full complement."

"You are good," I smile. "I just thought I'd pop up to check on everything and of course to wish you and Janie a happy new year. I hope it's a good one for both of you."

"I've a good feeling about it," he says enigmatically. "I'm going to go back in though, it's freezing out here."

"You've only just noticed? I'll see you in a bit," I smile, and, straightening up, I head towards the office.

Jon is right, it is cold, but in keeping with the rest of the last two weeks, it's another vivid, vibrant winter's day. A spider's web dances on one of the bird feeders, catching the low sunlight, and I startle a flock of pigeons from the short stubble of the wildflower meadows; they rise as one into the sky, circling to find the direction they want to head but settling instead for coming back down to the place they started. Clearly, it's too cold to fly. By my feet, the dog stands, unsure of why I have stopped, and seeming not to want to leave me.

"Job number one," I mutter to myself. I open up the building and go into the kitchen, getting a bowl for some water for her, and some cold cuts of Christmas turkey. It will need eating anyway. I suppose she needs more than this but it will do for now.

She tucks into the food and it's gone almost as soon as I've put the bowl down. A quick, thirsty drink, and a lick of the chops.

"We'd better get you home," I say, adding this job to my

list and going in. As before, she stays outside, and I have to close the door on her. It's too cold to leave it open.

With the heater on, the office soon warms up. I miss Julie's presence, which I'd quickly become used to over the short time she was back.

She sent me a lovely new year's message:

Have a good one, Alice and Sam. It has been lovely meeting Ben and I know he'll have changed so much by the time I see him again but then I'm not going anywhere. Ever. You're stuck with me. Thanks for letting me stay over Christmas, I loved every minute. Happy New Year xxxx

It was our pleasure, Julie, and you turning up at solstice was the best surprise ever. It's going to be an exciting year for you and Luke. I can't wait to have you back but make the most of your time out there. Happy New Year to you both. I love you xxxxx

I banish thoughts of loneliness from my mind, and phone Sam.

"Hi," he sounds out of breath.

"Everything OK?"

"Oh, yeah, just doing a nappy change. He doesn't want to stay still, the little bugger!"

I laugh. "You'll miss this when you're back at work."

"I'm sure I will. Maybe not the nappy changes, specifically."

"We've got an unexpected visitor here, Sam."

"Oh yeah?"

"Yeah. She's short and furry and has a very waggy tail."

"No! She's come back?"

"Yeah. Jon said she turned up last night, when all the fireworks were going."

"Poor little thing. I do think it's mean on animals, having fireworks. I guess we need to get her home again."

"Yes, I suppose so."

"I know you want to keep her with you forever and ever!"

"Don't laugh at me," I smile.

"Ahh, I'm not. I know she's your new best friend. It's fine. Even if she is a dog."

"Can you give Ron a ring, please?"

"Sure, just let me sort the boy out."

I don't hear back from Sam for a while, and I get stuck into some work, checking through payments and deposits, and expenditure. Not the most exciting work but it has to be done. And actually, from what I can see, we're doing OK, so it's not such a bad way to start the year. Jonathan brings me coffee, which I accept gratefully.

"Is the dog still outside?" I ask hopefully.

"Yep. Want me to get rid of her?"

"No!" I exclaim a little too loudly.

"Have you got a new friend, Alice?"

"Don't you start! Sam's already been winding me up about this."

"Alice and the dog, sitting in the tree, K-I-S- No, sorry, that is a bit too weird."

"Yep, just a bit. Anyway, can't you see I am busy and important?"

"Yes boss, sorry boss," he backs away, his head bowed.

"Thanks for the coffee, though!"

By lunchtime, I think I've done as much as I can for the

day. It is more than I'd planned anyway but predictably I had got sucked into things. This afternoon, though, Sam and Ben and I are going for a walk around town, and I want to get back.

There is no sign of the dog when I emerge from the building and I am disappointed, but hopefully she's headed home, and saved us having to get her there. I take a little walk around Amethi. There are muffled noises from the holiday lets, and the unmistakable smell of bacon frying for, I guess, a very late breakfast. Satisfied that all is well, I am about to head back to the car when I hear the sound of claws on gravel and there she is, trotting up behind me.

"What are we going to do with you?" I ask. I try Sam's phone but there's no answer.

"I've got to go," I say to the dog, giving her a good all-over rub, and as I drive away she stands forlornly on the car park gravel, watching me leave. It takes all my willpower not to reverse back and bundle her into the car.

After lunch, Sam gives Ron a ring about the dog, while I somehow manage to wedge Ben into his snowsuit.

"I think he needs a new one," I say when Sam returns.

"Already?"

"Yep. He won't stop growing, this boy."

"OK, we'll go shopping this week, when Mummy's back at work," Sam says to Ben.

Out into the new year we go. Cheeks soon glowing red in the biting cold of the seafront. The town is fairly busy but feels quiet, somehow; like the slightest noise will make the place groan in self-induced pain. The clean-up operation is well underway, and it's already hard to imagine that last night the streets and harbour were heaving with party-goers.

Those who are up and about today are, like us, young families, and the occasional older group dressed for a late lunch at one of the harbourside restaurants. The tide is out and the boats sit patiently on the rippled sand, waiting for the sea to return them to life.

Turnstones dart around, scurrying out of our way, while unruly seagulls strut about, gorging on food scraps that the street cleaners have not yet reached. Today, the town belongs to them.

Exchanging new year's greetings and smiles with people we pass, it feels like a special day.

"Fancy a coffee?" says Sam, seeing that one of the kiosks is open.

"I'd love one, please." Facing the harbour, I hold on to the pushchair, gently rocking it, Ben sitting semi-supine and ready to drop off to sleep soon.

Somewhere in the changing bag, Sam's phone begins to ring. I hasten to answer it, hoping it doesn't disturb Ben's sleepy state. If he is interrupted on his way to sleep, he can become quite irate.

"Hello?" I say.

"Oh, hello, I was hoping to speak to Sam." A man's voice I don't think I recognise.

"This is Alice, his girlfriend. He's just away for a moment or two, can I get him to phone you back?"

"Oh, Alice, it's Ron here. Calling about that little dog of yours."

"She's not ours," I remind him.

"Ah, yes, that's right. But listen, I guess Sam hasn't told you yet. I did hear back from the owner and he's not himself these days, poor old chap. I know him of old; used to look after his herd for him. Of course, he gave up that game some time ago. Anyway, that's by the by —" Does this man ever stop talking? "The long and the short of it being he knows he can't give that dog what she needs. She's young, and got a lot of collie in her, and she needs exercise, Alice. Stimulation. What I've said to him — Davies, his name is — is that I'll ask you and Sam if you want her. And I'll help him find a lapdog, some kind of companion, you know. Can't have a farmer without a dog, can we? Especially since his wife died. He'll get lonely. Probably already is…"

"Ron," I put my hand up to stop him, though he obviously can't see that as we are on the phone. "Hang on a sec. You're asking if Sam and I can keep the dog?"

"Well, yes, isn't that what you want?"

"Erm… well, yes, I suppose it is. I think. I need to talk to Sam about it."

"He seemed quite keen, when I called him earlier."

"Did he now?"

"Yes! Oh-ho, I hope I haven't got him in trouble."

"No, nothing like that, Ron! Thank you. I will get him to call you back."

"What?" Sam asks from between teeth gripped round a paper bag, a coffee cup in each hand.

"Have you heard anything from Ron yet?" I ask.

"No, nothing, he… did he phone while I was getting these?" Not much gets past Sam.

"Yes…"

"What did he say?"

"Oh, we had a very interesting conversation. I say 'conversation', it was pretty one-sided. He says that Mr Davies who the dog belongs to doesn't feel like he can give the dog the attention and exercise and *stimulation* that she needs. He wondered if we would like to have her. He's going to help find another dog for Mr Davies. According to Ron, this is something you've already discussed. I guess it must have slipped your mind."

"Oh yes, that's right, that does ring a bell," Sam smiles. "Do you mind?"

"No! I don't think so."

"I didn't want to say anything to you till I knew what the situation was."

"You are such a softy," I nudge him, and we walk to the nearest bench, facing the harbour and the slowly incoming tide. Ben is now asleep. We put the brakes on the buggy, our bums on the bench, our feet on the harbour railing.

"I know we need to get her checked out, and we need to know she's safe with Ben. But I can tell you're already attached and I realised how much I'd love a dog in my life again. What I was thinking was she could come to work with you and have plenty of space to run around all day…"

"As long as she doesn't run off."

"As long as she doesn't run off," he agrees. "But we can take her to training – one of us, or take it in turns. She'll love it. She's a clever dog, you can tell. Ron says so, too. And she can live with us, and…"

"That might be a sticking point," I say. "I don't think we're allowed pets in that house."

"Shit," says Sam, "I hadn't thought of that."

"But I want her now. I want that dog. And it feels like she's come to us, especially. I know that sounds a bit lame, but it really does feel like that."

"It does," he agrees. "Well, we can always ask the owners, of the house, I mean. And if it's a no, we will have to decide which we want more – the house or the dog."

I think we already know what the answer is.

28

"Watch out!" I laugh, plucking a bemused Ben from the sand and brushing him down. He is determined to walk, this boy, but finding the uneven surface a challenge. "Why don't you just crawl, eh?"

He won't be told. He's learned to stand up in the last week or so. To take a tentative step or two holding onto the furniture, and even to stand unaided in the middle of the room. The look of pride on his face is something to behold. The first time, he looked utterly astonished.

"Well done!" I said and he attempted to clap his hands too, but ended up back on his well-padded bum.

Now, he is full of himself. He's walked before, he'll do it again. He's not going to let any old beach stop him.

It's busy today; the first really warm day of the year. Not quite warm enough for a full-on beach day, in my opinion, but that doesn't stop some people. Wind-breaks, beach tents, the works; they set up a small fortress to catch and hold as much of the sun's heat as they can. Dressed in wetsuits, swimmers brave the winter-cold sea, shrieking as they enter but many giving it a good go. No doubt the sea at the surfer beach is swarming today. It's a bit wilder round there and I do love it but today I wanted to introduce Ben to days at the beach somewhere a bit more gentle – so he's not put off.

In just a couple of months, he is going to be one. It's hard to believe, and I feel a little lump in my throat at the thought of it. He's taken to Goslings like a duck to water (hmm) and I am sure he's gaining socialising skills, being with other babies and children every day. This is what I tell myself, and maybe I'm just trying to assuage the guilt, but needs must, and I needed to get back to work, as did Sam.

It does make these times we have together extra special, though. I love work but I look forward to my days off like never before. We have a little routine going, where the three of us – four if Sophie is visiting – have a lazy morning in our pyjamas, tucking into toast and tea (or milk in Ben's case) and playing with toys. Eventually, the shower calls for Sam then me, and soon enough it's lunchtime. Afternoons are spent out and about, as long as the weather's good. A wildlife park; a baby-friendly soft play place; the beach, of course; just a stroll around town. Anything is good for Ben, who is interested in everything. And it's so nice to have time as a family. It seems even more special now there is less of it.

Today, though, Sam is not with us. He is helping Dad take the furniture from the house: some to the Sail Loft, where Mum and Dad's newly extended apartment awaits it; some to an auction house near St Austell; some to a charity warehouse. It's hard to think how empty the place will be when we get back. And harder still to think that very soon we will no longer live there.

It's a house, I have to tell myself again and again. *Just a house.* But it is more than that, and it always will be. The new owners are a pair of local artists; the woman's star having recently risen, paintings and sculptures bearing large price tags, they are now in a position to move into town, having previously lived up and out of the way, not all that far from Amethi.

"I'll miss the fields," she said, when the deal was done.

"But I've wanted to live here since I was a girl. I grew up over Penzance way and my granny lived here but by the time I was old enough, there was no way I could afford anything."

She seems nice, and so does he, and I'm pleased for them. That's something else I have to keep telling myself.

So we've come out for a bit, Ben and I, and Meg. Yes, we have our dog. Ron gave her a good check-over, and we paid one of the guys at the local animal charity to do some behaviour training with us, to check she was as lovely as we thought. She was. She is. She dances around us on the beach, watching the sea with trepidation and letting out the occasional woof – trying to see it off. She had never seen the sea until we brought her to the beach; though she was living just a few miles away, her previous owner is firmly attached to the land he lives on, and so all of this is new to Meg. She has had a lot to get used to, including being allowed in the house, but to be fair it didn't take too long to break that habit. And she soon found a favourite place, on the end of the settee. Some nights, there is barely space for Sam and me as she sprawls out.

"Make yourself at home, Meg," Sam will say, but it's clear he's as smitten as I am. And Ben loves her, and she him. She's actually been a great support for him in learning to stand as he can rest on her to push him up. And she is as patient and gentle as she would be with a pup, even turning to lick him from time to time, which makes him laugh. They are already the best of friends. Now it's all going to change again and I hope she's happy and comfortable enough that she won't find it too stressful.

A secondary effect of Meg has been Karen and Ron. Ron and Karen. It may be a bit too soon to put it quite like that, but after we brought Meg home, Karen phoned.

"Hi, Alice, how's the new doggy?"

"Erm, she's brill," I had said. We'd literally been home only an hour or so. I know that the town is rife with gossip, but even so, surely gossiping about a dog is getting somewhere near the bottom of the barrel?

"You want to know how I know, don't you?"

"I guess."

"Ron just called."

"Did he now?"

"Yes, and he asked me out!" She sounded so happy, I couldn't help but smile. "We're going to the Cross-Section on Saturday. I've never been taken there before by a man. Or anywhere much, really, come to think of it."

"I'm really pleased," I'd said. "I hope it goes well."

And apparently it did. They have been seeing each other with increased frequency and so far, so good. It is a relief for Sam and Janie both to know that their mum is happy. And as a bonus it stops her interfering in their lives (and mine and Ben's) quite so much.

As for my own parents, they are happier, if not quite relaxed. Shona has been true to her word, her 'girl' Nicky working with them on the PR side of things, and helping them build their online presence. It seems to be working as their bookings have doubled at least and they are now nearly at full capacity for most of high season.

Meanwhile, Sarah and Mum have been planning a refurb for the guest quarters, which they hope can go ahead next winter, when things are quieter.

"Your mum is so great!" Sarah has said, more than once. "And your dad's so funny."

"Well, that's one way to look at it."

In fact, Sarah and Mum have had a couple of evenings out. A meal, and a trip to the theatre. It's a strange thought, and I have to put on my best grown-up's head about it. Sarah may be my friend but there is no reason she can't be my mum's, too. They did ask me along, to be fair, but Sam's working a lot of evenings at the moment and I haven't been able to go. Besides which, I'm so tired by the end of a long day at work, all I really want to do once Ben is in bed is lie semi-comatose on the settee, a warm, furry Meg at my feet.

Anyway, I have my friend. My best friend. For Julie and Luke are back, and she is at Amethi every day, just for an hour or two sometimes, but it is so good to have her back, though I have had to help her take a step away from the kitchen. And food orders. And menu-planning.

"It's Jon's now," I remind her. "You have to let him get on."

"But I wouldn't have done…"

"No, you wouldn't," I say gently. "But you've got to let him get on."

In fact, Jonathan is relishing this opportunity. "Now it doesn't feel like I'm babysitting for someone else, I can do some of the things I've been thinking about for years. If you and Julie agree to them, of course."

One such thing is opening as a pop-up restaurant in the Mowhay one weekend a month. "As long as it doesn't impact on our guests," I had agreed; Julie had, too, though slightly enviously, I could see.

"I learned so much when I was travelling, I always wanted the chance to do some different cuisines. I was thinking, we could make it a bonus for the guests who are staying that week; they can eat in the restaurant–" the communal area, dressed up "– or we can bring it to them.

I'm thinking Thai, Vietnamese, Indian – but I mean proper Indian, not Korma," he had scoffed.

"It sounds good," I had said. "In fact, it sounds great. What do you think, Julie?"

"Sounds bloody lovely," she had said wistfully. "I wish I could do something like that."

"Maybe you can help with it," Jonathan had said, in way that suggested he thought he was being very generous.

"Maybe," said Julie. I had kicked her under the table.

But she has bigger fish to fry, anyway. The adoption process is well underway, although it is still unclear quite how long it is going to take. The fact that Luke will be going out again soon for a month, to work with the charity again, might help a little. He is as excited as Julie, though they are both finding the process frustrating at times, and neither wants to be away from the other for so long.

"David and Martin have been brilliant," Julie said, "It's so good to know people who have been through it, too."

I couldn't help feeling, childishly, slightly left out. I pushed the thought aside.

"Though I think it was more straightforward for them as they were adopting in the UK." She has become quite an expert. "But now Luke and I are living on a reduced income, and still don't know when we'll have our baby. I shouldn't have been so hasty in giving up Amethi."

"You haven't given it up, and you need to be ready. And Jon isn't going to want to do this forever. One day, you'll be back here full time. But for now, enjoy this. You're still working, still involved, and you're getting the house ready for your new arrivals, don't forget."

"True."

Because it's not just a baby who Luke and Julie are welcoming into their home.

It's two babies, and two adults, and one dog.

"Live with us!" Julie had screeched on a video call while she and Luke were still away. Both Sam and I were sitting at the computer, and telling her how hard it was turning out to be, finding an affordable place where we'd want to live.

"We're never going to get a place of our own," Sam had lamented just prior to this. "Never mind get married."

"Come and live with us! We want you to."

I had looked at Sam. He had looked at me.

"Don't look like that. I know what you're thinking. But just take a little time to discuss the idea. You need somewhere to live. I'm going to be on my own in our house, a lot, while Luke's in London, or India."

"Don't make me feel guilty again," Luke grinned. "Seriously, you two, think about it. The house is big enough, and I know you want your own space, but this won't be forever. And you can save a bit, for your own place, or for your wedding, or both. And you can keep an eye on Julie for me, while I'm away. Make sure she's behaving herself."

Julie pushed Luke and he disappeared from view for a moment. He came back smiling.

"Seriously. I know you might think it's a bit weird. We're not in our twenties anymore and you've got Ben, and Soph of course. But we know each other well enough to make it work, don't we? You two can have the guest room with the en suite, and Ben can have the room next to it. There's another room for Soph when she comes, though at some point we're going to have to make it a nursery. But then there's the study downstairs, it has a sofa-bed. We can make it work. Honest."

He looked so earnest; they both did, and eager for us to

say yes. But I had my doubts. I want us to have our own place, Sam and me, and Ben – and yes, with a room for Sophie when she comes to stay. "We'll get back to you."

Sam and I had spent that evening talking it through; swinging first one way and then another.

"It's going to be a bit cramped," he said, "despite how bloody massive their house is."

"And what about time to ourselves? We barely get enough of that as it is."

"But it would mean we weren't destroying ourselves financially."

"We could save for our own place."

"And our wedding."

I had smiled at this. "The wedding will come. It will. We just need to get our lives a bit more sorted first."

"Tell you what, let's see what Soph thinks as well, shall we?" Sam suggested.

"Live with Julie?" Sophie had exclaimed. I'd almost forgotten how much she looks up to my cool, confident, stylish friend.

"Yes," I said.

"And Uncle – I mean, Luke?" She has stopped calling him Uncle Luke altogether these days. It doesn't fit her new, more grown-up identity. For she has grown up, a lot. And taken to life in Devon astonishingly easily. She gets a small school bus every day, taking her through those lush green valleys and over the hills, picking up other rural children on its way. And she works at the business at weekends, chambermaiding or helping in the kitchen; whatever is required. She is saving for a car, she says: "When I'm seventeen, I'll be able to drive myself places. And my mates."

Bloody hell. Sophie driving a car. How is this possible?

Anyway, her view on the situation was all positive, even when we pointed out she wouldn't always have her own room, when Julie and Luke's adoption transforms from a lovely idea into reality.

"That's fine," she said airily. "I'll kip in the study, and anyway by then you might have got your own place. We'll just have to take it as it comes."

It had taken all my willpower not to send a glance Sam's way. That's the problem with video calls; it can be very hard to hide a reaction.

"Alright," Sam had laughed. "If you're sure."

"I am."

Back on a call to Julie and Luke. "What about Meg?"

"The dog?" Luke asked.

"Hey! She's not 'the dog'. She's a member of our family."

"Well, I don't have any problem having Alice's furry second child at our place... do you, Julie?"

"No, as long as you promise not to call yourself Mummy, and Sam Daddy, not when it comes to the dog."

I shudder. "As if." Thinking, it may have slipped out from time to time.

"OK," I said.

"OK," said Sam.

"OK?" asked Julie. "You mean it's a yes?"

"It's a yes," I shrugged. Then smiled. "I can't believe we'll be living together again, Julie!"

"I know!" she shrieked.

Sam and Luke were a bit cooler about the whole thing.

"We'll see how it goes," Sam said. "Make sure it's working for everybody – and if not, we'll find somewhere else, with no hard feelings."

"Good thinking, mate," Luke agreed.

"*Good thinking, mate,*" said Julie, and we watched her fall, giggling, off camera, as Luke pushed her.

"Sorry about her," he grinned. "Well, this is great. I'm looking forward to getting back."

"But we must be honest," I said, earnestly. "If this is going to work. If you're fed up of us, you have to say. We're alright; we can leave if you two are as annoying as I think you're going to be."

"Thanks for the vote of confidence," Luke grinned, putting three fingers up in mock-salute: "Scout's honour, we'll be sensible, and we won't let it ruin our friendship."

When Ben has tired himself out, I call Meg and she sits patiently while I fasten him into the pushchair. We follow our time-honoured route back to the house. *For the last time*, I think. Of course, there is nothing stopping us walking this way whenever we want to, but I know it won't be the same.

By the time we are home, Ben has fallen asleep. I open the door to a very quiet house, and I push him in, tucking him out of the way, under the stairs. Meg runs through to the kitchen for a drink of water. I can hear her lapping and splashing away. Then she comes back, tongue lolling and a slightly wild look in her eyes. She knows something is amiss.

The dining room is empty of furniture but piled high with boxes.

"It's OK," I tell her, and she nuzzles my hand.

Planting a quiet kiss on my boy's soft cheek, I stop for a moment to enjoy the sound of his deep, earnest breath. Then I turn to go upstairs, Meg at my heel. We check each room in turn and I remember doing this when Mum and Dad were buying this place, and I was moving to Amethi.

Sam was still away in Wales then, and I had absolutely no idea what the future held. How could I have foreseen our beautiful boy, or wonderful Meg? Mum and Dad going on to buy the Sail Loft?

My footsteps seem loud in the fast-emptying house and I bypass Ben's room, and ours, which still both hold essential furniture which we will move with us next weekend.

Round the banister and up the next set of stairs I go, remembering the very first time I made this journey. Slightly shy and unsure, but buoyed up with Julie by my side. I push open the door to my old room, which went on to be Sophie's. It is empty. No bed. No chair beneath the window. It feels sad but somehow full of promise, too. This will become a studio, the new owners have told us – and Julie's original bedroom, next door. The pair of artists will work in rooms side-by-side, and though no artist myself, I can see how this could be the perfect set-up. Who knows what works of art will come from this space?

For now, just a short while longer, it is still ours. Meg paces out of the room and I hear her settle with a slight grumble at the top of the stairs. I hope she's going to be OK, moving home again so soon. It feels like something she might have to get used to, with us. Nothing ever staying still for long.

I open the little window, peer down the street. It is empty now and I imagine little trails left by all the times I have come up and down this road, my footsteps leaving imperceptible imprints. The image I can never shake is that shadowy figure I saw that stormy night, when Luke's mum had died and Julie was with him, and Sam had come in his grief to find me. The air had been thick and heavy that day, cracked open by the storm, which sent water rushing down the street, bouncing off roofs and gutters and windows, filling the night with noise.

Now, all is quiet. Save for Meg's panting just outside the door. I listen, to make sure Ben is not yet awake and trying to get my attention. But no. All is still. I breathe deeply. A gull calls from a roof across the street. There is traffic noise, but only a little. We have not yet reached silly season, when the streets are a slow, steady stream of cars and vans.

I quieten my own breathing, try to focus my hearing, and there it is. The sea. Calm today; soft, and reassuring. The thing which helps make this town so unique, so unbelievably special. Waves moving in, and moving out.

It never stops, is never the same, from one moment to the next. The ever-changing ocean, which gives life to this town; has provided livelihoods for the people here, since far before I ever came to this place.

In and out. In and out.

I try to match its pace with my breath. When I open my eyes again, see the empty room once more, I know that it's time to move on, and that everything will be OK.

While all good things must come to an end, there will be more ahead.

Acknowledgements

As some of you will already know, the Coming Back to Cornwall series was only ever intended to be a trilogy. It has continued largely thanks to my very lovely readers, who have offered so much support and positive feedback that it's made me want to keep going. I love all your messages, and the opportunities to get to know some of you better, and develop friendships despite never having met in person.

I also feel like I should thank Alice, and Sam, Julie and Luke, and the rest of the characters – they may not be real people but I have become very attached to them. As to the places. The townhouse... Amethi... the Sail Loft... the Cross-Section. I only wish I could visit them for real.

The experience of writing this sixth book has been unforgettable for me. The time in which it has been written has been unique, and very difficult for many of us. The lockdown of 2020; all thanks to the coronavirus pandemic. I still feel that everything seems so unreal, it's going to take some time to work through it all once things go back to 'normal', if they ever do.

For me, this time has been made even more difficult as all the time I have been writing this book, I've done so knowing that my mum, who *Something About the Stars* is dedicated to, is seriously ill. Diagnosed with cancer at the end of January, her treatment has not agreed with her and during April and May she has been in hospital and a hospice. She is now back home with my dad and showing such strength and determination.

I will be grateful forever to my mum and it felt very fitting to be writing this book, with its focus on motherhood, while she is so much on my mind. She has taught me what it is to be a mum and in some of my books I mention 'that type of mum' and by this I always mean *my* type of mum. I have never once doubted her love and support and I hope that I can offer my own children the consistency and security that both my parents have provided throughout my life.

I also have both my parents to thank for my love of books, and for their constant support of and interest in my writing. Dad has helped edit and proof the majority of my books and I'm very grateful for this.

As a family I think we are reeling – and in my own immediate family we are also grieving the loss of my mother-in-law, another Catherine – Kaye – Smith. Another voracious reader. Another strong and unforgettable woman, who we all miss dearly.

So it's been a sad year so far for us all and I've been so grateful for my writing and the chance to lose myself for a while somewhere else.

I must also thank my wonderful team of beta readers and I sincerely hope I have not forgotten to include anybody here (if I have, you must let me know). In no particular order: Jenny Holdcroft, Beryl Gibson, Rosemary Gibson, Claire Victoria, Denise Armstrong, Amanda Tudor, Pat Pearce, Mandy Chowney-Andrews, Joanna Blackburn, Shirley Blane, Clare Coburn, Ginnie Ebbrell, Tracey Shaw, Wendy Pompe, Holly Reeves, Helen Smith, Katie Copnall and Claudia Baker. I am so grateful for your time, your advice, and your positivity!

Thanks also to my proofreader Hilary Kerr, somebody else who has become a 'virtual' friend I hope I might meet one day, whose idea it was to rename the 'communal area' at Amethi.

And always, thank you to Catherine Clarke, my amazingly talented cover designer – for the covers, the laughs, the friendship, and the socially distanced walks, which I think we will remember for the rest of our lives.

The first five Coming Back to Cornwall books:

Book One:
A Second Chance Summer

Book Two:
After the Sun

Book Three:
As Boundless as the Sea

Book Four:
Sticks and Stones

Book Five:
Lighting the Sky

All books are available as paperbacks and ebooks, online and in store. Contact <u>enquiries@heddonpublishing.com</u> for further information.

Also by Katharine E. Smith:

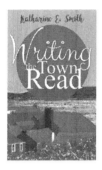

Writing the Town Read - Katharine's first novel.

"I seriously couldn't put it down and would recommend it to anyone to doesn't like chick lit, but wants a great story."

Looking Past - a story of motherhood, and growing up without a mother.

"Despite the tough topic the book is full of love, friendships and humour. Katharine Smith cleverly balances emotional storylines with strong characters and witty dialogue, making this a surprisingly happy book to read."

Amongst Friends - a back-to-front tale of friendship and family, set in Bristol.

"An interesting, well written book, set in Bristol which is lovingly described, and with excellent characterisation. Very enjoyable."